THE
BACHELORETTE PARTY

THE BACHELORETTE PARTY

SANDRA BLOCK

SCARLET
NEW YORK

To my
Aunt Karen
and
Uncle Sid
With love

—

THE BACHELORETTE PARTY

Scarlet
An Imprint of Penzler Publishers
58 Warren Street
New York, N.Y. 10007

First Scarlet Press edition

Interior design by Maria Fernandez

Library of Congress Control Number: 2024911610

ISBN: 978-1-61316-559-1
eBook ISBN: 978-1-61316-565-2

10 9 8 7 6 5 4 3 2 1

Printed in the United States of America
Distributed by W. W. Norton & Company

CHAPTER ONE

NOW

I yank off the crown.

Embossed with the finest plastic diamonds reading *Bougie Bachelorette,* the thing not only looks ridiculous, it's giving me a headache.

"Come on, Alex," Melody says, turning to me from the front seat. "You're the bachelorette. You have to wear it."

"Maybe later," I lie, since she took the time to buy the monstrosity.

Lainey turns the car key a few times, and the engine putters precariously before finally catching. "Gotta look at that starter," she says, with a grimace.

This does not bode well.

We're in Lainey's used Kia, which is about as sexy as it sounds. But Melody doesn't know how to drive and Jay needed his car, so we didn't have much choice in the matter.

Pulling out of my parking ramp, we make a few turns, then start crawling down the streets of Manhattan.

Tourists crowd the Saks Fifth Avenue Christmas windows, a kitschy throwback in this CGI-dominated world. A block later, a line snakes around the American Girl store, moms and daughters holding hands, dolls dangling everywhere. The soft snow has thickened into soggy flakes, clogging the air, making the city look like a postcard.

"This car sucks in the snow," Lainey says, frowning at the windshield.

"Come on," Melody trills. She's an actress—she trills a lot. "It's an adventure."

Lainey snorts, and I commiserate with her lack of excitement. It's only a month before the wedding, and I'm way behind on my 666 Killer profile. But Melody guilt-tripped me, saying this would be our last hurrah as single ladies, and Lainey didn't have many free weekends with basketball.

Oddly enough, it was Jay who made the final push. He's from Australia, where "hen parties" are more of a thing. "You've known them forever," he said. "They're your best friends. Go crazy. Do it up. Get the policeman strippers or whatever."

I had to laugh at that one. Melody would *possibly* allow male strippers in the name of female empowerment, but Lainey has zero interest in men, let alone naked men.

At least it's just the three of us. A blowout at some random bar would have been worse. I am not, and have never been, a party girl.

"Can you please just tell me where we're going?" I ask, leaning forward closer to their seats.

"Then it wouldn't be a surprise, would it?" Lainey answers.

I look to Melody, who answers with a zipped-lips motion. With a resigned sigh, I lean back again, fiddling with my seatbelt before remembering it doesn't work.

In the front seats, my friends look comical, Lainey's head well above the headrest and Melody's well below. Melody and Lainey are opposites. Lainey is White, skinny, boyish, and proudly six feet. Melody is Chinese-American, buxom with a Betty Boop quality, and proudly four feet eleven. Lainey has a low, gruff voice; Melody a high-pitched, incessantly cheerful one. Lainey would be Grumpy (if Grumpy were six feet), and Melody would be Happy (if Happy harped on intersectional feminism).

I don't think there's a suitable dwarf for me, since I'm not dopey or bashful, and sneezy and sleepy are hardly personality traits. I suppose I'm the median, in height and hair color, at least. I've always been the middle child, the peacemaker, ever since our first days as roommates at UConn.

Jay is right, I've known them forever.

"A hint," I say, butting my head in between their seats. "Just give me a little hint."

They exchange glances. "It involves your internship," Melody says. "Primary research."

"Primary research?" I ask, baffled. I drum my fingers on the cold velour seat. "For the 666 Killer?" I rest my elbows on the back of their seats. "Are we visiting him?"

"Um. No, Alex." Melody throws me a look. "We are not visiting your serial killer."

"He's not *my* serial killer," I correct her.

They answer with silence, which speaks volumes.

So, okay.

Ever since I took on the project, the tenth anniversary of the 666 Killings, I'll admit to being a tad obsessed with Eric Myers. Jay complained about the "disturbing" pictures covering our bedroom floor during my investigation phase. But I was just gathering clues from the murder scene, clues that were possibly (unlikely) missed by the detectives. Stab wounds, defensive wounds, a torn necklace, the butterfly pendant stained in blood.

I was hoping to uncover something new to springboard me from forever-intern to actual reporter on *Crimeline*. The pay would only be marginally less crappy, but reporter would be the next rung on the perilously long ladder up to TV journalist.

Melody finally settles on a pop station as the snow builds around us. We drive for a while, past the landmarks of the city, the skyscrapers, honking taxis, bodegas, and throngs of tourists. I love New York City, I do. But I always feel a sense of relief, somehow, leaving the city. I shouldn't complain. I have a great job. I have a great apartment (due to a great fiancé, who can afford it). Still, I was raised in Vermont. I yearn for wide open spaces. When I come back from visiting my mom, I sometimes feel an invisible net sucking me back into the city. I could never explain that to Jay. And they certainly don't have *Crimeline* reporter jobs in Vermont.

We crawl ahead, the wheels slipping in the snow. Lainey drives cautiously, hunched over the steering wheel. She turns the wipers up a notch, and the rubber squeaks and thumps with every swipe.

Squeak, squeak, thump. Squeak, squeak, thump.

"So, where was Jay, by the way?" Melody asks. She pops a stick of cinnamon gum in her mouth. "I'd thought he'd be here to give you a big send-off."

"He had Greg this weekend."

A family of deer trots by on the side of the highway, and one by one, they dart into the forest.

"Did you finally meet him?" Lainey looks at me from the rearview mirror, appearing fish-eyed in the reflection.

"Yeah," I say, but I don't elaborate.

Jay wanted to wait until the time was right, basically until after we got engaged. We had the clichéd "whirlwind romance," so it didn't take long. We only dated a few months before I moved in with him.

"How did it go?" Melody asks, playing with the radio again.

"Fine," I say, lightly.

I really don't want to get into it. I just want to enjoy our weekend and not ruminate over Greg. On the first "date" with his son, we went for sushi, followed by ice cream sundaes, and Greg barely said a word. Though I had no idea what to say to a twelve-year-old anyway. Jay assured me that I did fine. Afterward, I couldn't really tell if he liked me or hated me. Now I know it was definitely the latter.

"He's shy," I say. "Jay says it'll take time."

They both answer with noncommittal nods, taking my hint and dropping the subject. An hour or so passes, with Melody toying with the radio and Lainey white-knuckling the steering wheel, the wipers keeping up their hypnotic rhythm.

After another thirty minutes, Lainey leans over to peek at Melody's phone map. "Wasn't I supposed to turn left at some point?"

"Another mile," Melody says.

But the phone disagrees.

Left turn up ahead, the feminine voice informs us, sounding authoritative yet docile. Melody once skewered the Google Maps voice as "annoyingly subordinate." And don't get her started on Alexa.

"Up ahead where?" Lainey says. "You said a mile."

"Wait, no. I'm sorry." Melody peers through the blowing snow. "Here, right here," she says, pointing ahead.

"Right here? Or left here?" Lainey asks.

"Left, left!" Melody yells.

Lainey yanks the wheel, and a horn blasts at us from a passing truck. As the wheels spin, she overcorrects, then undercorrects, the back of the car fishtailing. Melody swings into the console and back against the window, possibly over-playing it, but then again, she *is* kind of small. Lainey keeps braking, gripping the steering wheel with her long fingers, the car juddering toward the curb before it finally stops.

We all sit there in silent shock, catching our breath like we just ran a marathon. Lainey looks even paler than usual, her hands trembling, while the wipers keep up their noxious rhythm.

Squeak, squeak, thump. Squeak, squeak, thump.

"I swear I thought it was another mile," Melody says in apology.

Lainey holds up her palm, indicating she should be quiet, and Melody answers with a subdued nod.

Squeak, squeak, thump.

Squeak, squeak, thump.

The defrost churns away, expanding the circle of clear glass in the foggy windshield.

"Listen," I say. "We don't have to go to . . . wherever we're going." I climb forward between the seats again. "We could just turn around and go back. Netflix. Wine. All good. We'll have a very wonderfully relaxed bachelorette party."

Melody turns to me. "With Jay and Greg?"

I shrug. "At one of your apartments, then."

In the ensuing pause, Lainey seems to consider this. I know she'd love to see Ruby, who happens to be in town to see her folks. Playing for the New York Liberty, Lainey's always on the road.

Suddenly, she smacks the steering wheel, making us all jump. "No. We've come this far. We're going all the way."

Melody claps her hands together. "Okay then," she says, pulling her seatbelt back on. "We go down this road for another ten miles before the next turn." She holds up three fingers. "Girl Scout promise." This seals the deal. Melody is twenty-six but mentions her Girl Scout days not infrequently.

Lainey puts the car back in drive, and I settle into the back seat again, yanking my seatbelt, before remembering it doesn't work. "*Now* can you tell me where we're going?" I ask.

"No," they both answer, sounding like annoyed parents, their toddler in the back seat playing with her crown.

CHAPTER TWO

SIX MONTHS AGO

JUNE

Bleary-eyed, I sit down at my computer.

My fellow intern, Wiley, wipes cream cheese off their chin, glossy with precisely grown stubble. When we first met, I was thrown off by the eyeliner and fake eyelashes paired with the perfect five-o'clock shadow. Now, it doesn't faze me.

"That kind of night?" Wiley asks.

"Mm," I answer, vaguely.

It's not the kind of night they mean, unfortunately, filled with sex or drunken revelry. I don't remember what happened. But I woke up with the lamp on the floor, my elbow smarting. I take a long sip of coffee to wake myself up. Intravenous delivery would be better.

Checking my email, I don't see any word from Greene County Prison. *Crimeline* greenlit my 666 Killer profile, but only for a six-month window, and my boss made it clear she wasn't enamored of the project.

"It can't just be a rehash," she warned me, flicking her long red hair. Toby has a beak-ish nose with her eyes set close together, giving her a perpetually puzzled look. For some reason, we don't mesh. Every time she calls me into her office, I'm afraid I'm about to get fired. "To even consider airing it," she said, "we'd have to discover something new."

But so far, said killer hasn't even agreed to be in it.

"I'd be up all night too," Wiley says, after swallowing more bagel. "Your fiancé is kind of a smokeshow."

"Uh-huh," I answer, turning to my stack of mail. "The word fiancé should be a hint. But I give you full license to try."

"No," they say, airily. "My fiancée would probably be displeased."

They're right. Josie would disembowel Wiley. Perusing my mail, I thumb through an official-looking insurance come-on, a bridal dress brochure, a special election flyer and—I pause. A hand-addressed envelope with a Greene County Prison stamp. With some apprehension, I rip open to the envelope to reveal a single handwritten page.

Dear Alex,

Thank you for your letter.

I'm thrilled to help you with your profile. You say I'm doing you a favor. But you're the journalist, so really, you're doing ME the favor. And believe me, I need all the help I can get. So . . . let me get this right out of the way.

I AM NOT THE 666 KILLER!!!!!

I did not kill those girls. I've done some really stupid shit in my life, but I would never hurt anyone, let alone kill anyone. I know everyone in here says they're innocent. But for me, it's the truth.

I'm hoping maybe your profile could help people see that. I got a guy working on my case from prison. He says he's using law books but I don't know. I tried to get the Innocence Project to take my case but they wouldn't.

Anyway, you can ask me anything. Anything at all. Hopefully you can get the real truth out there.

Sincerely,
Eric Myers

P.S. Feel free to use the ConnectNetwork prison email system. It only costs a small fee.

CHAPTER THREE

NOW

M elody bounces up and down in her seat. She has been quite vocal about her need to urinate.

We crawl the whole way, skidding on the unplowed streets. It's almost eight o'clock. We've been at this for hours now, and I still don't know where we're going. They won't even tell me if we're close. From what I can glean, we're either headed to the Catskills or the Adirondacks.

"We're almost out of gas," Lainey says, cracking her knuckles. "So tell me if you see a station."

"There's one in a couple miles," I say, referencing my phone map, since Melody is no longer trusted with navigation.

"Good," Melody says, still bouncing. "Because I really have to—"

"Pee," Lainey grumbles. "We know. You might have mentioned it once or twice."

The streetlights cast a sepia light on the snow, making the landscape appear Mars-like, unearthly. We pass a frozen lake, black in the distance.

I notice something moving across it.

With a jolt, I put my face right up to the window. "Did you guys see that?"

Melody turns to the window, scrubbing it with her mitten. "See what? I can't see anything."

"It looked like someone was walking on the lake," I say. I keep watching, but we drive past, the person fading away.

"Probably a shadow," Lainey says, glancing back.

"Yeah," I say. "Maybe."

"Or it could have been a bear," Melody mentions.

"Could be. They do have bears around here." I try to visualize it again. "It seemed smaller than a bear though."

A long beeping noise blares out of the radio, interrupting me. *This is a weather alert. Blizzard conditions with snowfall of up to twelve inches is expected in Delaware County. Unnecessary travel is not recommended.*

"Jesus Christ," Lainey mutters.

"You guys," Melody says, practically keening. "I'm going to have an accident in like two seconds."

"Gas station," I say, pointing. "Up ahead here."

Lainey slows down, softer on the brakes this time to avoid fishtailing. Pulling up to the pump, she lets out a sigh of relief. Meanwhile, Melody leaps out of the car, and I hand Lainey a credit card. "I got this one," I say. "Since you're driving."

Climbing out of the car, she performs a long, groaning stretch. "Want me to Venmo you?" she asks, grabbing the handle of the gas pump. Snowflakes cling to her ponytail, outlining her scrunchie.

"Nah," I say. "You'll get the next one."

But we both know I'll get the next one, or more accurately, Jay will get the next one. Melody is a working actress (read: very poor) surviving on her dual mothers' intermittent cash infusions. Lainey gets a pitiful wage from the WNBA, especially compared to what the men make. And as a *Crimeline* intern, I'm just as broke. Jay, however, is not.

"I'll get snacks," I say, opening the squeaky car door with some effort, the frigid wind pushing back against me. Snowflakes hover around the streetlights like moths. Hunkering down against the cold, I tuck my chin into my coat and walk into the shop.

After surveying the picked-over shelves, I grab some chips (to hell with my dress fitting), then check out the drink area. The refrigerated air chills me, and I grab a six-pack and a two-liter soda. Next to me, a good-looking guy about our age mulls over the beer section. He's got blondish hair and a medium build, wearing ripped jeans that appear genuinely ripped, not "distressed" to look that way, and a plaid flannel shirt with a Carhartt winter coat, unzipped.

The guy looks vaguely familiar somehow, though I don't know anyone out this way.

"Hey," he says, politely, noticing me staring.

"Hey," I answer back, quickly looking away.

He glances at my ring, which is difficult to miss, then back at the beer. Melody strides out of the bathroom, wiping her hands on her jeans. She clocks the cute guy with an eyebrow raise and goes back out to the car. Melody is currently "taking a break from asshole men," after her latest paramour, Mason the Med Student, dumped her. But she still can't help being heterosexual, a fact she bemoans as a personal failure. I love Jay to the moon and back, but I get where she's coming from, especially after what happened with Chris.

Peering out the misted windows, I see Lainey has finished pumping and make my way to the register, handing the cashier a fifty and stuffing a good tip into the "college" jar. The bells tinkle as I leave, and my phone sounds. I check it, hoping for a message from Jay. But it's not.

It's an Amber Alert. Immediately, I think of my mom.

AMBER ALERT. CENTRAL NEW YORK.

SUSPECT VEHICLE SILVER LINCOLN.

Glancing around, I realize I'm searching for a silver Lincoln. But of course I don't find it.

My mom said she wished they had the Amber Alert in her day. Then, her sister might have been found. I don't know much about Lissa, since she went missing before I was born and Mom doesn't like to talk about her, but she cries when her birthday comes around. It doesn't take Freud to trace this as the probable root of my true crime obsession. Someone like an Eric Myers probably took her, someone who slipped away and might still be out there. But they never found him, or her, so we will never know for sure. And that's what kills my mom.

I put the phone back in my pocket.

"Oh look," Melody says, pointing. "A farm. How rustic."

I barely see the farmhouse as we whip by. After a series of detours and missed turns, we are finally nearing our destination. The car shoots snow off in all directions, climbing the long and winding driveway. I keep thinking we must be there, and then we hit yet another turn. At last, an old wooden cabin comes into sight in the distance, dark and brooding.

"Surprise," Melody trills, jumping in her seat.

"Where the hell are we?" I ask, twisting to get a closer look. "It looks like the set of a horror movie."

"You'll see," she says, as we creep up the long stone driveway. Overgrown trees and bramble arch into an arbor over us. Branches scrape along the windows as we pull closer to what looks like a decrepit hunting lodge.

"Interesting," I say, since I have no idea what else to say. I put my nose against the cold window as we get closer and closer. The car finally reaches the house. Lainey cuts the engine, the wind whistling around us, rocking our car. We sit in silence a moment as I scrutinize the place.

"Oh my God."

"Right?" Melody comments, grinning.

"No way." I huff on the window to get a better look. "Is this really it?"

Lainey reaches over the seat to sock me in the shoulder, the punch both playful and unintentionally painful. "Happy bachelorette party."

"I can't believe this," I say, rubbing my arm from the punch.

Lainey gets out of the car, hurries to the trunk, and pops it open with a creak. "Come on," she barks. "It's freezing out here."

"I'm coming," I say. Though apprehension spirals in me as I open the car door, still staring at the lodge. Because standing in front of us is the very place featured on the glossy cover of *The 666 Killer* book.

The hunting lodge where Eric Myers stabbed a woman to death.

And scrawled 666 all over the walls in her blood.

CHAPTER FOUR

JUNE

The Unexpected Killer, Season 4, Episode #18, "The 666 Killer"

"Eric Myers denies it. To this day, he denies it," Fletcher Fox says.

"And we take a different perspective," Detective Connor answers, with an air of weary politeness. "As did the courts."

Fox offers a dramatic pause, a technique he employs more often than necessary. He leans forward in his painfully dated sky-blue jeans and a royal-blue suede vest, his posture suggesting earnest social worker. Meanwhile, Detective Connor sports the classic, never-out-of-fashion bedraggled detective look. He sits back in his chair, his top button straining at a bull-like neck, a fine lace of rosacea across his nose and cheeks.

I swallow the last piece of toast and jam, as Babushka tries to lick the plate. "Hey," I say, shoving her away, and she answers with an annoyed meow.

"Some have said you just homed in on Eric Myers, and that was that. You didn't bother to look at any other suspects." Fox bestows yet another long pause. "How would you answer that accusation?"

"I would answer that they were wrong," responds the detective, his politeness waning. "We did a very thorough investigation. And I stand by my department's findings, a hundred percent." He touches the knot of his tie. "And I'll say this as well. With everyone we asked, one name just kept coming up, again and again."

"And that was . . ."

Fun fact: Fletcher Fox's real name is Jerry Samuels, the most forgettable name that ever existed. I don't get why he gets $4.2 million every year, but ratings don't lie. Viewers love the guy. Toby says I could learn something from him, and she's probably right.

"That was Eric Myers," the detective confirms. "Again and again. Eric Myers."

"And why do you think that is? That people kept coming back to his name?" That's another Fox special, besides trademark cheesy clichés: his ridiculously easy questions.

"Well, there's the obvious, of course," the detective says, with a chuckle.

Fletcher Fox responds with a chuckle as well (though it seems in poor taste to be chuckling about a serial murderer).

"And then there was the eyewitness statement from the survivor. Leigh Jones," Detective Connor says. "An extremely reliable witness. More than most, I would say."

"So he matched the EFIT?" Fox asks, throwing another softball out there. Right on cue, the Electronic Facial Identification Technique appears on the screen.

There's something unsettling about these computer-generated faces. I have a certain nostalgia for the old-school sketch-artist caricatures. Now all the suspects look like video game villains.

"Perfectly. Matched it a hundred percent. Blue eyes. Tall," the detective says.

I jot this down, squinting at the EFIT. *Blue eyes. Tall.*

Babushka tries to bat my pen.

"And then, of course," Fox says, a smile playing on his lips. He literally somehow gets a smile to play on his lips. "That very crucial detail."

"Yes, of course," the detective answers. "Crucial."

A picture of a smiling Nicole White and then a frowning Eric Myers swoop onto the screen, followed by an overdramatic voice-over.

"What did Eric Myers have that clinched it for detectives? Find out. When we return to . . . *The Unexpected Killer.*"

I press pause on the ham-fisted cliffhanger, when suddenly hands are around my neck.

A hot whisper in my ear.

"Boo."

"Jay," I yell at him, jumping up in the seat. "You scared the hell out of me."

He half sits on the desk, facing me with a Cheshire grin. Babushka slides under his arm for some pets, and Jay obliges. "You watch too many serial killers shows."

I push away my breakfast plate, spilling toast crumbs, which Babushka pounces on. "Fletcher Fox is actually much more frightening than any serial killer."

Jay lets out a low baritone laugh. It's a lovely laugh. He crosses his arms, his shoulders straining the fabric of his soft blue shirt. He wears the shirt a lot ever since I told him it's my favorite. The bright blue color brings out the silver-blue in his eyes. Jay effortlessly nails the casually wealthy look, an understated yet bespoke button-down, and indigo creased jeans that cost more than my last paycheck.

Sometimes I still can't believe we're dating, let alone getting married, like characters in a novel, with an over-the-top meet-cute.

I had just gotten over Chris and wasn't looking for anyone. I was buying a round for some *Crimeline* interns after work, and a drunk asshole kept badgering me. To my right, I heard this uber-sexy Australian accent.

"Oi, mate. She's not into you. Move on."

The drunk buffoon puffed his chest up in one of those oh-yeah-what-are-you-gonna-do-about-it maneuvers, and then staggered back, stunned. I didn't even see the punch. The drunk guy's friends scuttled him away and, with my mouth open, I turned to look at this ridiculously handsome man. Smoldering, if I had to pick an adjective.

I said something witty like "Um, hi," and he rubbed his hand and said, "I know I'm supposed to act all macho and everything, but I think I just broke my bloody knuckle." So,

I dunked his hand in my Moscow mule, though it didn't fit very well, and said, "How's that?" And he laughed that musical laugh and said, "I'm thinking I should marry you."

Of course he was joking. At least, I thought so.

"You going to work?" I ask, feeling shiftless in my pajamas, even on my remote day.

"Meeting Eli for breakfast," he says.

"Mmph," I say.

I don't much like Eli, probably because he doesn't much like me. He's a glad-hander, always dressed in garish suits, his laugh as loud as his linebacker body. I wouldn't care, if I didn't catch his expression when we first met, his lips curling with disdain. He clearly saw me as beneath him (and Jay) and was unpleasantly surprised to learn of our engaged status a few months later.

Jay says Eli likes me fine, that I'm just paranoid about our age difference. Maybe he's right. But then again, Jay might be blinded by his own self-interest. They have a symbiotic relationship. Eli brings his hedge fund some heavy-hitting clients, and in return, Jay makes Eli a lot of money.

Jay leans in to kiss me now, and I notice the bruise under his eye has turned from eggplant to yellow-gray, the half-moon shape almost faded entirely now. I reach out to touch it, and he captures my hand.

"I'm sorry about that," I say.

Shaking his head, he kisses my hand with an air of chivalry, then stands up from the table. "See you later," he says.

CHAPTER FIVE

NOW

I stamp my boots on the frayed rug, then take off my gloves, wincing as the fabric catches my scabby knuckles. "This place is amazing," I say, gazing around.

"We know how much you love haunted houses," Melody says, blowing on her hands. "So we figured . . . why not a real one?"

She's right. I've dragged them to every spooky Halloween haunted house I could find, sometimes miles away. Nightmare Manor, The Haunted Screampark, The Headless Horseman's Farm . . . the bloodier the better. But I've never been to an actual murder house.

"How did you guys find this place?" I ask.

"Vrbo," Melody says, then makes a cartoonish *brrr* sound. She still has her hat on, a red-checkered hunting hat with earmuffs. I can't figure out if she wears it ironically or not. She rubs her arms in her oversized pea coat. "They actually mention it in the write-up," she says, putting on a spooky voice and waggling her fingers. "The haunted 666 house."

"Plus it was cheap." Lainey unzips her coat in a sharp motion. "Because it got mostly one stars."

"Yeah, well," Melody says, kicking off her boots. "It's the ghoulish thought that counts."

I take off my boots with some reluctance. The place is freezing. "You think there might be functioning heat at least?" I ask. I can still see my breath.

"Hopefully," Melody says, in a singsong voice. Smoothing her hand against the wall, she finds the light switch and flips it on with a *thunk*. The overhead light buzzes and flickers, lighting the room a dull, gloomy gray.

Lainey spots the thermostat. "Jesus. This thing was set at fifty-five." She twists the knob, the hum of the heating unit immediately sounding.

Walking on the knotty wooden floor in my thin socks, I pass the teeny square kitchen and venture into the great room. A chipped fieldstone hearth covers one wall, with a matted sheepskin rug on the floor. Two mismatched sofa chairs sit in each corner, and a forest-green leather loveseat, lined with cracks and scratches, faces the fireplace. I can't help but picture the black-and-white crime scene overlaid on the room, a woman crumpled on the floor, her limbs askew, a black slash over her eyes to protect her identity.

And blood on the wall, 666. The numbers dripping.

I shiver.

"It'll be warm in our sleeping bags at least," Melody says, misreading the gesture. She starts wandering around the room to investigate and grabs a heavy metal tennis racket that was leaning against the hearth for some unknown reason. "Tennis, anyone?" she asks, taking a swing. She examines the racket, plucking the strings. "This is so random."

"It is that," I answer.

She puts the racket back down with a clunk, wandering about again. "There's supposed to be a bedroom too somewhere. With a bathroom and a shower."

I plop onto one of the sofa chairs. "Bachelorette Girl calls the bedroom," I say.

Melody opens one of the doors and peers down. "This one's the basement," she says, her voice echoing. She keeps walking, then opens another door with a creak. "And here's the bedroom." Then she pauses. "Oh my."

With that intro, Lainey and I hop up to join her, crowding the doorway to see a small room with a twin bed, a rough, gray flannel blanket tucked in with military precision around it. There is indeed a shower in the corner, with a childish plastic curtain decorated with bright yellow ducks. The curtain hangs half open, revealing rings of rust on the concrete floor.

"On the other hand," I say, stepping out of the doorway. "Bachelorette Girl doesn't really want the bedroom."

"Yeah," Lainey says, retreating as well. "That's gonna be a hard pass for me too."

"We'll just sleep together in the great room," Melody says. "OG slumber party."

But the thought makes me stiffen.

Almost unconsciously, I check my phone to see if Jay has texted. But he hasn't. Then again, I don't have any signal right now. If he had called or texted, I probably wouldn't have gotten it.

Lainey flops onto the sheepskin rug. "I can't believe vegan Melody got a place with a dead animal rug."

"I checked," Melody answers. "The owner said it was ethically sourced."

Lainey snorts. "I doubt the sheep thought so."

"Why don't we get a fire going?" Melody suggests, pointedly changing the subject. "Now, let's see . . . where are the matches?" she says, surveying the pile of logs stacked against the hearth. A rusty axe leans against it, next to the tennis racket. A few charred logs remain on the grate. Her eyes rove around the room. "Matches . . . matches . . . matches . . ."

"I'll find some," I mutter, climbing off the sofa.

Wandering around, I pull out a side table drawer, which sticks, then squeaks open. A flat, old-fashioned compass slides around. Pens. Random keys. Rubber bands. No matches. So, I check out the small cube of a kitchen, the hardwood floor scratched and warped. Two schoolhouse wooden chairs crowd the butcher block table. The appliances feature a grimy minifridge and a grimier electric stovetop. I open one of the wooden cabinets, revealing a few random cans of soup, and on the shelf above, mismatched cups, bowls, and plates.

"Any luck?" Melody calls.

"Not yet," I answer, opening another drawer to find cheap cutlery, and yet another drawer with a spool of twine and more pens.

"Come on," Lainey yells from the family room. "It's freezing in here."

Opening another junk drawer, I find a Swiss Army knife, various coins, random keys, rainbow-colored rubber bands, and . . . matches. "Got them," I call back.

I check one more drawer for more in case we run out, but it holds just one object—a long sharp kitchen knife. A vision breaks through of Eric Myers grabbing it. Stabbing Nicole White over and over again.

I slam the drawer shut.

CHAPTER SIX

JUNE

Dear Alex,

Thanks for using the messaging system.

In answer to your first question, yes, I would love to do an interview. I understand that it has to be virtual. If you can set it up, I'll be there. (It's not like I have anywhere else to be, lol.)

Now, onto your other questions, which are certainly reasonable.

I do know about the The Unexpected Killer episode. I saw it on television here. (Bizarre, right?) One of the guys told me that was meta. I have no idea what that means. But anyway, I decided not to even be in it. They asked me. But it was going to be a frame job, I could tell that right away. Let's just say, the show got a lot of things wrong. So here are the facts, okay?

The EFIT picture. WHAT A JOKE! That was their big piece of evidence, right? I'm really sorry for Leigh Jones and all she went through. But she was in shock, right? You can't really trust what you see in that situation. Even so, let's take what she said as valid for now. She said he had blue eyes. BLUE. She was definite on that point.

My eyes are not blue, they are green. The lawyers said that in the right light they might look blue but that's just complete bullshit. They don't look blue at all. They are definitely green, I repeat. Green.

I consider this argument, which seems wanting. From the courtroom close-ups, his eyes appeared a sort of blue-green, more blue in some, more green in others. And this isn't exactly an Elton John song. In the shadowy light, Leigh Jones picked the best color she could. So no, I'm not buying that.

1. She also said the killer was tall. I'm not short, but I'm not that tall either. I'm five-eleven. They booked me at six feet but they didn't even measure me. That's just what they booked me as. I know I'm not six feet. Most of my friends are over six feet so I know that for sure.

This argument seems similarly lame. First off, I highly doubt they didn't measure him. His mugshot probably shows his exact height. And anyway, Leigh Jones said he looked *about* six feet. It's not like she was carrying a ruler.

2. THE GUY WAS WEARING A BALACLAVA!!!! How could she really even tell what he looked like when she couldn't see his face. (I don't own a balaclava by the way).

Yeah, okay. He might have a point about the balaclava.

So you may be wondering why didn't I tell my lawyer all this, well I DID tell my my lawyer all this but he sucked. He just wanted me to plead guilty so he could move on to another case. But I couldn't afford a real one, you know?

Anyway, you sound really smart—being a journalist and all. I never graduated from high school, but I'm working on my GED for when I get out of here.

Because believe me, Alex. One of these days, I will get out of here.

Sincerely,
Eric

P.S. I just wondered if you would have any interest in giving a little money to my prisoner's account. It's just for little things, toothpaste, Doritos, stuff like that. No problem if you can't. Just thought I'd ask!
P.P.S. They take Venmo.

CHAPTER SEVEN

NOW

We sit on the freezing cement hearth.

"I'm not sure the heat's even working," I say, rubbing my stiff, cold hands by the starter-fire. The flames lick up strands of an old newspaper we found, strategically placed by Melody between the logs.

Lainey holds out her palms to the fire as well. "I guess you get what you pay for."

For a minute, I think of what Jay could have paid for a swanky hotel with a Methuselah of rose-gold champagne, and probably Beyoncé coming by to personally sing a few songs. But then again, that isn't the point. Bonding with my friends is the point. And I love them for their morbid choice of accommodation. Even if it is below freezing in here.

Gazing ahead at the wall, I once again picture the numbers crudely drawn in blood.

666.

"That's where the numbers were," I tell them, sitting on my hands to warm them.

"What numbers?" Melody asks.

"The 666. He wrote them in blood. From . . . the victim. Nicole White."

A pause follows this morbid observation.

"I thought you said her name was Leigh Jones," Lainey says.

I'm both touched and surprised that that she's actually been listening to my ramblings.

"No, he *tried* to kill Leigh Jones, but she fought him off." I don't mention that the police suspect him of killing two more who went missing around that time, Angela Adams and Amelia Atwood, the so-called *A*-girls, the alliterative pair becoming a footnote in the story.

"Well, on that cheerful note," Melody says.

"Who's hungry?" Lainey asks, interrupting my thoughts.

I'm guessing the answer is Lainey, since she's always hungry. My ever-suggestible stomach growls though, reminding me I've only had coffee today. I check my phone. Nine o'clock.

"Didn't you bring the cookies?" Melody asks her.

"Yeah," Laine says. "I sort of might have eaten those already."

Melody pops up to a stand. "Never you worry. I brought provisions aplenty. I have a cheese and cracker tray in the trunk."

Lainey does not appear consoled. "Let me guess, vegan cheese."

"Of course."

"And the crackers . . . are gluten free."

Melody looks offended. "You know I have gluten issues."

My stomach growls again as smoke slithers between the logs.

"I got beer and chips in the car?" I suggest.

By now, the fire is humming along, if not roaring.

It hearkens me back to my childhood home, the rough wedge of wood on my fingers, heat suffusing the air, the scent of burning logs. I remember our cozy family room, lit up orange inside, buffered against the blackness outside, the frigid Vermont nights. This was before the divorce, when things were still cozy, when we could still afford the old, drafty house.

Now, we all lie on top of our sleeping bags on the sheepskin rug, passing around chips and sipping beer. Pine trees sway in the distance as wind pummels the windows. Jay's borrowed sleeping bag smells faintly of mildew.

"So, what should we do?" I ask. A log pops in the fire. "Anything good on Prime?"

"Wi-Fi's not working," Melody reminds me.

"Oh, right. And no signal." I tried calling Jay three times, but nothing went through. I froze my ass off on the porch trying to get some coverage.

"Charades?" Melody asks, in all sincerity.

We both give her a look.

"Fine, fine." She sits up on the sleeping bag with a grunt and starts knee-walking over to the cabinet. "So, let's see," she says, opening the door with a squeak. "Okay, folks. We got Life, Trivial Pursuit, Monopoly." She rifles around some boxes. "Yahtzee."

"Or . . ." Lainey says, pulling something out of her overnight bag. "We could have a little White Widow party." She holds up a bag, displaying three nicely rolled joints.

"White Widow." Melody scrunches her nose. "They didn't have Maui Wowie?"

"Jesus Christ," Lainey says, with a huff. "Do I look like a fucking dispensary?"

"Okay, fine. Whatever. It's better than this beer," Melody grumbles, taking a last sip. She grabs a blunt and hands me the other. "White Widow makes me itchy though."

Lainey puts her joint into the fire to light it, then inhales.

The unmistakable skunky smell flutters through the room as Melody lights hers up too. "Don't you get tested?" she asks Lainey, which I was wondering about as well.

"In six months," Lainey says, holding in her breath.

Melody nods and takes a hit, but I sit there, still holding my joint in a pincer grip. I think about what I read on my research. "They say THC might make it worse," I say, staring at the fire.

"Make what worse?" Lainey asks, waving smoke away from her face.

"The dreams."

This is met by silence. Melody takes a thoughtful drag, but neither of them speaks.

They both know about my sleep problem, acting out my dreams. The first time it happened, I dreamed I was running away from Chris, and leaped off the bed and into the nightstand, busting my lip. The next time, it was Eric Myers lunging at me and stabbing me. I punched him as hard as I could. But it was actually Jay I punched. He jokingly called me a husband-beater, and I started sleeping in the office. I felt guilty every time I looked at his black eye.

I hadn't done it for a while until recently. Eric Myers appeared again on my bed, so real I could feel the weight of his body, the outline of his leg, against mine.

My punch left four knuckle-sized dents in the wall.

"Do you know why it's happening?" Melody asks, her voice husky from smoke. "Just like stress or something?"

"Probably," I say. But I'm not telling the whole truth.

"I'm sure it'll be fine," Lainey says, exhaling after holding a lungful of smoke.

"Yeah, I'm sure," Melody agrees. She's usually good at acting, but she sounds a little nervous to me. Turning, she swishes against my sleeping bag. "You don't have to smoke, you know. No peer pressure. We'll still be your friends," she jokes.

"Yeah, I know," I say, with a forced laugh. I dip my joint in the fire to light it too, then take a sweet puff, the paper warm between my fingers.

What the hell, it's my bachelorette party.

CHAPTER EIGHT

JUNE

"Anything new with your Doritos serial killer?" Wiley asks.

"Nah," I say. Though I did Venmo him some money. I figured five dollars here or there would be well worth it to keep him talking. But I haven't uncovered anything new. I've scoured the Armchair Sleuths, a true crime chat room, for any leads on the 666 Killer and find the thread disappointingly quiescent. My brief Twitter survey was dead on arrival as well.

Everyone seems to agree that Eric Myers did it. End of story.

"How about yours?" I ask, drinking from my water bottle. "What did they call him . . . the Monogram Killer or something?"

"Yeah. He liked to carve his initials in his victim's skin." They click on their mouse. "Postmortem, at least."

"Nice," I say. "Devious and yet self-incriminating."

"Yeah. Not the sharpest psychopath in the toolbox."

My phone pings with a text, and I check to see it's from Lainey.

"Wedding stuff?" Wiley can't get enough wedding talk, the opposite of literally anyone else I know.

"Yeah, looking at dresses for Lainey," I say, typing in the address of the place.

Wiley raises an eyebrow. "Lainey's wearing a dress?"

"No," I say. "Not exactly. She's wearing a suit in the same lavender of the dress that Melody is wearing." I pause. "If that makes any sense." She and Melody are my maids of honor, though Lainey bristled at being called a maid of anything. So, of course, Melody referred to her as a maid-a-milking for a full day.

"Ooh," Wiley says. "I have to take that down. I can see a suit in periwinkle for my maid of honor." Wiley is also planning two maids of honor, one for them and one for their fiancée, Josie. It's confusing.

Getting nowhere with the research, I consider plunging into the 666 podcasts again. But I can't take listening to any more right now, some of which barely deserve the podcast moniker, consisting of two people saying "um" a million times and apologizing for their dog barking, which descends into a discussion about their unfortunate bowel habits (the dog's) requiring a low-protein diet. I'm about to hit the break room for a coffee when I spot the usual delivery guy heading our way. He's holding a dozen red roses. "Alex Conley?" he asks, looking at Wiley (who could pass for an Alex).

"That's me," I answer, standing up to sign for the delivery. The velvety smell rises from the bouquet. Smiling, I flip open the card, wondering if Jay sent them. He does this occasionally, just out of the blue.

Reading the card, my smile disappears.

"Jay?" Wiley asks.

I shake my head, showing him the card.

Wiley's eyes open wide. "What the actual—"

"I know," I say. Because the card has no words and no signature.

Just three numbers in black, standing out against the blank white card stock.

666.

"I'll keep digging," Juanita says, as we walk up the stairs with Toby.

Juanita serves as *Crimeline*'s main private investigator. Handling threatening letters for lowly interns falls well below her pay grade. But I helped her niece on her college essay (which didn't really need any help) and she got into Brown (which had nothing to do with me), so now Juanita basically loves me.

"But I don't get it," I say, embarrassingly short of breath as we climb another floor. It's pathetic. I've only gotten to the third floor, and still have two more to my office on the fifth. At a solid two hundred pounds, Juanita hasn't broken a sweat. She works on the tenth floor and doesn't like elevators.

"Probably just a troll," Toby says, with an unimpressed shrug, her collarbones rising. She's junior-sized small and wears oversized clothes and high heels to hide this, which only accentuates it, making her look like she's playing dress-up. Toby brings to mind Minnie Mouse, but with long red hair and freckles. She also happens to be a marathon runner and can climb ten flights no problem.

"I suppose it could be a troll," I say, trying to hide my wheezing. I did the basic investigatory grunt work, calling the flower delivery service, but the sender apparently used a PayPal account connected to a burner cell number and a fake name. "Who knows I'm doing this profile?" I ask, clinging to the handrail. "I mean, no one from *Crimeline* is gonna send this. My fiancé's not going to send this."

Toby and Juanita slow down their pace for me. "So, you're telling me you haven't done any internet research?" Toby asks, with an eyebrow raised.

"I guess I have hit Twitter, Facebook, and a couple crime chat rooms." I think for a second. "So basically anyone could have sent this."

Toby gives me a patronizing smile. "As I said, a troll."

"But we'll follow it up," Juanita says, perhaps just to pacify me.

Finally, we reach my floor. I'm envisioning opening the door and just dropping straight onto the carpet. "This is me," I say.

"Me as well," Toby says, shooting past me.

"Let me know if you get anything else," Juanita says, her voice trailing up the stairs. "Hopefully it's a one-off."

CHAPTER NINE

NOW

F ueled by White Widow, the evening flies by.
We sit in a loose semicircle facing the hearth as if
around a campfire, mesmerized by the flames. Hot air flickers
against my face.

"Alex?" Melody asks, still looking into the fire.

"What?" I pluck a piece of fuzz off Jay's sleeping bag.

"We just had one question for you." She chews on her lip,
looking oddly, uncharacteristically nervous.

"Okay . . ." I say, drawing out the word.

A piece of a log crumbles onto the grate and sizzles.

"It's just . . ." Melody turns to me, her eyebrows furrowed.
"You're sure about this, right? Absolutely sure? No doubts
whatsoever?"

Lainey watches me too, in rapt attention. I have a feeling
they've been waiting a while to ask me this. Like this might

have been the "spring the question on Alex" part of the night, or even the whole reason for the night. The idea irks me.

"Yes. I'm sure," I say, maybe too brusquely. Then I pause. "Why, are you trying to tell me something?" I think back to my first college boyfriend, Tariq, who Lainey saw cheating on me.

"No, no," Melody says. "Nothing like that." The fire crackles, and she puffs her pillow up. "It's just . . . it was so fast. After Chris and everything."

"Yeah," I say. "I suppose so." I know where they're coming from. My mom has interrogated me over it too, thinking I'm just jumping into a rebound.

Almost unconsciously, I stretch out my hand. The diamond catches the light of the fire, glittering. The stone juts out, maybe a little *too* big, if I'm honest. But I am definitely sure.

"Yes, I love him. I put my engaged hand back in my sleeping bag. "I promise you. No doubt whatsoever."

"Okay." Melody exhales, as if the question were weighing on her. "That's all we wanted to know." But Lainey still watches me, wary.

"Oh my God!" Melody shrieks, out of nowhere.

"What?" I jump up, looking around for Eric Myers. Then I realize this makes no sense. The White Widow must have hit me pretty good.

"We almost forgot about the cupcakes," Melody says, gasping like this was the worst oversight ever. The White Widow must have hit her pretty good too. She leaps up and jogs to the kitchen while Lainey unzips her gym duffle. As Melody returns with a plate of cupcakes, Lainey pulls out a gift and hands it to me.

I hold what appears to be a hardcover book, ripping off the satiny red wrapping paper to reveal the title. *The Real 6-6-6 Killer.* Flipping through the book, I focus on the thick photo section in the middle, the smell of new paper rising up from the pages.

"I didn't even know about this one."

"Yeah," Lainey says, biting back her smile at my reaction. "It's out of print."

"Oh," I say, cooing. "That's so thoughtful, you guys." I lean over to give them kisses, hitting Melody's neck and Lainey's ear.

"Ugh," Lainey says, wiping it off. "You gave me a wet willy."

"You loved it."

"Girl," Lainey says. "You are so not my type."

"Cupcake time," Melody sings out. "Made by *moi.* Vegan and gluten free, of course." She grabs one, licking blue frosting off her fingers. Two more cupcakes sit on the plate, one blue and one red. "You get the red one since it's your favorite color."

"Aw. You guys rock so hard." I hold up the cupcake, admiring the puffy, pompadour-shaped red frosting. Then we're quiet, wolfing down our cupcakes. "Thanks, you guys," I murmur, swallowing. "This is really good."

"Mmph-mmph," Lainey says, nodding while chewing. "Not bad."

Melody starts laughing then, pointing at me.

"What?" I wipe crumbs off my lips.

"Your teeth are red," she says. "You look like a vampire." Her shoulders shake with laughter, the vision surely funnier with some White Widow on board.

"And you look like you've been fellating a Smurf," I say, pointing back at her.

"Anatomically implausible," Melody says, then pulls her phone out of her pocket. "Selfie," she announces, and Lainey and I lean into her, baring our red and blue teeth. The flash lights up our faces. Half blinded, I finish off the cupcake.

After we're done, Melody starts yawning. "I'm hitting the hay, you guys."

"Yeah," Lainey says, pulling her extra-long-but-still-too-short sleeping bag up. "Me too."

Grabbing my phone, I consider trying to call Jay one last time. But then I realize it's already eleven o'clock. He'd usually be up, but sometimes he goes to bed early when Greg's over, and it probably wouldn't get through anyway. I put the phone back down.

After a while, Melody turns in her sleeping bag. "Happy bachelorette party," she mumbles, the words slurring into sleep. Lainey has already fallen quiet, her eyes fluttering shut.

My eyes remain resolutely open. I'm afraid to fall asleep.

Because I don't want to dream.

I don't want to hurt them.

CHAPTER TEN

DID HE DO IT? PODCAST: EPISODE #187, THE 666 KILLER

Shardai: Come on, Trayvon. This one's just too obvious.

Trayvon: No, no. That's why I picked it out. It's *not* so obvious.

Shardai: Other than the fact that he wrote it on—

Trayvon: Hold up. Hold up. We'll get to that later. Let's tackle the witness statement first. You can pretty much throw out the EFIT picture thing, right? I mean, the guy had a balaclava on, right?

Shardai: Yes, I'll agree that's a problem.

Trayvon: And you would also agree that visual identification is problematic in and of itself, especially in traumatic situations.

Shardai: Sometimes, yes. I would agree on that too.

Trayvon: But there's another problem that no one's really pointed out. (Pause.) Race.

Shardai: What about race?

Trayvon: Leigh Jones is Black.

Shardai: Um . . . that's not news, Tray.

Trayvon: Yeah, I know. I know. But the point is, we all know White people are crap at identifying Black people. And vice versa. Cross-racial identification has loads of problems. That's been well validated, right?

Shardai: Yes, I suppose that's true.

Trayvon: You suppose? Come on now. We've had more than one show where the victim ended up being just plain wrong, have we not? And it cost someone his life. Usually a Black person. Some of them executed, in fact.

Shardai: Sadly, yes. We have.
Trayvon: I'm just saying. Maybe it happened in this case too. To Eric Myers.

Shardai: Yeah, but wait a second, here. We're not just talking about facial recognition, Tray. We're talking about something much more obvious than that.

Trayvon: But that's the thing. How valid is that either? I mean, Leigh Jones was in shock. It's not her fault. I'm not trying to blame the victim or anything. I'm not saying she's *trying* to lie.

Shardai: No, I get that. But how could she have gotten something like that wrong? I mean, she might have been in shock. She might be bad at identifying White folks.

Trayvon: Yeah, yeah. I know what you're saying.

Shardai: But this piece of evidence is rather distinctive.

Trayvon: True. It is. (Pauses, then laughs.) Aren't you going to tell them what it is?

Shardai: Oh, Tray. You know we have to have a cliff-hanger for the next episode, don't you?

Trayvon: Indeed, we do.

Shardai: Check us out next week, when we'll talk about the key piece of evidence that Leigh Jones brought to the police.

CHAPTER ELEVEN

NOW

Fighting to stay awake, my brain skates in circles.

My dream problem has a name per Dr. Google: REM Behavior Disorder.

It turns out you're supposed to be paralyzed when you dream, which makes evolutionary sense. Lying down like prey for a third of our lives seems foolish enough. But jumping out of a window while dreaming of skydiving takes it a step further.

Dr. Google blames my Zoloft, which I coincidentally started when the dreams did. First, I had to get the restraining order against Chris. Then Toby wanted to discuss why I seemed "distracted" lately, forcing me to explain my teeny, little concern about getting murdered by my ex and ending up on our show. (A *Crimeline* intern on *Crimeline*? That pitch would definitely fly.) Then came friction over the wedding with Jay, my mom worrying, his ex-wife sniping, and his son as solemn as a funeral. Suffice it to say, I got a lot of shit going on. If I tell my doctor about the dreams, she'll take me off the Zoloft. And I really need it right now.

The fire crackles, and I stare up at a crack in the ceiling, trying to stay awake.

The crack goes blurry, then double, and I blink my eyes again to straighten it.

My so-called "dream enactment" has been fairly standard fare thus far. I've researched much worse cases. In fact, *Crimeline* covered one case where a man drove to his in-laws' house in his sleep and bludgeoned them to death. He got off, as it actually *was* due to sleepwalking. (Supposedly.)

So far, I haven't done anything too dangerous in my sleep, but I've come close. I once grabbed a pair of scissors, which means I opened the drawer with no recollection. Luckily, we don't have any guns in there. I woke up with feathers wafting around me, and realized I'd stabbed my pillow. Shamefully, I threw away the scissors and the pillow, as if they were to blame somehow. From then on, I slept in the guest room, with wind chimes on the door handle to alert me (and Jay) to any wandering. We even hid the car keys, just in case.

The crack in the ceiling doubles again, and I blink my eyes and pinch my thigh, hard. The crack straightens, then slithers on the ceiling, twisting into an S-shape as I start drifting off.

Sitting up abruptly, I decide maybe reading would help keep me awake.

I grab the book, leaf through the photos, and land on one of Noah Thompson. He was a friend of Nicole White, and one of the key witnesses in the trial. One picture shows Noah in the courtroom, looking nervous in an ill-fitting suit.

His eyes are striking, even in black and white. I remember them from the trial photos, a root-beer–hazel color, with flecks of gold in them. I flip to another more casual photo of him in his bedroom, shy but smiling with the usual boyhood accoutrements: cans of Mountain Dew, car posters, a video game console, and his wall stenciled with an outgrown sports theme, a row of soccer balls, footballs, and baseballs. I try to read through the captions, but my lids keep closing, as if drawn closed by weighted pulleys.

I try to hold them open but must have failed.

Because I startle, with a vision of Lainey, blood coming from her mouth like a vampire. My hands clench, ready to fight her, but I wake up before I can even take a swing.

Glancing over, I see my book on the ground, and Lainey lightly snoring, without blood-dripping fangs. I notice the screen of my phone lit up, and I'm shocked to see it's not even eleven thirty. It felt like I was asleep for hours. Then I see the text, which must have woken me up in the first place. I don't know how it's possible since we have no coverage. But maybe we had signal just long enough for a text to slip through.

Have a nice bachelorette party, it says.

I hope you fucking die.

CHAPTER TWELVE

JUNE

"Thanks for seeing me," Eric Myers says, sounding almost bashful.

Butterflies float in my stomach as I adjust my computer screen. The prison finally gave us the approval for the interview. "Thank *you* for seeing *me*," I say, hearing the nerves in my voice. It feels weirdly like a first date. But if so, it's a cheap one, as *Crimeline* will only pay for a virtual date.

I'm home on my hybrid day, and he's obviously in prison.

The guard, a beefy guy with enormous veined biceps and a shaved head, leans against the wall with a bored expression. Eric clears his throat.

Eric Myers has aged from the trial photos, where he had certain cocky swagger, good-looking in a Jim Morrison way, with wavy brown hair and a wild animal energy, his body rangy with muscles. Now, his muscles appear gym-bought, his hair an institutional brush cut, brown mixed with gray,

and wrinkles fanning around his eyes from too many cigarettes. I can almost smell them over the screen. In other
words, the years have not treated him well.

My mind runs through possible starting lines. How was
breakfast? (Inedible.) Have you had any visitors lately? (I
know the answer is no.) Beautiful outside today, isn't it? (He
doesn't have a window.) The usual rules of small talk do
not apply in prison. In the awkward silence, "I can hear the
washer shifting gears, and the whine of the dryer from the
mudroom.

"You say you're innocent," I say, deciding to plunge right in.

"That's because I *am* innocent."

I don't respond, allowing him to fill the silence, and he
watches me, perhaps doing the same. I'm not sure if this is
more of a first date or a chess match. I double-check the red
recording button, and watch the timer count out ten long
seconds of silence.

"I know it doesn't look that way," he says, breaking first.
"But everything they have against me is circumstantial.
Everything."

A scramble of footsteps sounds out behind him, a man
yelling, a tirade of fury and expletives. We both wait for him
to pass, the guard barely glancing up. The outburst jars me yet
doesn't seem to affect Eric Myers. Just another day at the office.

"I talked about the problems with the picture they used
to identify me in the email, right?" he asks. He pushes his
orange sleeves over his elbows.

"Yes," I say, "we did."

My eyes are green. I'm not that tall. Blah, blah, blah.

"I feel bad for Leigh Jones and all. I really do." He shakes his head, with a mixture of disbelief and frustration. "But, come on, the guy was wearing a balaclava." He throws up his hands, emphasizing the point. "A balaclava!"

The washer in the mudroom bangs as the machine rocks, the drum off balance with sheets twisting around it. "She did see something else though, right?"

His expression hardens then, his gaze dropping to the table.

"I think before we go much further, we have to talk about it," I say, gently. The washer thuds now, shimmying like it might pull away from the wall. "The elephant in the room, so to speak."

Eric licks his lips, then takes a hard swallow. "I thought you were here to help me," he says, his tone plaintive, soaked in self-pity. "To tell everyone what really happened."

"Not exactly," I push back, lightly. "I'm here to do a profile on the ten-year anniversary of the killing. But I'll go where the facts lead me." The washer hums now, madly spinning. "And hopefully, you can help me with that," I add, as an olive branch. I muse at the tightrope act, trying to befriend Eric Myers without being manipulated by him. Fletcher Fox is better than I give him credit for.

The dryer in the mudroom lets out three beeps, followed by the sudden silence as it stops. A crystal-clear meow emerges from the kitchen.

We both look toward the sound.

"What's that?" he asks, peering at the screen, as if trying to see around the corner. "A cat?"

I'm about to lie when she meows again. "Um, yeah," I say. I have to remember to put her in the bedroom next time. I don't like him knowing anything more about me than absolutely necessary.

"What kind?" he asks, conversationally.

"Oh. Um. A torty," I say.

He nods, smiling. "What's her name?"

"Her name is . . . Whiskers," I say, my face flushing. I'm sure he knows I'm lying. I'm stupid enough to have several Babushka-themed passwords, but not stupid enough to tell him the name.

"I used to have a cat," he says, half smiling at the memory. "Named Marty." Then his face darkens. "Some kids in the neighborhood killed him though."

I shiver, and can't help but wonder if Eric Myers killed the cat and projected the act onto others. This would be classic sociopathic behavior, a little practice before moving onto more advanced mammals. "That's awful."

"Yeah, it was." He nods in agreement, twiddling his thumbs. "Some people are just evil like that." He stiffens then, seeming to realize this term could apply to him. "I'm not like that though." He shakes his head. "I could never hurt someone like that."

"Yes, I'm sure." I would love to coddle him, to draw him out of his cocoon before pummeling him with the first obvious question. But Toby laid down the law. I have six months to decide if he's truly guilty or not.

"Let's talk about the tattoo," I say.

CHAPTER THIRTEEN

NOW

I can't open my eyes.

My knees ache, cold and wet.

Wake up, I yell at myself.

I try to move my fingers, but they barely twitch. Numb. My eyes cannot open—glued, stitched shut. I try to yell through dry, cracked lips, making only a weak, scratchy sound. My eyes stay closed. But I'm not fighting or running. I'm not punching. Just paralyzed, frozen.

Wake up. You are dreaming. Wake up.

Open your eyes.

WAKE UP.

Slowly . . . they open.

I gaze around, disoriented. Automatically, I reach out for Babushka, looking for Jay, but then realize I'm not in my bed, not in our apartment.

Then it all comes back to me.

The party, the hunting lodge. 666 on the wall.

White Widow.

But I'm not in my sleeping bag either, not in the family room even. There is no fire. No Lainey or Melody. Lying on a cold, hard floor, I can barely see anything. I touch chipped tile, a drain. As my eyes acclimate to the darkness, I can see the outline of . . . a yellow duck.

A yellow duck?

Reaching out, I push away the plastic curtain as the realization crawls too slowly into my head. I'm in the shower.

The familiarity of this provides some measure of relief. I must have sleepwalked into the bedroom. Slowly, I sit up, my head dizzying. Every muscle feels worn down, exhausted. But then a memory whips through my brain, unfolding in stuttering frames.

Whispering, screaming. A flash of a knife.

I squeeze my eyes closed, and open them again. It must be the White Widow playing tricks with my mind. I try to stand up, my hand on the freezing porcelain. My thighs burn with the effort. I stagger one step out of the shower, nearly slipping on my wet fuzzy socks as more memories insert themselves.

Screaming, running.

Am I dreaming? Is it possible that I'm still dreaming, but with my eyes wide open?

But no, I am not. I am in the dreary bedroom. In the window, the moon slips out behind a cloud, lighting the room gray. The bed sits untouched. Subconsciously, I pat my pockets for my phone, then realize I'm in my pajamas. My hands feel sticky, maybe from the shower. Wiping them on my pajamas, I walk toward the window and stand there in a daze.

The wind howls, banging against the glass. Black-green trees shiver outside. A blistering white moon shines a perfect circle in the sky, the icy tree branches glistening in the light, eerie and beautiful.

I open and close my hands, stiff and numb, caked in dried sweat.

That's when I see it.

Bewildered, I look closer. For a confused second, I think they are not mine. They must be someone else's hands. But with horror, I realize they are my hands. They are attached to my wrists. My wrists attached to my arms. My arms attached to my body. Me.

Yes, they must be my hands. And I have dipped them in something. In the brash moonlight, I can see it. Not from the shower, not sweat.

My hands are covered in blood.

CHAPTER FOURTEEN

JUNE

E ric Myers rubs his hand over the ink as if trying to erase it.

But obviously he can't. He can't hide the blue tattoo on his wrist. The numbers have grown fuzzy and blurred with age but remain unmistakable.

666.

The same numbers written on the wall. The same numbers Leigh Jones described to the detectives, the tattoo revealing itself as his sleeve slipped up off his wrist. The same numbers that maybe Nicole White saw in her final minutes on this earth. The numbers that gave him the catchy serial killer moniker, beloved by *Crimeline* shows.

The 666 Killer.

He hangs his head. "That's when everyone stops listening, when they hear about the tattoo," he says. He tents his hands on his lips a moment, then looks up at me, desperation shining in his eyes. "But here's the thing. That's all they have, right? This one little thing. That's all. Nothing else sticks."

I tap my foot on the kitchen tile. "How do you explain it though?" I ask. "That Leigh Jones was attacked in the exact same way as Nicole White, with those numbers written on the wall. And that Leigh Jones saw your tattoo?"

He stares down at table, tracing a hieroglyphic with his finger on the surface. "I can't explain it. That's the problem." His blue eyes loom over the screen. "But it doesn't change the fact. I still didn't do it."

Something in his eyes (blue, not green) gives me pause, makes me want to believe him.

The evidence couldn't be any more obvious. But part of me wonders if it's almost *too* obvious. Then again, maybe he's just convincing. Sociopaths often are.

He raps his fingers on the table. "I have some theories on it. Not that you'd believe them."

I move closer to the screen. In truth, I would love to believe him. I would love a theory that makes sense, that would get Toby to reinvestigate the case for the show. "Try me," I say.

"Okay, well." He crosses his arms, leaning back in his chair. "Number one is this. Maybe Leigh Jones is lying for some reason. She got someone to attack her, just so she could blame me for it."

I stifle an incredulous laugh. "You're saying she got herself scarred for life and nearly killed just to mess with you?"

She met him briefly at a party per the court files. But she didn't really know him and didn't recognize him during the attack. She would have no reason to pretend he did this to get back at him.

The guard at the wall moves, jangling his keys.

"Or," Eric says, putting both palms on the table. "She was attacked as she says, but someone *else* had the tattoo, and then they left town."

"Uh-huh," I say at this equally ridiculous theory.

Checking my expression, Eric Myers registers my skepticism and moves on. "But what makes most sense, in my opinion, is theory number three. That someone framed me. They just drew the numbers on their wrist before attacking her."

Of any of the theories, this seems the most plausible, but still doesn't make a whole lot of sense. "Why though?" I ask. "Why would they do that?"

"I don't know," he mutters, with a pronounced shrug. "Someone with a grudge against me. I don't know why that would be. But it's possible, right?"

The clock ticks on the wall of the kitchen as I think this through. "She described the tattoo perfectly though," I argue. "Every little detail. That would have been quite a feat to copy."

Leigh Jones had focused on the tattoo during the attack with an almost photographic memory. She drew it out for the detectives, including a pale line at the wrist crease, where the ink had faded, and little nubs at the top of each numeral. The imposter would have to have copied these exact details.

"What made you get it in the first place?" I ask, with genuine curiosity. "Does it have any specific meaning for you?"

He lets out a sardonic laugh. "Do *you* have any tattoos?" he asks, turning the question around.

I notice the guard listening now, with a prurient interest. It's none of their business, but I don't see any harm in responding.

"Yes," I say but don't elaborate. I got my tattoo freshman year. We all did, Lainey and Melody and me, bright orange-red-yellow sunbursts on our ankles. Chris used to trace his fingers over mine, sending almost painful shock waves of desire through me. Jay calls it my youthful indiscretion. He doesn't have any tattoos.

"Does it have any specific meaning for you?" he asks, his intonation mocking the words.

I don't answer.

"Yeah, me neither," he says, the words resigned now instead of angry. "I was seventeen, and I thought it looked cool. That's it." He lets out a long sigh. "I just thought it looked cool."

I consider the tattoo on my ankle, etched one drunken night with my friends. It has no deep meaning. But my tattoo connects friends in a sunburst of energy and light. His connects him to evil, and more directly, to a crime.

It's not the same. He shakes his head in dejection. "I understand, the tattoo looks bad. But that's it. That's all they have. Nothing else. No DNA or anything. Not even one hair." He looks up at me. "Think about it. If I stabbed her like that, over and over and over." He balls a hand into a fist, smacking it into his other open hand. The 666 tattoo blurs in the movement. "Again and again and again and again," he says, each slap echoing in the room. The guard throws him a look, and he stops, unclenching his hand. "I would have been cut. There's no way I would have gotten by without a scrape. It's practically hand-to-hand combat. Blood is slippery, right? I would have cut myself at some point," he argues. "They'd find my blood on her. They'd find my sweat on her. They'd find something." His volume elevates with each claim.

The smacking sound rings in my ears.

For a man claiming innocence, he seems to have an intimate knowledge of the experience of the crime, down to the slickness of the blood on the knife.

"The tattoo guy said I shouldn't do it," he says, with a grimace. "That I'd be marking myself, inviting the devil in. 'Hell is hot,' he said, 'and you'll get burned.' I thought it was some voodoo shit. But he was right."

He looks straight into the computer camera. "Hell is hot. And I got burned."

CHAPTER FIFTEEN

NOW

I run into the family room to see the fire, the flue sucking up the smoke.

The room remains silent, other than the grandfather clock ticking monstrously loud. It takes me a second to realize what is wrong with the silence. I should hear something, mumbling or soft snores. Shuffling in sleeping bags. Sounds of life. But I don't.

I take another step in and reach along the wall to find the light socket. As I flip the switch, light flickers over the scene.

And my breath goes out.

Blood stains the sheepskin rug in calligraphy loops. My friends' puffy sleeping bags appear sloughed off, like molted skins, while mine lies pristine and flat. I kneel down on the rug on my sodden, freezing knees. Blood polka-dots the pillow, like some decorative tribal design. Shaking Melody's sleeping bag, I can smell her rose perfume.

"Lainey," I call out. "Melody." My voice trembles with fear and cold. The memory of that old *Crimeline* episode worms into my head. The man driving across town and bludgeoning his in-laws, and waking up covered in blood, his memory blank.

Did I do this? Please God, no. Say I didn't do this.

"Melody?" I whisper. "Lainey?"

No one answers my call. But then, a creak sounds from the basement.

I hold my breath, straining to hear another sound. I stand there waiting out long seconds, but silence remains. Maybe the killer is down there. Or maybe Lainey and Melody are lying down there, hurt and bleeding. I pull closer and put my ear against the cold wooden door.

Silence.

I don't want to go down there. Every fiber of my body screams at me not to go down there. But I can't abandon my friends, especially if I'm responsible. They could be bleeding out, waiting for me to save them.

Quietly, I open the door.

My eyes blink in shock. A grisly trail of blood leads down the stairs.

So they've been down there, or still are. A flash of me chasing them into the basement plays over my eyes. I blink again. No, that's impossible. I'm just imagining things.

Following the trail like a bloodhound, I tiptoe down each stair. With each step, the room darkens, the light above fading away. My breath comes in spurts. I cringe at every moan from the warped wooden steps. My hand grips the rough railing, my ear tilted down to catch any sound. But I hear only my own breathing and my own heartbeat swishing in my ears. "Lainey," I whisper. "Melody."

Finally, I land on the cement floor. The cold room smells of dust and starchy mildew. I venture into the room taking small, light steps, allowing my eyes to adjust to the total darkness. Every few steps, I pause to listen.

But I hear nothing. Cavernous silence.

Blindly, I keep walking until I come to a block window. A swath of moonlight cuts across the floor, revealing a pool of dark water, or maybe oil. As I take another step, a light web brushes against my cheek, making me jump back. Reaching to brush it off, my finger grazes a loop, and I realize it's a string, not a spider web. I loop my finger through the hangman's noose of the drawstring and pull. One click, and the room is doused with gray light.

The puddle lights up, and I step back in horror. Bright red. Not water or oil.

Blood.

Footprints surround the dark puddle. Bits of *Crimeline* true crime shows float through my mind, the ominous voice-over: *The luminol revealed a size eleven men's boot, the same size as her husband's foot.* But these are not man-sized. Three sets of footprints surround the pool of blood, one small and wide, one long and lean, and one that looks smudged and smeared.

Without thinking, I am searching for bigger shoes, for Chris's huge basketball sneaker prints, for the star in the middle of the rundown Chuck Taylors he always wears. I don't see any. But I do notice another amorphous, furry print, smudged and spindly. With a sense of dread, I put my foot over it. The print made by a fuzzy sock.

Mine.

So I must have been down here. And it strikes me what I don't see. Scattered footprints, but no *shoe* prints. So if someone else was down here, I don't see his mark. The faint memory whispers through my mind, like an audio track playing, clomping down the stairs, crying, shrieking.

Then I see it.

On the floor lies a long knife with bloody prints all over the handle. Is it the kitchen knife? I picture it in the drawer, when I was looking for matches. I knew where that knife was, no one else did.

Suddenly, I feel the knife in my hand, gripping the handle, swinging. The memory feels dream-like, inserted maybe. One frame on a flickering reel. My arm rising and falling, the oak handle solid and warm in my hand.

Was I fighting someone? Please, God. I must have been fighting someone, whoever attacked us. I must have been fighting him.

I peer in closer to look but don't pick it up. I'm not that stupid. If I did this, my prints will be on there anyway. If not, I do not want to mess up a crime scene or implicate myself.

Then I notice something next to the knife. A little pink puffy blob, like a slug. I move closer to examine it, but my head dizzies. Because I recognize the puffy thing. It's the scrunchie from Lainey's ponytail, with a clump of her bloodied, flaxen hair. My knees tremble uncontrollably.

"Lainey!" I scream, as loud as I can, my voice breaking. "Melody!"

Still screaming, I race up the stairs. But no one hears me.

CHAPTER SIXTEEN

PODCAST:
DID HE OR DIDN'T HE DO IT

Trayvon: Yeah, yeah, yeah. He had the tattoo. But we still have the misidentification problems. Maybe she didn't even *see* a 666 tattoo. Maybe she just imagined it.

Shardai: (Groans.) That is *such* a stretch, Tray.

Trayvon: She had met him at a party, right? So maybe she knew him and was just thinking of him subconsciously when she got attacked.

Shardai: Also a stretch. But okay . . . let's go with your theory for a moment. Let's say Leigh Jones misidentified him *and* his tattoo because he's White or she's in shock or whatever . . . then how do you account for the other witness?

Trayvon: (Pause.) What other witness?

Shardai: The one who saw him around the lodge a few days before Nicole White's murder.

Trayvon: Who? (Pause.) Oh, the farmer's wife?

Shardai: The farmer's wife? Did you really just say that?

Trayvon: (Laughs.)

Shardai: What . . . did she cut off his head with a carving knife?

Trayvon: Okay, okay. (Laughing.)

Shardai: Yeah, Tray. I think we can safely assume the farmer's wife might have an actual identity in her own right. Esther Thompson is her name. The farmer's wife, even though her husband's been dead for some time now. But, yes, he was alive back then. And she saw Eric Myers *loitering* . . . I'll repeat that . . . *loitering* around Hobbes Lodge earlier that day. She said, and I quote, "It looked like he was casing it."

Trayvon: She did. She did say that. But . . . they also mentioned that she had cataracts. So . . .

Shardai: Oh, please Tray. Don't even.

Trayvon: I'm just saying . . .

Shardai: And Esther Thompson is *White*, so it's not a cross-race issue. And we can't claim she's in shock or anything. So . . . now that's *two* witnesses that place Eric Myers at the scene. How you gonna explain that one away, Tray?

I take off my heavy headphones, my ears stinging.

I already tried calling Leigh Jones twice now, obtaining her number too easily off WhatsApp. I left messages announcing myself as a *Crimeline* reporter, which often triggers an immediate call back, but not in this case. And I don't want to cross the fine line between investigation and harassment.

But Shardai gave me another lead.

She's right. It wasn't just Leigh Jones who identified him.

I decide to reach out to the farmer's wife herself, Esther Thompson. I search social media sites for her, but nothing comes up. She's in her eighties, so I figured she might at least be on Facebook to show off her grandkids or decry Democrats or whatever. She's not. But searching Whitepages on the computer, I get a hit on Esther right away. Jotting the number on a Post-it note, I pick up the receiver on my bulky office phone and make the call.

After four rings, Esther Thompson answers.

"Hello?" She sounds short of breath, as if she ran to pick the phone up.

"Hi," I say, shifting in my chair and playing with my lanyard. "My name is Alex Conley. I'm a reporter at *Crimeline* and wondered if I could ask you a couple questions about an old case." *Crimeline* usually pops up on the caller ID, so people trust my identification.

"What old case?" Esther asks, a wobble in her voice.

"Yes. It's about the murder of a young woman named Nicole White, which took place about ten years ago. I understand you were involved in the naming the—"

Click.

The dial tone floods into my ear. I glance at the screen on the office phone to make sure the call wasn't dropped. But it looks like the obvious occurred, she hung up on me.

Undeterred, I call her back.

"Hi," I say, as soon as she picks up. "I'm sorry. I think we got disconnected and—"

"No, we did *not* get disconnected," she says. "I hung up on you. Because you're a despicable person."

The accusation floors me. "I'm sorry . . . did I say something that—"

"Goodbye," she says.

"Wait, wait," I call out, then duck my head down as a few interns look my way. "I'm sorry. I really don't mean to upset you. I'm just reviewing some of the facts and—"

"I'm hanging up now," she announces.

"Wait," I say again, in desperation. "Do . . . do you have Noah's number at least? Can I speak with him?"

A long pause comes over the phone then. When she speaks again, venom pulses through her words. "Don't you dare drag my son back into all that. He's finally put his life back together and you're trying to pull him down again?"

"I'm . . . I'm sorry," I stutter, taken aback. "I really didn't mean to—"

"Don't call back here," she hisses, and hangs up again.

CHAPTER SEVENTEEN

NOW

With trembling hands, I search through the family room for a phone, any of our phones. If we have a signal, I can call 911 even without their passwords. But first I need to find a phone.

I shake out the sleeping bags, sticky and heavy with blood, the room smelling like an abattoir. I comb through the soaked sheepskin rug, then rifle through my book bag, though I know I didn't leave my phone in there. I dump out Lainey's bag, Melody's bag.

No phones.

Then I remember an old, faded yellow landline in the kitchen, attached to one of the cabinets. Running into the room, I pick the receiver up, the mouthpiece sticky and smelly, but no dial tone emerges. I stab at the buttons, flicking the receiver button up and down. It's useless. The phone isn't working.

Pacing around the kitchen, I reason with myself. Okay, so I can't call 911. But what if he comes back? If I stay here, I'll be dead.

But who? Who is *he?* Who could have done this?

Chris?

He did threaten Lainey once. He violated the restraining order multiple times. Somehow, I still don't see it. I fully believe he could shoot me. But I don't think Chris would have hurt my friends.

Who else?

The answer comes from in my head. *You. You could have done this.*

A montage passes before me. Jay's horrified face. Serious-faced police. Miranda rights. Handcuffs. Funerals. My mom hugging me before I'm taken away. My father's disappointed expression.

"No!" I yell. The word reverberates in the silence. I couldn't have done this. Yes, I've grabbed scissors. Yes, I've crept from the family room up to the bedroom without remembering it. But this is something else altogether. I couldn't have stabbed my friends like that and never woken up. If I had done it, they would have woken me up, not run away.

It couldn't have been me. It must have been someone else.

But I feel a flash of it again, the thick knife handle in my palm.

The tactile memory makes me think of something. I walk over to the drawer that held the kitchen knife. My heart rate elevates, and I take a quick breath and jerk it open.

Empty.

"No, no, no," I say, in a panic. I slap my forehead to wake myself up. But I can't wake myself up. Because I'm awake, just living in a nightmare. "You couldn't have done this," I murmur, like an incantation. "You couldn't have done this."

What if the White Widow pushed me over the edge?

A tree branch slaps against the window, making me jump. *Calm down,* I tell myself. *This isn't helping. Think. Think.*

But I can't think. My brain feels empty as a husk.

I walk over to the fire, which has held up remarkably well. It seems impossible that this could be the same fire we slept by just hours ago. How many hours? I glance around for my phone to see, then remember. No phone. The ticking sound again sounds out, amplified in the silent room. The meaning of this ticking remains somehow cleaved from its source until it lands into my addled brain.

The grandfather clock.

I charge into the front room and turn on the light. The serene scene remains bizarrely unchanged, our coats hung up on the rack along with the *Bougie Bachelorette* crown, hats and mittens strewn haphazardly on the floor.

The brass pendulum reflects a warped image of the hung coats.

Ten after one.

It's only one AM? How is that even possible?

But then the fact of this heartens me. If someone took my friends, the sooner I can find them, the better. Every hour lost decreases the chance they will be found. Alive, at least.

"I need to find them," I say to myself.

I know I sound like a lunatic, but I don't care. I need my own voice to steady me right now. I take a deep, fortifying breath. "You didn't do this. There's no way you did this. So, get ready, and go look for them." I nod to myself. "Okay. We have a plan."

With that, I run to the kitchen to wash off my hands, then I peel off my pajamas and damp fuzzy socks, laying them on the hearth to warm them.

My toes feel numb and stinging, the skin purply blue. The beginning of frostbite? *What if I get frostbite?* "You can't worry about that right now," I answer myself. I throw on dry clothes from last night. I hadn't bothered to pack extra for the ride home. I put on fresh socks with a sense of relief. "Okay," I say, "now how do I get out of here?"

Lainey's car.

If I can just find her keys. I embark on another search around the room. I check everywhere. The kitchen, under the rug, in every pocket of their bags. Between the cushions on the couch, every spot on the hearth, behind the radiator. I even check the bedroom, though we haven't stepped foot in there. I double-check, triple-check. No keys.

A thought flips into my head. *I could hotwire the car.*

Except for the minor fact that I don't know how to hot-wire a fucking car. Then I think maybe I can Google it and remember for the hundredth time, *I don't have a phone.* "Then you will have to walk," I say, reprimanding myself. A log falls and smoke puffs into the air, as if the fire is breathing. "Okay, so what do you need to go out there?"

This is a hunting lodge, after all, which means there might be useful items. I check all the places that I remember from my matches search, like some twisted game of memory. First off, I grab the matches themselves from the hearth, then go back to the drawer with the compass and pick that up too. The glass face is cracked, but the spinner appears to be working at least. The patina of the metal leaves a soft residue on my fingers. Trying to channel Melody's inner Girl Scout, I search through all the other drawers and find a few useful items, a Swiss Army knife, some twine, rubber bands. I dump them in my backpack along with my toothbrush and toothpaste, though clean teeth seems the least of my worries.

"Food," I say. I probably won't need it, but I've seen enough survivor shows to know that if I get lost in the cold somehow, I might. In the kitchen, I scoop up the few cans of soup and toss them into the bag. Another drawer reveals a rusted can opener. Then I fill up my "True Crimes Junkie" water bottle from the tap, ignoring the in-your-face irony of the faded logo. Patting down my backpack, I feel something hard and rectangular in a side pocket, and remember then the Hershey bar in there. I got it from a vending machine at work last week and completely forgot about it. The item seems so innocent, so simple, an artefact from my before-life.

I go back to the family room to check the drawers one more time. Something sticks as I try to open one of them. Feeling in the back of the drawer, I grip the pointy corner of paper and manage to slide it out, revealing a rectangular map.

I open the accordion folds, the paper thin and ripping at the seams. Two regions around the lodge have been circled in red. I'm not sure of their significance, though they seem elevated on the topography. Hunting stands?

Squeezing my eyes closed, I try to visualize the drive up here, wishing I had paid attention instead of joking with Lainey and Melody the whole time. But no landmarks stick in my memory, just wafting snow and black ice roads. Trying to put myself back in that moment, I hear the scratchy sound of the AM radio, the weather alert, Melody's musical laugh, and Lainey arguing with her. Then I remember one more thing: the frozen pond, with someone crossing it.

Maybe that was real, then. Maybe that was more than a shadow.

Or it could have been a damn bear for all I know. In any case, it doesn't help me orient myself. There's the gas station, of course, but that's about ten miles away, if it's even open.

"Then go there," I say. "You need to find help. Call 911."

Or call Jay at least. The thought soothes me. Jay can help me. Of all people, he will have a plan. He always knows what to do.

I'll head for the gas station. Or if not, at least I can get to the street. The thought of the crazy long driveway disheartens me. I smack myself on the forehead again. I can't give up before I have even started. I can do it. Of course I can do it. I just have to make it to the small country road. Not a thoroughfare by any means, but it's a long road. Someone might be driving on it. And I'd get to a main road eventually. I examine the map, trying to locate the biggest road. I'm not good at reading paper maps though, spoiled with Google. I trace a line with my finger, which might be a road. Or maybe a river.

Disgusted with myself, I throw the map in my bag and step in the doorway to grab my hat and mittens, slipping on my boots. Melody and Lainey could be out there somewhere, freezing, bleeding out. And I'm playing with a stupid map.

I know I'm just procrastinating here, delaying the inevitable. Because I really don't want to go out there into the cold. But any idiot knows I have about forty-eight hours here to find them. It's the name of the damn television show. I can't stay here.

And anyway, he could come back. Unless . . .

"No," I tell myself. "That's impossible. I couldn't have done this." Even with the guy who drove off and bludgeoned his in-laws. That was just one crazy case. That's not me.

With my outer gear on, I feel dressed and ready for battle, or for the cold at least.

"Okay," I say, slapping my hands together to ready myself. "Let's go."

CHAPTER EIGHTEEN

JUNE

Twitter
#The666Killer

Wokebro: Come on, dude. Of course he did it.

Alex33: There are discrepancies. That's all I'm saying.

Wokebro: What discrepancies? Seriously.

Alex33: There are issues with the main witness, Leigh Jones. Cross-racial misidentification being one of them.

Daddy-oh: "Cross-racial misidentification being one of them." LOL. Okay, you're the smartest person alive, we get it.

Wokebro: LOLOLOL

Alex33: I've been communicating with him. He makes some valid points. None of his DNA was on the scene. And he was wearing a balaclava, another factor that brings the whole eyewitness testimony into question.

Wokebro: Communicating with him? Why would you be communicating with him? That's not normal.

Alex33: It's called research.

TNT: Nicole White was high off her ass on drugs. Play stupid games. Win stupid prizes.

Alex33: So . . . she deserved to be stabbed to death for getting high?

TNT: Just sayin'. If she didn't do drugs, she would still be here today.

Alex33: Hmm . . . that reasoning seems flawed. There are lots of people who get high and yet nobody murders them.

Wokebro: Yeah. Alex has a point there. The guy is one messed-up individual. I mean, it's one thing to have sex with that Nicole girl when she was a little wasted. But he didn't even do that. Dude fucking stabbed her to death.

Alex33: Well, having sex with her when she was a little wasted would have been RAPE so, I guess it's good he didn't do that at least.

Wokebro: Dude, stop with the virtue signaling.

Daddy-oh: Yeah, who took your balls?

Alex33: I'm a woman. So no one took my balls.

Wokebro: That actually explains a lot.

Alex33: Like what?

TNT: Like why you're such a bitch.

Alex33: Deeply original.

Wokebro: I bet this isn't research at all. I bet you're just pen pals. You're probably one of those sicko weird girls who want to marry the guy.

Alex33: Or just find out the true answer.

Wokebro: Other than the 'oops I tattooed myself with a 666' thing. He CONFESSED. Let me say that again for the slower (Alex) people among us. He confessed.

Alex33: I just don't think it's that simple.

Wokebro: As simple as you are, you mean.

TNT: Maybe you should just marry the guy.

Daddy-oh: Have little psycho babies.

TNT: ROTFLOL.

Wokebro: Alex? Alex?

TNT: I don't think Alex is playing anymore.

Wokebro: Ah, she went home crying because her feelings got hurt.

Daddy-oh: I hate it when girls come on here and then just leave when the going gets tough. If you can't stand the heat, get out of the kitchen.

Daddy-oh: On second thought, she's better off staying in the kitchen.

TNT: Hahaha. LMAO

Jay comes into the apartment, dropping his keys in the dish with a clink.

His entrance surprises me, since it's only 5:00 PM, early for him to come home. Standing there, he lets out a momentous sigh. "I am going to have a drink," he announces.

"What happened?" I ask, closing down my computer at the table. I'm done reading the "Top Ten New York Serial Killers" article anyway. Babushka jumps off my lap.

"Nothing a Tooheys can't fix," he says, grabbing a schooner from the refrigerator. He opens the bottle with his hand, the metal cap skittering on the marble island. "Want one?"

"Nah." I haven't acquired a taste for Australian beer. "But I might just help myself to some merlot." We have some left over from dinner last night. I pull a large wineglass from behind the frosted glass cabinets and give myself a generous pour.

We clink glass to beer bottle and each take a long sip, the rich plum taste coating my tongue.

Jay swallows, wipes his mouth off, and exhales. "That's a start," he says.

"Shit day?" I ask, leaning an elbow on the island. I circle the sharp rim of the wineglass with my finger.

"Shit day," he agrees, taking another long sip. Then he moves closer to me, the smell of starch coming off his shirt. "How about you?" he asks. "Any more creepy letters?"

"Nah, I just got in a war with a bunch of misogynist Twitter bros. So that was fun." Babushka tries to sip the wine, and I give her a little shove.

"Idiots," Jay mutters, after another drink. "I don't know why you even bother with them."

"I'm not *trying* to bother with them," I say, piqued. I smooth my hand on the marble island. "I was just plumbing the mines out there to get information."

"On Twitter? Or X? Or whatever the hell you call it?" He snickers good-naturedly. "More like mining the cesspool."

"Yeah, I suppose you have a point." Babushka licks my knuckle with her sandpaper tongue, then darts in to attempt another taste, which I block. "And what irks me most is that they actually have a point. Eric Myers did confess."

"Wait." Jay makes a face. "He confessed? And you think the guy is innocent?"

"I think that *I don't know.*" I grab *Cabin in the Woods* from the kitchen table, then crack it open to the page with his signed confession, which starts with a simple sentence.

I killed Nicole White.

"You want to hear it?" I ask.

He raps his knuckles on the island. "I'm assuming the correct answer is yes?"

I don't bother to answer the moronic question, just clear my throat and start reading.

I killed Nicole White. I stabbed her multiple times at Hobbes Lodge. We were both high and started kissing, but then she told me that she had a boyfriend and did not want to date me. She laughed at me like it was a big joke and I got angry. I should not have got so mad but I did and then things got out of hand. I grabbed onto her heart necklace and broke it. She got upset and slapped me and that really set me off. There was a knife on the kitchen table and I grabbed it. Then I don't even really remember what happened but I kept stabbing her. When I realized that she died, I got scared and wrote 666 on the wall. I thought someone would think it was some satanic thing and not suspect me. I threw the knife in Cooper's Lake. I threw it really far, but you could try to find it. I admit to killing Nicole White.

I look up at Jay.

"And?" he asks, apparently waiting for more.

"And that's it."

"So, what's the question?" he asks, taking another drink of beer. "The guy is guilty as sin."

CHAPTER NINETEEN

JUNE

"They made me write that," Eric Myers says.

The next day, I decide to tackle the confession head on. "Then why didn't you tell anyone about that right away?" I straighten my chair, squeaking against the gray kitchen tile. Babushka is locked away in our bedroom for the moment, with her scratching post and fake mice to keep her company until I'm done with the interview. "Why wait until after the verdict?"

"I *did* tell people that," he says. "I told my lawyer." Out comes a bitter laugh then. "That guy was a waste of space."

Having read the court transcripts, I can't say that I disagree. "So you're saying that your lawyer didn't tell anyone? Make a complaint?"

"Nope," he says, gravel in his voice. "Too much of a bother, I guess. But that doesn't mean it isn't true." The guard snorts in response, and Eric Myers glares at him, bristling. But there's not much he can do about it.

"Okay, then. Tell me what happened," I say, pulling up a new notebook page. "From the beginning."

Eric Myers steeples his hands, resting them against his lips. He stays this way for a long moment. Then he asks a question. "Have you ever stayed up all night?"

I sit up in the chair, taken aback by the non sequitur. "Well . . . sure . . ."

I went to college. Of course I've stayed up all night.

"Okay." He chews on his lip, pausing for another question, and unease glides through me.

I'm breaking a cardinal rule of journalism, letting the interviewee ask questions. As my college professor said, *You own the interview. Once the subject takes over, the interview's over.* I'm about to speak again when he beats me to it.

"How about two nights?" he asks.

I think back to our family trip to Ireland, right before the divorce, which might have been a last-ditch attempt to save the marriage. I remember little about the trip, except waiting in a long line to kiss a stone, and my parents softly arguing in the next room every night. We were up nearly forty-eight hours coming over. So, the answer would be yes. I have been up two nights.

"Three nights?" he asks, without waiting for my answer.

I pause. "What are you trying to say, Eric?" I ask, trying to wrest the interview back.

He taps his fingers on his table, not ceding an inch. "Have you ever been screamed at?" he asks. "Not yelled at, screamed at. Constant, nonstop, screaming, screaming, screaming." His pitch rises with every word, and the guard throws him a warning glance. He lowers his volume again. "So you can't hear your thoughts."

I don't answer. Maybe he thinks that represents a negative response. But, yes. I have been screamed at, by Chris. So loud, so furious, that I could barely hear my own thoughts. *I fucking love you, don't you understand that? I don't exist without you. You don't exist without me.* So loud, so furious, that I needed a restraining order to keep that voice away. That I needed antidepressants to leave the house.

"So you are saying they kept you awake and screamed at you?" I ask. The question comes off as belittling, though I don't mean it that way. Screaming at someone for three days may not be torture but at least falls under "enhanced interrogation techniques." It could force a confession.

"Have you ever been smacked in the ears?" he asks, the question soft, almost a whisper. I have to lean toward the computer to hear it.

I shake my head, uncomfortable with somehow becoming the interviewee again.

"Doesn't sound that bad, does it?" he asks, with a half smile.

I don't answer, but no. Being kept up all night, screamed at, and having your ears hit doesn't sound that bad. Not in comparison to being sliced and stabbed. Not in comparison to what Nicole White and Leigh Jones went through. And maybe Amelia and Angela as well.

"The first slap isn't so bad," he says, resting his elbows on the table. "Kind of a surprise that the cops are actually hitting you. But then, that's not so surprising, is it?"

I don't admit it but, no, it's not all that surprising.

"The second one hurts a bit more though," he says, his eyes glazing over. "And when you're getting over it, they hit the other side. And the screaming gets louder." His fingers play on the surface of the table. "The next time, the room starts spinning. So hard that you throw up. And they keep hammering you, screaming. *You did it. You know you did it!* But you keep saying that no, you didn't do it. You swear on your mother's life that you didn't do it."

Silence takes over the room, sucking in every sound except for his voice. I want to say something, even just an okay, or go on, but I can't. It would be wrong somehow, like talking in the middle of a play. Or maybe I'm afraid to break the spell.

"At some point, you stop counting the blows." He stares off in the distance, no longer looking at me, maybe not even talking to me. "The room won't stop moving. The buzzing in your ears turns louder than the screams. And it hurts. It fucking hurts. Ringing, buzzing pain. And you just want them. To. Stop."

His head drops into his hands for a second, then he looks back up. His eyes redden but shed no tears. "So finally I just said yes, I did it. Whatever they told me that I did, I agreed with them. I just copied whatever they said, word for word." His voice sounds low, dejected. "I wrote it down, even though my eyes kept going double from being so off-balance. They had some story about how I got mad because she laughed at me or whatever." He shakes his head. "And that's it. I wrote it all down and signed my name."

Now, outside noises seep in again. A horn beeps outside my window. From his room, keys rattle, a corrections officer making the rounds. The beefy guard coughs into his fist.

The spell has broken.

Eric rubs his eyes with the heels of his hands. "By the time they were done, I didn't even know what day it was. I remember looking out the window when the light came up and trying to figure out if the sun was coming up or setting. I barely even knew my own name." He shrugs out of weariness, the gesture shorthand. He has no story left in him to tell. "Finally they let me sleep," he says, in a dead voice. "And in the morning, I woke up, and I regretted taking that pen." His jaw clenches. "And I will regret it for the rest of my life."

CHAPTER TWENTY

NOW

My hand's on the door when I notice it.

Lainey's black and teal New York Liberty winter coat hangs on the rack.

I pause. It couldn't be that easy, could it? Probably not, but there's only one way to find out. I reach into the side pocket, without any hope of success, but my fingers recognize it right away. A miniature flip-flop. It was Ruby's first gift, a silly beach-vacation souvenir, which has been on Lainey's keychain ever since. I could kick myself for wasting all that time instead of looking there first, but better late than never. Keys gripped tight, I venture outside.

After the warmth of the fire, the sudden cold shocks my system.

Like walking into a freezing shower.

My scalp muscles tighten under my hat, cold air squealing against my face, needling into my skin. Awkwardly, I walk through the mounding snow toward the car and hit the remote. The thing doesn't even chirp. I push the button over and over with the same result.

"Okay," I grumble to myself. "So you just have to use the key."

Stepping through the heavy snow to the car, I try the key in the door, my fingers cold and clumsy in my mittens. The key doesn't go in. I jam it in a bit but don't want to break it. The key seems to fit the slot, but it's frozen over.

"Come fucking on," I yell at no one, trying to scrape the ice out with my mitten, which doesn't work. I bend down and blow hot air on it, which also doesn't work. I doubt there's deicer in the cabin and don't want to waste any more time. In frustration, I start banging the iced-over driver window with my fisted hand. A chunk of ice flies off the window, but I'm not close to breaking it. I could find a hammer or something from the lodge, but that should be my last resort.

Then I have an idea. Taking the backpack off, I rest it in the snow and unzip the side pocket, rooting around for the box of matches. I finally nab them and am about to strike the first one when the match stick drops from my fingers into the snow.

With a groan, I dig around the snow a bit, not seeing anything. I hate to waste matches I might need later, but it's going to be a needle in a haystack, or in this case a match in a foot of snow, so I grumblingly take out another match. Holding it carefully this time, I strike it and get a flame.

Which immediately dies out in a flash of wind.

"Damn it." I try again, carefully shielding the match with my cupped hand and holding it up to the lock. I hold it as long as I can before the flame burns my fingers, then quick jam the key in, and . . . in it slides.

Smooth as butter.

I almost can't believe it; something finally worked.

I don't have time for a victory dance in case the damn thing freezes in there. I twist it and have to yank the handle a few times to wrench the door open, as the frame iced over as well. "Finally," I mutter to myself, and put the backpack in the seat next to me.

After adjusting the rearview and pulling the seat forward from Lainey's ten-foot distance, I slot the key in and turn.

Nothing.

Not even a putter. Not even a squeak.

"No, no, no, no, no . . ." I squeal. I turn the key again. And again.

I bash the wheel with the heel of my hand, but only a pathetic soft bleat emerges from the horn. Feeling tears coming, I lay my head on the cold, stiff wheel.

My breath comes out in puffs. Pocketing the keys, I grab my backpack off the seat and reluctantly climb out of the car. I don't have the luxury of self-pity right now.

I have forty-eight hours.

I have to get to the street. That's my only plan, and it's not a great plan, but it's all I got. If I can get to the street, maybe a car will pass me, or I'll find a house along the way. Just get to the street. Get to the street.

I tell myself this with each grueling step, and it hasn't even been that long yet. Twenty steps, maybe thirty steps. I'm in terrible shape. My sporadic yoga has not helped my stamina. My heavy thighs ache, and I'm absurdly short of breath.

I wish I had Jay's self-discipline, waking up at 5:00 AM to run every day. He urged me to come along with him, promising to take breaks and only go for a half mile. Lainey tried too. To help me after breaking up with Chris. She took me to buy running shoes and jogged next to me, keeping up encouraging patter and running backward, while I could barely breathe. It was my first and last time. After that, I gave her my go-to line: "I'll run if there's a bear chasing me." My running shoes sit in the corner still new and unused, chastising me.

Lainey's pillow, soaked with blood. Her hair on the knife.

"No," I yell at myself.

I keep walking, my toes tingling and frozen.

Don't think about her. Don't think about her.

Think about something else. Who could have done this?

Of course, there was the text from last night sweetly wishing me a nice bachelorette party and hoping I might die. I know who must have sent it, but that's a dead end. There's no way they could have done this.

So Chris shoots to the very top of the list. The ex.

It's always the ex.

I'm ashamed to admit that Chris was my first true love. And he fooled me for a while. Narcissists are like that, con men. I saw him as intense, misunderstood, my very own James Dean. Things were always up and down with Chris, and that volatility sucked me in, intoxicated me. And the sex was off the charts.

The coercion was more subtle, baked into his bad-boy persona. It was never physical, not at first. He would text me all the time or call during meetings. When I would complain, he would say I was reading too much into it. He'd send me flowers and we'd have ferocious sex, and things would work out again. The word *gaslighting* is overused nowadays, but he could teach a master class. I was imagining it, always.

I took it upon myself to fix him somehow, to make him more loving and less jealous. But that never ends well, and in this case, it ended with him choking me after one particularly vicious argument, leaving a swath of purple bruises on my neck.

That very day, I was examining *Crimeline* crime photos for a different case and noticed the bruises, the almost flowery, florid fingerprints. I looked at my own bruises on my neck and realized that could be me one day. A *Crimeline* story.

So, I finally broke up with him.

Lainey and Melody told me I should have dumped his ass way before. They were right, of course. I know about abusive red flags, and they were everywhere. Then he stopped bothering me. Not after the restraining order, but after I got together with Jay. There are certain rules of engagement, after all. Abusing a woman is one thing. Abusing another man's property is another.

And anyway, this wouldn't be his MO. Chris loathes me, every single cell of me. Still, he once puked during a gory movie scene. He would be too squeamish for knives. If anything, he'd buy a gun and shoot us, and then himself. Then he could be both dramatic and consequence free. That's Chris.

Could it be Chris? Yes, it could be. But I don't think it is.

Who else could it be though? I would blame Eric Myers, but he's in prison.

Which means maybe he is innocent after all, and the real killer has been out there this whole time. Maybe I was right to doubt his guilt, even after his slipup, and it's another suspect from my investigation. Or maybe it's someone new, a copycat killer.

Or maybe it was you.

You should never have smoked the White Widow.

"Nonononono," I murmur, and keep walking.

Walking and walking.

CHAPTER TWENTY-ONE

JUNE

T he view dizzies me.

It should be romantic, the skyline over sherbet-colored clouds. But it unsettles me somehow, miles of concrete, glass, and metal, the buildings haphazardly scrunched together.

Flying into Vermont, you can see the earth, vast fields and trees underneath you. Gradients of white in the winter, a hundred greens in the summer, and in the autumn, clusters of reds, oranges, and yellows that almost look artificial, like trees from a model train. But you know you are landing on earth, solid earth.

Up here from the sixty-fifth floor of the Rainbow Room, you cannot see even a speck of land. The buildings appear to have sprouted like a strange cement fungus, taking over the earth and the sky. We sit at an oversized round table, too big for two but perfect for a tasting. Caitlyn, Jay's executive assistant, arranged it, having taken it upon herself to become our wedding planner, much to my (and my mother's) chagrin. On some level, I know my fear at this height may be a metaphor for my fear of something else, i.e., getting married. But I suppress the thought. A tasting at the Rainbow Room for my wedding should be cause for celebration, not panic.

"You think it's true?" Jay asks, a flake of spanakopita landing on his plate.

"What?" I ask, turning away from the window, yanked back into the room with the gaudy chandelier, shifting pink lights above us, and the parquet wooden floor beneath us.

"What you said," Jay responds, his eyes scrunched in question. "About the confession. You really think it was forced?"

"Oh, yeah. Sorry." I sip the champagne, bubbles tingling on my tongue. "I don't know, to be honest. The only thing is . . . his ears weren't swollen at all."

Jay nods, appearing to think this through. "What did he have to say to that?"

I debate another spanakopita triangle, but with imminent bridal dress shopping, hold off. "He said they knew how to hit him *just right*, so they didn't bruise or swell or anything."

Jay downs the rest of his champagne. "Sounds bloody convenient."

"Yeah, I know. And he said the doctor basically lied because she didn't like him. So she said his ears looked fine."

He snorts and I agree, it sounds fanciful.

A waiter comes over with merlot, showing Jay the maroon-black bottle with a simple and elegant white label. Simple doesn't mean cheap though. I caught a glimpse of the price on the menu. Two hundred seventeen dollars. (Let me repeat, two hundred seventeen dollars!) To Jay, that isn't all that expensive. He goes through the tasting rigmarole. After twirling the red wine, Jay takes a sip and nods in approbation, then the waiter nods smartly back and pours, the wine glugging into the glass. I spread my hand over my own glass. The champagne already has me lightheaded.

Jay takes another sip as the waiter leaves. "Cracking," he says. "I'll have to tell Caitlyn to get the name of this one."

"Uh-huh," I say, sick of hearing her name in any association with the wedding. Lainey and Melody call her the c-word. Not the actual c-word, just "the c-word."

"How are things with you?" I ask, to change the subject from Caitlyn. The sherbet clouds turn muddy outside. "I always bore you with my stuff. You never talk about your stuff."

"My stuff?" Jay puts the wine down, leaving a rim of red on his lips. He looks oddly like an oversized toddler who's been playing with Mom's lipstick. "My stuff is fascinating. You wouldn't *believe* how predictive analytics set up my bid-ask spread today."

I have to laugh. "Yeah, that does sound exciting."

"Almost as thrilling as serial killers," he says, then looks up as two plates are delivered to the table. Salmon with a beurre blanc and risotto, and a filet mignon with asparagus and creamy, mustard-colored béarnaise. A trickle of blood pools under the steak.

"Hey," he asks, picking up his fork and knife. "Did you look at the invitation samples yet?"

"No," I admit. The smell of fish mixed with béarnaise turns my stomach. "You know, with the profile and everything but . . .

I will. I promise. I will." I don't tell him Caitlyn has already emailed me twice about it.

"We still have some time," he says, the knife squeaking on the plate. He takes another sip of wine, then looks around the room with a searching gaze.

"Straight back and to the left," I answer his unspoken question. I already hit their impressive bathroom full of marble and mirrors, copper trough sinks with country club paper towels, and everything buffed just so.

"Cheers," Jay says, then stands up and heads that way.

As he strides off, women from two tables away check him out. They meet my eyes briefly and smile, caught out. But I understand the look, the unspoken question.

What is he doing with you?

And I get it. I once asked him point blank what he sees in me, not as a fish for compliments, just a genuine question. I'm not eye-candy material, more muscular than thin, pretty, but not the pretty that he could afford.

Objectively, he could have done better.

He gave me a look and said, "You have no idea how fucking sexy you are, Alex." I still smile when I think of that.

While I wait, classical music plays overhead, mixed with the tinkling of cutlery. A shriek of drunken laughter shoots across the room from a table full of women wearing crowns—a bachelorette party maybe. Lainey and Melody have been hinting about that, but so far I've held them off.

He seems to be taking a while, and I'm checking my watch when his phone rattles on the table, vibrating with the ringer off. Eli's name scrolls across the top of the screen. After a spate of angry buzzes, the phone silences.

Then a text shows up, again, from Eli.

Did you take care of her?

I stare at the screen, my *Crimeline* brain going into overdrive. *Did you take care of her?* The text fades away.

My mind blazes as Jay appears back at the table.

"Those bathrooms are something." Settling back in his chair, he looks at me. His eyes flicker a marble blue in the candlelight. "Is everything okay? You look like you just saw a ghost." He rests his hulking elbows on the table.

"I'm . . . I'm okay." I rub my chin, nervously. "Someone called you though."

"Oh," he says, grabbing his phone.

Just then, the waiter returns with a huge tray of desserts. "Are you ready for the best part?" he asks, with a fawning smile.

"Wow. That cheesecake looks good," I say, injecting enthusiasm into my voice. "Doesn't it?"

Jay looks up from the text, his frown morphing into a smile that doesn't quite reach his eyes. "Cheesecake," he says, pushing his phone to the side. "My favorite."

CHAPTER TWENTY-TWO

NOW

I walk, sweat dripping into my eyes, the salt stinging them. The backpack strains my back, digging into my shoulders. I decide the Hershey bar can be my treat, my incentive. If I can get to the street, I'll allow myself one square. Okay, two squares, I think, negotiating against myself. I'll allow myself two squares, but that's it. And only if I can get to the street.

This idiotic agreement keeps me going.

I let my mind wander, fly above me, watching me. I can hear my boots crunching the snow, my ragged breathing and the wind whistling in the trees. The snow drifts up sometimes, and I keep walking through the whiteout. It feels like I'm in outer space somewhere, on the moon maybe. It almost confuses me then that a full moon hangs above us, not below us. The wind rolls the snow, wheeling across the fields like prairie grass.

I flip out the compass without using my flashlight, the face just visible in the moonlight. The light is already dim and iffy, and I want to save the batteries as much as I can.

Northeast.

The compass has become a trustworthy friend in my hand, a security blanket, even though I don't really know how to follow it. I know what northeast means, but not intuitively, not in my bones. I've done hikes, too many with my bird-watching parents when I was younger (and they were happy watching birds together). But I never really paid attention.

Jay and I went camping in the Adirondacks one weekend, strapped down with all his expensive gear. He would flip out the compass and make subtle direction changes to get to our campsite. He'd been trained in survival, living in Australia. *You don't mess around in the bush,* he told me once. So I didn't worry about it. I trusted him, implicitly. In the back of my mind, I knew we always had Google Maps, should we get really lost. I never followed a compass for real, when my life depended on it.

Wind swoops in, tearing my eyes. Sweat slicks my shirt. My head aches with cold, my scalp tense and sore. My body feels worn, dragged down by a heavy load. I don't remember the driveway being this long. Sure, long for a driveway, but a half mile at most. Then again, we were driving, not trudging through snow in zero-degree weather.

I look back toward the lodge, catching my breath, the cold air singeing my lungs. The tips of my fingers tingle and throb. Maybe I should just go back. I got this far, I can just go back. Then I could wait out the night and search for them again. The weather will be better in the morning. I turn to face the other direction, eying the road back to the lodge. My knees wilt, my energy sapped. I take a step of surrender back toward the lodge.

But then I stop.

Forty-eight hours and they are dead, if they aren't dead already. And if I did this, I can't run away from it. I need to own up to it and find them. Either way, there is nothing for me in the lodge, except blood and carnage. I have no choice but to keep going.

Hunger grips my stomach, and I decide to have a square of chocolate. Just one to help me continue. Flipping my backpack off, I start unzipping the side pocket. But I stop again.

No. That was not the deal.

I think of Jay talking to his son. *That was not the deal, bud. Xbox after your homework is done.* I remember thinking, how will I know that? I'm twenty-six. How will I know how to raise a twelve-year-old? Jay said I'd be a natural, but I wasn't sure. The specter of years with Greg—summer vacations, first crushes, school plays, SATs—riddled my nerves. I figured I would get a book on it, but I haven't gotten a chance to do that yet.

Stop, I tell myself. *That's not important right now. You have to get to the street. That's all that matters right now. And you will not back down. You will not stop until you get there.*

I stomp my feet and slap my hands together to get the blood moving again.

And I keep walking.

CHAPTER TWENTY-THREE

JULY

"You're quiet today," Wiley observes, typing with lightning speed. Wiley was an administrative assistant at a law office before this gig and boasts an eighty-words-per-minute rate.

"Am I usually really loud?" I ask, searching for Noah Thompson's phone number without any success. He's not on any social media, though he could be savvy, using an alias. I might have to dig through some of my secret people-search sites to find him.

"Well, you're usually verbal at least," Wiley says, and I snort-laugh at this.

I don't say any more, however, having decided to put Eli's text out of my mind for now. It's none of my business anyway. The question sounds nefarious, only because I have a *Crimeline* brain and because it comes completely out of context. *Did you take care of her?* could refer to anything. "Take care of" doesn't have to be a euphemism for threatening or killing. It could actually mean helping someone. It could refer to a client from the hedge fund with outstanding questions. It could be asking about Caitlyn, or some regulator with concerns. It could mean anything. Plus, I don't trust Eli. So whatever he's asking Jay to do, it doesn't mean Jay would actually do it.

And it *definitely* doesn't have to refer to me.

Why would Jay need to take care of me?

I don't have time to worry about it anyway. Toby already nudged me about the profile. I was embarrassed to say I still hadn't spoken with the main witness, only gotten bullied by Twitter bros and a farmer's wife.

I check my phone to see I have an hour before my planned lunch date with Lainey and Melody.

Since I can't reach anyone on the phone, I decide to peruse the court files.

Lawyer: "Can you state your name for the record?"

Noah: "Thomas Noah Thompson."

Lawyer: "Thank you, Thomas."

Noah: "Noah."

Lawyer: "Excuse me?"

Noah: "That's my full name. But everyone calls me Noah."

Lawyer: "Oh yes. My apologies. *Noah*. Can you tell the jury how you know Ms. White . . . Nicole?"

Noah: "She was my friend."

Lawyer: "Thank you. Were you . . . in classes together or . . ."

Noah: "Yeah. Math class."

Lawyer: "Great. Okay. Could you describe the victim for us?"

Noah: "Sure. She was blonde. Um, sort of medium height and—"

Lawyer: "No, I'm sorry. Not her physical description. We can all see she was a beautiful girl. I mean, what was she like? As a person?"

Noah: "Oh. Yeah. She was . . . well . . . she was really nice."

Lawyer: "Great, could you go into a little more detail there?"

Noah: "Um. Sure. She . . . was cool to everyone. You know? She was, like, really popular. But she still was nice to everyone. Like, she stood up to bullies. But not, like, physically or anything. She just kind of like . . . shamed them into being nicer. Yeah, so. Not everyone's like that."

Lawyer: "You're right, Noah. Not everyone is like that. Not by a long shot. So . . . how well did you know her, would you say?"

Noah: "Not real well at first. But then, when she was tutoring me, I got to know her a little better."

Lawyer: "As in . . ."

Noah: "Not like that. Just . . . better friends. She would even . . . confide in me. This made me feel, like, special. Like, she knew she could trust me."

Lawyer: "Okay. Did the victim ever talk to you about the accused?"

Noah: "You mean about Eric Myers?"

Lawyer: "Yes. I'm sorry. Eric Myers."

Noah: "Yeah. She did."

Lawyer: "And what did she say about him?"

Defense Lawyer: "Objection, Your Honor, that's hearsay."

Judge: "I'll allow it."

Noah: "She . . . she was afraid of him."

Lawyer: "She told you that?"

Noah: "Yes, she did."

Lawyer: "And what exactly did she say? Can you tell us her words?"

Noah: "She said he asked her out a couple times. She went to a movie with him once, I think. But then she found out how old he was, and she didn't want to see him anymore. Because she was like, only sixteen, you know. And he's like . . . a lot older."

Lawyer: "Twenty-five."

Noah: "Right. And she said he was sort of stalking her. He would come up to her after school. More than once. And he texted her a lot. She showed it to me. Like fifty times or something crazy like that. She finally had to block him. She was afraid of him, I think."

Lawyer: "Did she say anything to make you think that?"

Defense Lawyer: "Leading the witness, Your Honor."

Judge: "I'll allow it."

Noah: "Yeah . . . she . . . said he was creepy. Like he was the type of dude who would shoot up a school."

Lawyer: "Those words?"

Noah: "Those words. And . . . she said . . . she was joking, I think, but also kind of serious. She told her friend Talia if I ever get killed, Eric Myers did it."

Defense Lawyer: "Your honor. That is definitely hearsay."

Judge: "Agree. Jury, please disregard that statement."

Lawyer: "Thank you, Your Honor. Thank you, Noah. That will be all."

CHAPTER TWENTY-FOUR

NOW

Finally, I get to the street.

It probably took an hour, which means it's about 2:00 AM.

I've never run a marathon, but I can see how the runners feel, endorphins spent, crossing the finish line. I want to cry with relief.

Standing under the dim streetlight, I can finally fulfill my promise to myself. I unzip the side pocket and rip out the chocolate bar.

I can't stop at two squares. A monster takes over.

I am stuffing half the bar in my mouth, chewing without breathing, barely even swallowing, when I think of Chris, looking at me with unveiled disgust when I grabbed a candy bar at a Halloween party. *You sure you need that?* he asked, pinching my hip, a bulge of fat, pretending to be playful. I remember how the chocolate stuck to my tongue then, cloying and sickly sweet. A circle of friends saw what he did and looked away.

I once told Jay that story, after he saw me fretting, pinching a roll of fat on my stomach. *If I ever see that guy,* he said in a low voice, with muted fury, *I'm going to kill him.*

I wrap up the rest of the chocolate bar and shove it into my backpack before I can be tempted again. Flipping out my compass, I can see it better now in the faint streetlight.

I have a decision to make.

I'm not just following a driveway east anymore. I have to choose a direction. Should I turn to the right or the left, north or south? South should be toward home since we're in the Catskills. But we went for miles without seeing signs of life. Going that way might be a miscalculation. Maybe there are more stores or houses to the north. I glance down one direction and then the other, as if that might steer me. Neither appears promising, both sides an equally bleak landscape of dark forest, monotonous snow, and endless pavement.

Then a memory strikes an off-handed comment that Melody made on the way in. *Oh, a farm. How rustic.* Could that be the Thompson Farm? Or if not, at least someone could be living there who could help. Though I only caught a glimpse. It might not even be active anymore. Either way, it's worth a try.

So that means going back in the direction we came from. But for the life of me, I can't remember which way that was. Again, it should be south, coming from home, but there was a detour. Did we take the road south for a bit before going north again? Is that where the farm was?

I look both left and right again, but nothing sparks my memory.

Then I remember the map and grab it out of the back-pack, the paper waving gently in my mittened hands and snowflakes landing on the paper in little starbursts. I wipe off the scads of sticking flakes but can still barely see the map in the streetlight. When I take the flashlight out, I almost drop it while trying to push the worn-down rubber button on and hold the map. Finally, I manage it all, holding the trembling light over the map, which the wind keeps trying to close.

After a while, I locate the teeny line which might represent this street. The map flaps in my hand, the flashlight flickering. North appears to have more hilly regions, two of the circles embedded deep in there. The other red circle is far flung out in another elevated region in the south. I search every square inch of the map but don't see any sign of a farm, which of course isn't surprising.

With a sigh, I fold up the map and put it away with my flashlight. My best bet would still be heading south, back toward home.

Turning to the right, I'm heartened to have a plan. A pseudo-plan. Turn right, walk south. I reach for my phone to check the time, before remembering I don't have it. Still, I don't need to know the exact time to know that precious hours are falling off the night.

And Lainey and Melody are out there somewhere.

South, south, south.

The word repeats in my head as I plow forward.

The walking goes easier on the street at least, less strenuous than the slog through foot-deep snow on the ground. As I walk, the snow squeaks under me, my heel slipping at times. After righting myself, I slow down a pace. I have to be more careful. Things are bad, but they could be worse. If I turn an ankle and get stuck out here, that would be worse. If I hit my head and lose consciousness on the street, that would be worse.

Snow keeps filling the sky, which remains dark still, though I know it's well past midnight. We're far out here, away from the gray skies of the city that literally never sleeps, the light pollution reflected in the clouds. Piling snow weighs down my hat and flickers in my eyelashes. It seems impossible, the fact of even more snow, like the sky should be empty by now. But it's not. Still, I'm from Vermont, where snow is a fact of life. We could be in a blizzard with three feet of snow and whiteout conditions. A travel ban, with no one on the road to help me. All of these would also be worse.

But I won't let myself think of the *worst* worst thing.

If I can't find my friends. If they're already dead.

I shun the thought, banish it. I need every ounce of mental and physical energy in me right now. I can't afford such soul-sucking thoughts. So I keep walking, mumbling the word with every step. "South. South. South."

I imagine myself back home, thinking of Jay, maybe ordering pizza for Greg. Maybe they are watching television, or playing video games, Babushka sprawled out on the couch next to them. I don't know what Greg likes on his pizza—another thing I'll have to find out.

When I hint at my uneasiness to Jay about all the things I don't know about his son, or even parenting at all, he gently scoffs. *It's just a little thing,* he'll say, trying to bolster me. *You'll be great.* But all these little things accumulate into a mountain, threatening to overwhelm me.

South. South. South.

Then I stop.

I see something.

Straining my eyes through the snow, I see the barest glimmer of light coming down the road. I squint through the dotted air, afraid my eyes could be tricking me, and quicken my steps, careful not to fall. After a little bit, though, no doubt remains. A beam of light shines through.

Desperate, I start waving my arms around and yelling, even though the car would be too far off to see me. But I can't help myself.

"Hey," I scream, as loudly as I can.

The soft rumble of the car sounds in the distance, and the light shines brighter through the snow. Now I start waving around like mad. "Over here," I scream, so loud my voice hurts. "Over here!"

The rumbling grows closer, louder, the headlights shining bright halogen-white through the snow. I inch just little closer to the street. Getting hit by the car, that would be worse. I wave as high and fast as I can, windmilling my arms, stretching my shoulders. *Please see me. Please see me.*

"Hey!" I bellow out again. "Hey! Hey!"

The car engine growls, the headlights blinding bright, and the vibration of the wheels rumble under my feet. I lean into the street, screaming and waving my hands. It happens fast, like a dream. The car emerges through the snow, showing itself for a window of just seconds, like the prow of a ship though steep fog.

Then it's gone.

The mammoth car roars and flashes by me. Snow thuds off the wheels in pellets, stinging my face like an insult. As fast as the car flew by, it disappears, slipping into the distance. I run after it, screaming. For minutes, I keep it up, running, crying, and screaming. But finally, slowly, I give up. I'm just yelling into wind. The car is long gone.

I slow down even more now, staggering. Either the driver didn't see me or didn't want to see me. Yelling after them won't change that; it merely wastes energy stores I don't have.

The street appears calm again, only a ghost of the car remaining. Like it never happened, like it was all in my imagination, the empty street seems to mock me.

Suddenly, I'm enraged.

I yell out in frustration, clenching my fists. I scream out a string of swear words, jumping up and down in fury. Then my heel slips.

This time, I don't catch myself. My hip hits the ground, my elbow cracking on the pavement, then my head, and pain hurtles through me. My cheek swells as blood drips in my mouth from biting my tongue. I try lifting my head, but the pain concentrates whooshing into my skull. Overwhelmed, I close my eyes, trying to catch my breath.

A word repeats in my head, but I don't remember what it means.

South, south, south.

Maybe I should just rest, conserve my energy. Rest.

Just for a second.

CHAPTER TWENTY-FIVE

JULY

"That's really freaky."

"Agree," Lainey says, wiping off a mustache from her hot chocolate. We came here for our planned coffee-lunch, but Lainey has never developed a taste for coffee. I didn't tell Wiley about the text, but as soon as I sat down with my best friends, the truth slipped out.

"What do you think it means?" Melody asks, her knee jiggling from her three shots of espresso. Unlike Lainey, Melody has been mainlining coffee since age twelve.

"Probably nothing. I'm sure it's just some business thing and I'm overreacting."

Lainey taps her long fingers on the table. "What did Jay say about it?"

I pause.

Lainey raises her eyebrows. "You haven't asked him?"

"Not . . . yet," I say, staring into my cold chai tea. "I don't want to be making a mountain out of a molehill."

"Yeah," Lainey says, blowing on her hot chocolate. "You're right. It's probably nothing."

"Yeah, but what if it's not?" Melody insists, her face lined with worry. "What if it's like some Bernie Madoff thing? Or he's being blackmailed or something?"

Lainey answers with an eye roll. "You're being overdramatic."

"No, I'm serious," she says, pushing aside her empty coffee cup. "You have to ask him."

I look at Lainey, who shrugs but then nods in agreement.

"Yeah, I guess you're right." I stand up then and start clearing my napkin and cup. "Maybe I'll ask him tonight."

Melody gets up too, putting on her denim jacket, which smells faintly of weed. "Doing anything fun for the Fourth?"

"Oh," I say, throwing my cup away. "I think we're having drinks on some yacht or something."

"Oh, we're having drinks on a yacht or something," Melody copies, in a rich lady voice.

"Shut up," I say, laughing. "What about you? What are you all doing for the fireworks?"

Melody grins. "Mason got us tickets to the Empire State Building," she sings, doing a sort of side-to-side jig, her voice bouncing.

"Mason the Med Student?" Lainey asks.

Melody rolls the sleeves on her jacket. "You don't have to call him that, you know. It's not like I'm dating more than one Mason."

Lainey stands up with a stretch, making other patrons look over. An exceedingly tall woman always attracts attention. "Ruby and I are going to Coney Island," she says.

"Old school," Melody says. "Respect."

"Hey," Lainey says, turning to Melody. "Did you call the place yet?"

"It's on my list."

"The place for what?" I ask, grabbing my purse.

"I shall not disclose," Melody answers, pulling her satchel over her shoulder. "Under the penalty of death."

"This better not be a bachelorette party thing," I warn her. They exchange wry grins.

"I will kill you both," I say. "I really and truly mean it."

Armed with the files from Noah Thompson's courtroom appearance, I decide to see what Eric Myers has to say about the accusations.

I've signed up for an actual office this time for our interview, instead of intern row. It still doesn't afford much privacy, however. After some high-profile sexual harassment cases, all of the offices became see-through, walls converted to glass. (Though I'll note, Fletcher Fox still has an office with actual walls.) Looking around the glass walls, people surround me on all sides, like I'm in a fishbowl. Maybe like how Eric Myers feels, being watched twenty-four hours a day.

I adjust the chair down with a pressurized hiss.

"Tell me about Esther Thompson," I say, soon after he gets on the screen.

Eric Myers appears genuinely confused. "Esther who?"

Someone hums a tuneless song in the hallway, and I focus back on the screen. "Esther Thompson. The woman from the Thompson Farm. She claims she saw you earlier the week of the killing around the lodge. Casing it, is what she said."

He stares off for a second, then the recognition seems to hit him. "Oh, yeah, her. The farmer's wife."

The podcast comes back to me. *What, did she cut off his tail with a carving knife?*

"She lied," Eric says. "Through her teeth. I wasn't anywhere near that lodge."

I adjust my seat down again. "Any idea why she said that, then?"

"No idea. The woman just hated me." He backs away from the table, tipping his chair on its hind legs. I have a vision of him falling backward and smacking his head on the hard floor, blood slowly pooling. "She had it in for me for whatever reason."

A guy in jeans and a T-shirt peacocks down the hall, looking like someone born on third plate who thinks he hit a triple. He's dressed to unimpress, but I recognize him as the executive director's son. He gives me a peace sign, and I smile, unsure how to appropriately respond to that.

"Her son said Nicole White was afraid of you."

"Her son? Right. That's just because *he* had a thing for her," he says, with an indignant huff. "I don't even remember the kid's name. He was only like fifteen or something—"

"Noah," I say. "Noah Thompson is his name. And he was fourteen."

"Yeah well," he says, crossing his arms, his thumbs in his armpits. "He's wrong. I barely knew the girl, like I said. A couple of dates is all."

"Uh-huh," I say, prepared for this oft-stated argument of his. "Fifty-seven."

He watches me with misgiving. "Fifty-seven what?"

"Text messages," I say, pausing to let this land. "Seems a bit much, doesn't it? Like a little more than barely knowing her. Or dating her just the couple times?"

His head lowers an inch. "Listen. I know that looks bad but . . ." He tugs on the neck of his undershirt. "I was really into her. I'll admit that. And she was . . . too young, I'll admit that too. But . . . that doesn't mean I killed her," he says, knocking on the table with each word.

The beefy corrections officer throws him a look, and Eric flattens out his fist.

"Here's the thing," Eric says, softly, in the tone of a confidant. He moves closer to the screen. "Everyone in town knew about Esther Thompson. The woman was crazy. Nuts. And she hated Nicole too. Hoo-wee, did she hate her."

This development surprises me. "Why would she hate Nicole?"

"I don't know. But I'm telling you. She looked like this nice little old lady."

His chair legs crash down to the floor, and I jolt back in my seat.

"She wasn't. She was a fucking psychopath."

The lights sparkle on the waves, shimmering, as we lean across the ship railing.

A light wind picks up, and I pull my cardigan tighter. It's not a cold night, but the ocean breeze cools the night a good ten degrees.

"You want my coat?" Jay asks, already taking his blazer off.

"No, that's okay," I say. "You need it."

He holds it out for me. "You'd be doing me a favor. I hate wearing these things."

He's not lying. He never would have worn the blazer without the dress code specifically calling for it. I loop my arms in, relaxing into the warm heft of the coat. "Thanks," I say, as he puts his arm around my waist.

A white-gloved server passes us with champagne glasses of prosecco. I've already had two, but they were so refreshing that I take another. Jay takes one too.

"Cheers, mate," he says to the server, who nods back. I notice a lot of the (rich) people on this boat don't make eye contact with the waitstaff. But Jay used to serve at a country club near his house, where he now has a membership for his parents. He doesn't treat the waiters like they're invisible.

"Oh," he says, turning to me. The wind ruffles his hair. "Did Caitlyn email you? About the wedding favors?"

"I'm not sure," I say, not mentioning that I autodelete whatever she sends.

"She was thinking cashmere pashminas," he says, loosening his arm on my hip.

"Hmm," I say, to be polite. "That sounds kind of . . . expensive."

"Yeah, maybe," he says, with a shrug. "Just an idea. She just wanted to bounce a few things off you. Since you haven't done much on it yet."

I don't respond to the subtle barb. Then again, maybe he's just stating a fact.

A shot of laughter comes out from the cabin of the yacht, where people are dancing. The bass thumps so loud I can feel it through the railing. I thought I recognized a couple of models, and maybe a C-list actress. *It's the ones you don't recognize that* really *have the money,* Jay told me once.

The sky darkens a shade, the barest of stars poking out. My watch says ten more minutes until showtime. I realize I'm running out of time here. I should ask him about the text before the fireworks begin. In the distance, the sound of the orchestra tuning up floats over the ocean. A cacophony of bleats, chimes, and strings follows, then a silence. The music on the ship stops too, the buzz on the railing disappearing. Partygoers from the cabin file out now, crowding around the railing, where Jay has adroitly staked out the best spot.

Did you take care of her?

I swallow and take a deep breath. "Jay, I wanted to talk to you about something."

"Oh yeah?" He turns to me, but then, in an instant, the music swells up, lustrous notes building, flowing into the sky. Jay closes his eyes. "The *Pastoral*," he says.

"What's that?" I ask, like an idiot.

"Beethoven," he answers, pushing closer to me on the crowded deck. Excitement flurries around us, tittering and whispering. People call over to each other: *Come on. You're gonna miss it. It's about to start.*

A spattering of pink-red and powder-blue fireworks bounce up. The amuse-bouche of fireworks. The ship goes quiet.

Then the music grows louder, instruments blending together, as the fireworks surge up to oohs and aahs. Loud pops turn into splayed-out reds and greens, a starburst spreading then sizzling out, worms whistling across the sky. The air smells of smoke.

The music carries the fireworks, moving together almost spiritually.

I realize the third prosecco must have gotten to me and turn to Jay to find him gone. Addled, I glance around but just see beaming faces around me, all fixated on the sky. I turn back around myself, to see the fireworks popping up again, rapidly now. One after the other, layering on top of each other. Smoke covered by light covered by smoke then light. Around the ship, people murmur, *The finale!*

I look away again for Jay and see him in the cabin of the yacht arguing with Eli. Jay is shaking his head, and Eli is throwing his hands up. I don't know Eli well, but it's definitely him. He's three hundred pounds and wears snazzy suits. He's hard to miss.

Did you take care of her?

What are they fighting about? Me?

Did you take care of her?

The music screams in a climax, then stops as the final cannon sound explodes.

The boom echoes, pounding into my ears.

CHAPTER TWENTY-SIX

NOW

E ye level with the street, I see snowflakes piling, like icing on a wedding cake.

My brain struggles with the simile, and I am half wondering why I decided to lie here and watch the snow when the throbbing in my head reminds me. The reel plays backward to the scene of me throwing a tantrum like a toddler before falling. I acted like an idiot, and I fell.

"So get up," I mumble to myself, my tongue tasting blood.

But it takes strength. Part of me wants to just lie there. Maybe close my eyes again, just for a few minutes, hitting the never-ending snooze button that Jay complains about.

Jay.

Lainey. Melody.

I need to get up. I'll get hypothermia or get hit by a car, not getting up ever again, one way or another. I need to get up.

I try to move, pain shooting through my body, clawing at my hip and my shattered elbow. The side of my tongue feels sliced, like a pound of beef. But at least I can move everything. My arm and hip may be bruised, but they're not broken.

Gingerly, I try to turn over onto my other hip. The streetlight bangs against my eyes, my vision swimming with the movement. I work myself up to a sitting position, then take a break, catching my breath and waiting for the spinning to stop.

The sky still looks dark, so not too much time must have passed. Slowly, I stand upright, using the strength of my good arm and leg. I take a careful, testing step, the pain in my hip bowling me over. I stop, gather myself, and breathe again. My elbow throbs in rhythm with my head and my tongue, but I force myself to take another step, and another. I have forty-eight hours to find them.

Less now. So I have to keep moving. I have no choice.

The car seems like an improbable dream now, shooting by me and leaving me stranded. But something about the car needles me. The vision of the car, the brief glimpse through snow, floats up in my head. I try to clutch the picture before it slips away again. As I walk, I rewind time, slowing down every second to focus on details. A flash of silver—yes, it was silver. Boxy and powerful. The vision solidifies. It was a sedan.

Okay, fine, it was a sedan. But it's gone, so dwelling on it won't help. I can't shake the image, my brain still batting it around, when the memory weaves through my muddled brain.

The Amber Alert.

I grab my pocket to check the alert on my phone before remembering again—no phone. Searching my memory, I retrace my steps in the parking lot of the convenience store. I was thinking about Lissa. I was looking for . . . a silver Lincoln.

I'm almost positive it was.

I don't remember the license plate number and couldn't have seen it anyway with the car flying past. I couldn't say it was a Lincoln for sure, and there are a lot of silver sedans out there. But maybe that was the car.

I keep trudging ahead.

A silver sedan. Okay, so let's say it was the same car. Is that even related to my missing friends? Probably not. In most of these cases, the captor is most likely the "noncustodial parent," i.e., the father. Which is cold comfort, because sometimes the father would rather kill his children than lose control of them. We don't feature too many of those on *Crimeline*. Pretty White women—that's our demo. Dead kids aren't as popular.

In any case, most likely no relation to whatever happened to Lainey and Melody. But then again, my *Crimeline* mind would say, there are no coincidences. I lick my lips, my tongue sore and dry. *Just keep walking. Just keep walking.* I click open my compass again, brushing falling snow off the face.

South. Keep walking south.

I let my mind take over. *Walk, walk, walk.*

A memory springs up of cross-country skiing with my father while my mom stayed in the lodge doing crosswords since she hated skiing. I remember the swish of our long skis, which looked skinny compared to the downhill ones I would rent. We would ski and ski, my head sweating into my hat, until we hit a rhythm. A flow. Just me and my father. The world felt big and small at the same time.

I am entering this rhythm now, this flow.

Walk, walk, walk. South, south, south.

But then I stop.

I come upon a sign on a wooden gate, which opens to a long driveway. And at the end, if I squint through the snow, I can see the barest outline of a farmhouse. Maybe this was the one Melody commented on.

A hanging metal sign swings, creaking in the wind, the design obscured by the snow. I reach forward and knock off the snow, revealing the black silhouette of a horse jumping. And stenciled above this black iron design is a name.

The Thompson Farm.

CHAPTER TWENTY-SEVEN

JULY

I'm on the subway on my way to work, my jean jacket looped over my arm. I didn't need it after all, the morning already sweltering and hotter in the subway. A drip of sweat glides down my back, and I breathe through my mouth to escape the overwhelming body odor all around me.

I've decided to forget about the text for now.

Jay's obviously going through something with Eli, but it's none of my business. And between my job and the wedding, I don't have time to worry about it. To kill some time, I flip through one of the true crime books and come on the autopsy report.

NAME OF DECEDENT: NICOLE WHITE
DATE OF BIRTH: 7/4/1996
DATE OF DEATH: MAY 3, 2012
AGE: 16 YEARS OLD

DATE OF AUTOPSY: MAY 4, 2012
SEX: FEMALE

MANNER OF DEATH: HOMICIDE

CAUSE OF DEATH: Exsanguination due to multiple stab and incised wounds (torso, neck, arms).

EXTERNAL EXAMINATION:
The body was that of a well-developed, well-nourished sixteen-year-old Caucasian female fully clad in one bra, underwear, one pink T-shirt, one pair of jeans, two green socks, red sneakers. The clothing was bloody, with multiple punctures as described below. Near the victim was a black leather purse with contents spilled out onto floor. On the floor was a black cell phone, opened pack of gum, four tampons, three sanitary pads, one lipstick, a scrap paper with Revelation 13:18 ADAM written in blue ink, letters stained by blood. Car keys with metal keychain reading "Hawaii Forever" and pink nail file. Near the victim's head was found a torn gold necklace with butterfly pendant.

The body weight 133 lbs. with a height of five foot six and appeared consistent with her reported age. The body was cold. Rigor was broken to an equal surface on all of the body. The scalp hair was long and brown. The irides were brown, and corneae were cloudy. One tattoo of a blue butterfly was noted on the left wrist, with an apparent laceration.

FINDINGS:

1. Generalized pallor and evidence of exsanguination.

2. Multiple stab and incised wounds

      1) Penetrating base of left lung,

      2) Penetrating middle lobe left lung,

      3) Penetrating superior vena cava,

      4) Penetrating left fifth rib,

      5) Penetrating spleen

      6) Penetrating left iliac crest

3. Incised wounds. Multiple, consistent with defensive wounds.

4. Toxicology is positive for ethanol and cannabinoids in peripheral blood. A urine drug screen is positive for cannabinoids.

Opinion:

The sixteen-year-old female, Nicole White, died as a result of multiple stab wounds resulting in exsanguination. The autopsy reveals no gross evidence of significant natural disease processes. The toxicology was positive for ethanol and cannabinoids. With the information available to me at this time, the manner of death, in my opinion, is homicide.

Signed:

Aaron Goldberg, MD

I suck in air as a shock of pain makes me look up from the book.

A man in hiking shoes has stepped on my sandal, scrunching my pinkie toe. He apologizes, appearing mortified.

"It's okay," I say, but grit my teeth in pain, tears filling my eyes. The toe tingles, already swelling up. A spot of blood pops up under the nail.

The car screeches to a stop, the calm voice announcing the station. And the man apologizes again, then escapes into the throng of people leaving. I wipe off my toe quickly, telling myself to stop being such a baby, as a mass of people file in, searching for seats or places to stand. I turn back to the page again to take my mind off my throbbing toe.

It jars me, the juxtaposition of the cold words on the page with the white-hot rage of the crime. Yes, she had on a pink T-shirt, bra, jeans, and red sneakers. But they don't paint the true picture of Nicole White, who was alive before she was dead, a young woman becoming a senior next year, not just a victim requiring an autopsy. She lived a life in those listed clothes, the pink T-shirt emblazoned with a sunburst Old Navy logo, the pale boyfriend jeans with the cuffs rolled up, the lime-green socks, the old-school red Converse sneakers with a blue-inked heart on the cracked white rubber on the left toe.

The list of wounds underscores the horrific, lurid photos. Penetrating, penetrating, penetrating—a testament to each excruciating blow. And in the end, it all boils down to one obvious sentence.

The manner of death, in my opinion, is homicide.

With a sigh, I'm about to close the book, when one detail catches my eye.

The blood-stained note reading Revelation 13:18 ADAM.

The *Crimeline* episode delved into this briefly, as did the police reports. Her stepfather's name was Adam, but that lead didn't go anywhere. No one managed to decipher this juicy piece of evidence, which essentially fell by the wayside when Eric Myers fell into their lap. I can't help but wonder at it. The curious note doesn't quite fit, like a leftover puzzle piece, with too many nubs for the remaining slot.

Pondering this, I almost don't hear my station called, but manage to slap the book shut and limp off the train at the last minute.

ARMCHAIR SLEUTHS:

Kathy: The Revelation thing? I don't think they ever figured it out.

Colby: And who's Adam?

Insook: Not to be negative here, but isn't this a waste of resources? Why does it even matter? Eric Myers is in jail already.

Alex: But what if he's innocent?

Colby: Yeah, not to be "that guy" but I don't think he's innocent.

Mark: Seconded.

Kathy: 100%

Alex: Adam is the name of her stepfather. But it seems he was ruled out.

Tom: Yeah, I heard that.

Insook: Not surprised. Why would he have attacked Leigh Jones?

Colby: And he has no connection to the A-girls either.

Insook: Not to be a jerk, Colby, but I hate when people call them that.

Kathy: Yeah, it bugs me too. Amelia and Angela. They have names.

Insook: Otherwise, they just become like, not even real people.

Colby: Apologies. Didn't mean it that way, of course. L

Insook: Oh, no! I know you didn't. Just wanted to point it out. J

Mark: I still don't understand how they never got him to admit to killing them. He signed the confession. Why not help those girls too?

Kathy: That was effed up. They had the death penalty on the table and took it off before even trying to negotiate with it.

Insook: Death penalty? In New York?

Kathy: They were trying to make it a federal crime, due to the violence. But it didn't stick. So, state crime. No death penalty. No info on Amelia and Angela.

Mark: Sucks.

Kathy: Yeah, sure does.

Colby: So, what is the note, then? Revelation?

Mark: One of the podcasts said the police thought it was a password.

Colby: Which podcast?

Mark: Don't remember for sure. *Murder, He Wrote* maybe?

Tom: I heard that too. That it was a password. I don't remember from where though. Maybe one of the books.

Colby: But why would she have his password written on a paper in her pocket?

Kathy: Or anyone's password for that matter?

Alex: And what kind of password is that? It's like two different things. A Bible passage and a name.

Insook: Yeah, you're right. It doesn't make sense.

Colby: It obviously still has to do with Eric Myers though.

Kathy: For sure.

Insook: You know what it refers to, right? The Bible passage?

Tom: Definitely. "Let the person who has insight calculate the number of the beast, for it is the number of a man. The number is 666."

CHAPTER TWENTY-EIGHT

NOW

An old woman in a thin bathrobe stands half hidden by the door, her gray hair in curlers. I don't know what I was expecting, but it wasn't this. In the few photos of Esther Thompson from the trial, she is sitting, appearing doddering and frail, even ten years ago. Her hand on the Bible as she glared at Eric Myers. At a full stand, though, she is nearly six feet, with a gargantuan torso, like a female linebacker. Shardai was right to scoff at her being some "farmer's wife."

"Hi," I say, still catching my breath from the trek down the driveway. My feet have turned from tingly to thoroughly numb, as well as the tips of my fingers.

She doesn't open the door any wider, eyeing me with suspicion.

"I'm . . . my name is Alex." My lips don't work right though, as if shot with Novocain. "I'm a little lost . . . um . . . can I borrow a phone maybe?" I try to peek inside, but she blocks the doorway. "I just need to call someone if I could. Please."

A voice floats out from inside the house. "Who's there, Mom?"

"Some girl," she croaks, with disdain, as if I were selling cleaning supplies.

A young man appears beside her at the doorway, in boxers and an undershirt, rubbing his arms. Shadows cover his face. "Jesus, Mom. Let her inside. She's about to freeze to death."

"Okay, okay," she says, sheepish at being called out on her poor hospitality. She opens the door an inch wider, and I slip in before she can change her mind. In the small foyer, the overhead light accentuates her abundant wrinkles—superabundant wrinkles branching off into more wrinkles, unlike the Botox-smooth faces of all ages in New York City, especially in my line of work. Rheumy blue eyes stare at me.

"Thank you," I say, stomping my feet.

"Hey," the young man says. "I'm Noah."

I do a double take. Now I know why the hot guy in the convenience store looked so familiar. His handsome face appears like the age-progressed image of a missing child, the adult version of the boyish young man in the book.

In truth, he looks boyish still (twenty-four years old by my calculation) with fair features, and standing at about five nine or ten at the most. And in this light, the peculiar color of his eyes shines through, hazel with flecks of gold. He looks slight next to the form of his hulking, ogreish mother.

"And this is my mom, Esther."

"Hi," I say, awkwardly. We don't shake hands. "I'm sorry. I know it's late. It's just . . . I'm in a little bit of trouble here."

My eyes search the room for a phone. "I just needed to call someone if I—"

"Noah," Esther interrupts. She points upstairs. "Go put some clothes on."

"Oh." He looks down at his underdressed self, abashed. "Yeah, I'll just . . ." He vaguely motions upstairs and then heads up.

"You," she says, dispensing of her next burden. "Take those wet things off."

So I do as she says, shedding my coat, boots, mittens, and hat in the front room, hanging everything up on corroded brass hooks. Then she leads me through the vinegary-smelling kitchen and into the family room. A toasty fire crackles by the handsome brick hearth, and I catch a glance at a brass clock on the wall.

A quarter after two.

Above the hearth, a deer head stares at me accusingly, like maybe I put him there.

Esther catches my gaze. "Oh, don't mind him," she says, as if the deer head were performing hijinks. "My husband is a big game hunter." She turns toward the stairs, putting her hands in her deep bathrobe pockets, with the hem frayed. "Noah," she calls up. "Get our guest some new socks."

"Yup," he answers, the sound of drawers opening and closing echoing above us.

Esther looks me up and down, seeming to find me unworthy, then points to the hearth. "Sit," she commands.

And like the family dog, I sit, pleasantly surprised by the warmth of the concrete seeping into my wet, heavy jeans. I'd love to take them off too but don't see a way to modestly do that. But I do peel my socks and sweater off, quickly warming myself by the fire.

"All right," she says, sitting down heavily across from me on the fabric couch, adorned with faded roses. "Now, what exactly is going on here?"

I start explaining the situation of the bachelorette party with my friends, but she stops me as soon as I mention the Vrbo.

"Hobbes Lodge?" she asks, sounding both agitated and irritated. "What are you all doing in Hobbes Lodge?"

"It was . . . sort of for research," I say. "I'm doing a profile on the case for my work." I decide whether or not to mention I actually already spoke with her, since she did refer to me as despicable. She obviously didn't like me then and doesn't like me now.

But maybe it would lend some credibility to my situation.

"I actually called you some months ago. Maybe you remember? Alex Conley?" I wait for some recognition but get none. "I was calling from *Crimeline* about the Eric Myers case?" I add.

Her suspicious countenance doesn't alter. "No one ever called me from *Crimeline*," she says, her tone accusing. "I'd sure as hell remember that."

I blink in confusion. She actually sounds like she's telling the truth, that she doesn't remember it.

"Okay . . . it's just . . ." I stammer, unsure which direction to go at this point. I decide to just plow ahead. "Anyway, as I was saying, I woke up in the shower, and my friends were gone. So . . ." I swallow.

She's clearly unhappy with me for some reason and looking for any excuse to throw me out. I just have to call 911 before that happens.

"I really just need to call someone about my friends." I gaze around the family room for a phone. They must have one *somewhere*. Though maybe not. I don't pay for a landline anymore myself. "Your cell phone maybe? Do . . . could I borrow it?"

Instead of answering, she fixes me with a dark stare. "Okay," she says, in a low voice, in a cut-the-crap tone. "Now, why did you really come here?"

"I'm . . ." But I don't know what else to say. The question literally leaves me speechless.

"You came to see him, right?" she prods.

Again, I sit there with my mouth wide open, which she seems to take as a yes.

"Well, you can forget all about that," she says, smirking. "Noah isn't interested. He's got enough to worry about without you girls chasing him all the time."

"Um," I say, feeling like I'm being punked here. "No, I promise. It's not that at all."

But she frowns and shushes me at the sound of his footsteps. He reemerges from the darkness of the stairs, wearing the same beat-up jeans from the store and clean gray T-shirt. "These should work," he says, handing me a thick pair of white tube socks.

"Oh, thanks," I say, holding up the socks. But . . ." I lower my voice, to avoid the ire of his Mrs. Bates of a mother. "Do you have a phone I could borrow?"

"Oh yeah, sorry. It's charging." He combs his fingers through his mussy hair with an apologetic glance up the stairs. "Shouldn't be long though."

I look up at the stairs too, as if that might hasten the charging. "Do you have another phone in the meantime?" I ask, wondering which phone she answered when she hung up on me.

"No landline," Noah says. "Sorry. We gave it up. Mom has a cell phone too though."

"I have no such thing," she argues.

"You do, Mom," he says, sounding perturbed. "I bought it for you, remember? With the big buttons?"

"Oh, that." She flicks her wrist in dismissal. "Who knows where that thing is."

Noah shakes his head in annoyance and sits down next to me while Esther glares at us. I can smell the fresh scent of detergent from his shirt, feel the warmth off his body. Glancing at him, I notice something then. Faint traces on his arms, scarred over.

I think of what Esther said when I called her, though she claims not to remember this. The anger simmering in her words. *He's finally put his life back together and you're trying to pull him down again?*

Track marks.

I glance away before he can see me looking.

CHAPTER TWENTY-NINE

JULY

Since the Armchair Sleuths had no further insight on the Revelation question, I'm hoping my scheduled interview with Eric Myers might shed some light on the matter.

I'm in the fishbowl office again, my pinkie toe still aching from the stranger's hiking boot. Eric Myers has a new guard today, not the beefy one. This one is skinny and tall, and sort of looks like a giraffe with tattoo sleeves.

"I wanted to talk to you about the note in Nicole White's pocket," I say, opening my notebook.

"No clue," he says, before I even give any more details.

"The note about Revelation," I say, wincing as my toe hits the garbage basket. "You know what it means, right? What the passage refers to?"

"Yeah, yeah, yeah. The beast. Six, six, six." He lets out a bored exhale. "I've already told you. It's got nothing to do with me."

I tap my pen on my pad. "How about the name Adam, then? That ring any bells?"

"No idea," he says, yawning and stretching up his arms. "I mean, except for the stepfather, obviously."

He was supposedly investigated but wasn't in the court files. Though I recall him briefly mentioned on the *Crimeline* episode. It never made the final cut after a threat of legal action. *Crimeline* has high-priced lawyers, but the segment apparently wasn't good enough for the bother.

"They say he was ruled out."

"That's bullshit though," he says, with a cackle. "She was petrified of him."

I hesitate, aware of him trying to hijack the interview again. But I take the bait anyway. "Why do you say that?"

"She told me," he says, to my quizzical look. "Remember? On our couple dates?"

"Oh right."

The dates. The finding of his fingerprints on her purse changed his story rapidly from not even knowing "that girl" to having just the one date and holding her purse at the movies, absolutely not realizing she was under eighteen. Of course, the fifty-seven texts skewered this rendition of dating her once almost by accident. And stalking her *high school* might have clued him in to her age.

Eric Myers twiddles his fingers on the table. "He was just like . . . really overprotective. But weirdly so. Like, he wanted her to wear a purity ring." He puts purity in air quotes. "Promising she would remain a virgin until marriage." His face puckers with the memory. "It was kind of gross, to be honest. So, honestly, if someone was going to be quoting the Bible, it would be him."

"Okay," I say. An intriguing angle, if actually true.

"He used to check up on her too . . . like . . . if she said she was going to her friend's house, he would come by to make sure she was telling the truth." Eric adjusts himself in his chair, the legs scraping against the tile. "That's probably why she rebelled so much."

Someone swears outside the office, the sound muffled. It's Tammy, Fletcher Fox's personal assistant, holding three half-spilled coffee cups. She looks up at the ceiling, sending prayers up and mouthing imprecations.

"Listen," he says, just above a whisper. The tattooed-giraffe guard glances over and then back at the bars. Eric bends toward the screen as if telling me a secret. "I don't know how to say this without sounding like an asshole but . . ."

I wait him out.

He throws up his hands in resignation. "No matter what, I'm going to sound like an asshole, so I'll just say it. Nicole White wasn't this perfect little angel that everyone thinks she was." He gnaws on his lip though, uncomfortable with the statement. "I mean. I know that sounds bad. But I just had to get that out there."

"Okay," I say, leaving him plenty more rope with which to hang himself.

"She just . . . everyone thought she was a saint. But she had a wild side. She would get drunk, and high." He chews on the hangnail now. "She wasn't this blessed virgin like her stepfather thought. She had boyfriends besides me. So, if it's always the boyfriend, then fine, but I wasn't the boyfriend."

I don't recall reading about another boyfriend, but I may have missed it.

"Noah?" I ask.

He answers with a scornful laugh. "That kid? She was *way* out of his league."

"Who, then?" I pick up my pen.

"Ryan Johnson," he answers, peering into the screen again, ready to spell the name out if necessary. He leans back with a grin now, having successfully commandeered the interview again. *Way to go, Alex!* "He's the one you should be questioning."

I write the name down, figuring it to be a dead end, but worth investigating at least. I vaguely remember him making an appearance in the old *Crimeline* episode as well. I don't think he made the final cut either. Maybe he could be a true suspect, a new angle that would entice Toby to invest more in the project.

"He used to live in Brookside. The trailer park," Eric Myers adds, oh-so-helpfully. "Might still be there, I don't know."

Tammy marches by again, now with three new coffees and a brown stain on her blouse.

"Hey." Eric tilts his head down. "You getting married?"

I freeze, following his gaze to the desk, with a bridal brochure lying there, and jerk the camera away from the view. "No," I say. "It's for a friend."

"Uh-huh," he says, his grin indicating that he doesn't believe me.

I feel sick about it all the way home.

I don't want to give Eric Myers any more information on my personal life than he already has. Jay worries about me "getting too close" with him as it is, and I haven't disclosed my Venmo contributions to his prison fund. Mentioning I accidentally revealed our engagement definitely won't go over well. I plan to come clean about it right when I get home.

But when I open the apartment door, I hear him on the phone.

"She doesn't know anything, Eli," he says. "Calm the fuck down." He's upstairs in our bedroom. I close the door softly, walking a few steps to hear better.

"I'm telling you," Jay says, his voice ice cold. "I will deal with it."

I take another step, and he stops talking.

"Wait a sec," he says, just above a whisper.

I open the door again and slam it shut. "Hey, I'm home!" I call out, and clomp around the family room, forgetting about my toe for a second and grimacing with pain.

"Gotta go," he whispers. "Hey, hon," he calls back, in his sunny Aussie voice. His feet start bounding down the stairs. "How was work?"

"Fine," I answer. Suddenly, my faux pas with Eric Myers seems trivial. "I thought I heard you on the phone up there?"

He reddens a touch. "Oh, it was just Eli. Doing some damage control. You know how he gets."

"Uh-huh," I say. At least he didn't lie about that. But I also don't think he's telling me the whole truth.

She doesn't know anything.

Who is she? Who is the person he is supposed to take care of? I watch him for any more clues, but his face remains closed. In *Crimeline*-speak, the *she* in texts and the phone calls always refers to the wife. Or the fiancée, in this case. Still, this is Jay, not someone from my *Crimeline* research. I just need to ask him. I drop my purse on the coffee table in the family room, and Jay slips his phone into his pocket.

"How was work?" he asks, leaning with one hand on the couch. "Anything new?"

"Not really," I say.

She doesn't know anything.

I drop onto the couch, feeling like I can barely keep myself up.

Then Jay makes a sudden, sharp sucking noise. "What happened to your foot?" he asks, wincing.

"Oh, that." I examine the toe, which has turned an ugly purple, and on second glance looks askew. "Someone stepped on it. On the subway."

"Yikes," he says, affectionately. "Hate to tell you. But it looks like you broke it, darlin'."

"You think?" I look down again. "It's not too bad." Though now the pinkie seems to be throbbing from the attention. "Maybe I just need some ice," I say, starting to stand.

He motions back to the couch. "You sit. I'll get ice. We need to tape it to the other toe. I crunched a few in my rugby days. It'll be right as rain in no time." He lifts a one-minute finger. "Don't move."

I sit there, listening to him hum and gather supplies for my toe. Maybe he's a great actor, but he couldn't seem less guilty if he tried. In fact, he seems quite wonderful, as usual.

She doesn't know anything.

I just have to ask him.

CHAPTER THIRTY

NOW

Noah rubs his temples like he has a headache. "I don't get it. Someone attacked you guys and like . . ." He looks up at me, squinting. "Abducted your friends?"

"Yes," I say, without hesitation. "I know it sounds crazy, but . . . yes, that's exactly what happened." As I pull the tube socks on, the fabric sticks to my skin. My wet jeans smell of smoke, drying stiff and warm on my body.

Noah sits a foot away from me on the hearth. "And you were there just for research, you said? For *Crimeline*?" He sounds, not suspicious, but not fully convinced either.

"Yes," I say, then backtrack. "Sort of. I didn't know they were taking me there. It was . . . a weird surprise."

"I'll say," Esther grouches.

"It's just . . ." His jittery knee bounces. "Hard to believe. Like . . . how do you not remember?"

"I don't know," I admit, with embarrassment. "We were pretty drunk though." I don't mention the White Widow. Esther would definitely throw me back in the snow for that one.

"Eric Myers is in jail though," he says, half to himself, blinking hard. "He couldn't be back."

"I agree," I say. "But from my interviews—"

"Who are you working for?" Esther interrupts.

A long pause follows this question.

The heat from the fire pushes against me. "As I said, *Crime-line*. That's why we even—"

"No, no, no," she crows, pointing an arthritic finger at me. "Someone put you up to this. And I want to know who it is. Right now."

Tears pop into my eyes, and I try holding them back. "Nobody. I promise you. I'm telling you the truth. It's honestly what happened."

"Mom," Noah says, with a weary sigh. "Why don't you make us some coffee?"

"Coffee?" she warbles. "What, am I your servant now?" She huffs but gets up from the couch, wincing, her huge bulk diminished somehow. With a waddling, aching gait, she walks into the kitchen.

We wait her out in an awkward silence.

Once she's out of earshot, Noah moves to her seat on the couch across from me. "My mom has memory problems," he explains, embarrassed. "So she's a little . . . off sometimes."

I nod, surreptitiously wiping the tears sticking to my lashes. At least her odd behavior makes more sense now, and why she didn't remember me calling her.

"I was going to college in Ithaca for a few months, but then I had to come back. I had some . . . issues . . ." Noah scratches his ear. "I guess I don't need to hide it. Basically, I messed up. Got hooked on H. Ended up in a rehab a couple times."

I nod, figuring his "issues" had to do with addiction. "I'm sorry to hear about that."

"Yeah well. I blamed Eric Myers for a while but . . . I've learned that I have to take responsibility for things I done myself." This definitely sounds like rehab jargon.

He nods to himself. "Yup. Just me. No one else is to blame . . ." Then he digs into his pocket and pulls out a coin.

When he hands it to me, I see it's a bronze chip, not a coin.

"Three years sober," he says, with a little smile.

I give him a genuine smile in return. "That's great," I say, handing it back.

He stuffs it back in his pocket with some embarrassment. "Anyway," he says. "By the time I got my shit together and moved back home . . ." He frowns, looking toward the kitchen. "I didn't realize how bad she got."

A spark pops off a log, and I rub my hands by the fire, still fighting a chill running in me. A cuckoo clock ticks loudly on the wall. When he turns away from the fire to look at me, shadows dance on his face, lighting up the gold in his eyes. "Do you really think he could be back?"

I don't answer.

"Maybe you should check on that phone."

CHAPTER THIRTY-ONE

JULY

I keep wanting to ask him. But somehow, the night passes without me doing so.

I know I should just do it, ask him and get it over with. But I feel bad even bringing it up, considering how lovely he's been with my foot. It reminds me of me icing his knuckle when we first met. But he nursed my toe with tenderness and offered me "paracetamol" (otherwise known as Tylenol). We've gotten through dinner, a Netflix binge, and now bedtime together, and I still haven't said a word about it.

Jay flips through some boring financial magazine on his tablet, while I half read my thriller, but find myself stuck on the same paragraph, my throbbing toe distracting me. And still, the phrase keeps running through my head.

Did you take care of her?

"Caitlyn said we're well ahead of schedule, by the way," Jay says, still flipping pages on his tablet.

"Yeah, she told me that too," I say, glancing up from my book.

She did so with a patronizing "good girl" intonation, like she might throw me a cookie-treat. Though she's still been banging on about the invitations, and despite multiple entreaties from Jay, I haven't done my homework of looking at them yet. I make another attempt at the paragraph when I feel a warm hand on my knee.

"Hey," he says, with a bashful grin.

"Hey," I answer back, smiling despite myself.

Desire tugs at me. I felt a jolt of it when he carefully taped my toe. I just can't help it. Looking down the length of him, I notice the hair on his chest, his hard-won six-pack abdomen, and his muscled legs. And his navy-blue boxers that I bought him, which have apparently come to life. I touch his chest, the soft hair on warm skin, and he shifts over to my side, climbing on me.

"You're so fucking hot," he says, and starts kissing my neck.

Did you take care of her?

His weight pins me down now, suddenly smothering me. I feel myself stiffen, and immediately Jay stops kissing me, his face looming over mine.

"Everything okay?" he asks.

"Yeah," I lie. "I'm just . . . my foot kinda hurts."

"Oh, yeah," he says, his expression abashed. "Sorry. I should have thought about that."

I feel guilty at the lie and tousle his hair. "We can keep going. I'm sorry."

"No," he says, climbing off. "No worries." He arranges the blankets over himself. "Sleep in here tonight though, okay?

You haven't acted out the dreams for a while now. I think it'll be all right."

I swallow.

"Okay?" he asks.

The words sit in my mouth, ready to bubble out. I need to ask him about it.

Did you take care of her?

She doesn't know anything.

"Okay," I answer, instead.

With a contented smile, he turns off the lights, and pulls me toward him in a spooning position, his arm heavy around me.

And I lie there in the darkness, wide awake.

I have to find out.

I trust him, of course. And I'm probably overreacting. But I need to find out.

Which is why I'm in his office, snooping around his desk with my phone flashlight. He sleeps deeply, so I'm not worried about him waking up. And if he does, I have the perfect cover story. I was just dreaming.

So far, I haven't made much headway though. I've pored through some hanging files, but they seem in order. The files are sparse anyway, most of his stuff on his computer or the Cloud, I'm sure. I sift through legal contracts that I can't decipher, a copy of his car title, and a folder stuffed with various sizes of Greg's school photos. I don't bother checking his fireproof safe. After all, he gave me the code once, asking me to grab his passport for a trip.

If he's a master criminal, he sucks at it.

I move onto his mess of a desk now, flipping through junk mail, an invitation to his son's chorus concert, a highlighted *Financial Times* article. I'm about to call it quits when the flashlight catches the metallic sheen of an embossed paper.

Peering closer, I see the United States government eagle crest above the header, "From the U.S. Securities and Exchange Commission." My heart ticks up a notch, and I scan the long letter, mostly full of incomprehensible legalese.

"We note excessive redemptions and withdrawals of crypto assets within your company. Please describe actions taken to identify material concentrations of risk . . ."

An arrow points to this, along with blocky blue ink reading:

THIS IS YOUR MESS. CLEAN IT UP.
—EJB

Eli Jason Banks.

I lean in closer, and just then, the light flicks on.

"What are you doing?" Jay asks, his gruff voice booming across the room. His laid-back Aussie smile has vanished, replaced by a cold, suspicious stare.

"I . . ." I'm so shocked that I forget entirely about my dreaming cover story and just grab the first thing my fingers land on. An invitation.

"I couldn't sleep. So I was looking at invitations and . . ." I add a spry, wholesome lilt to my voice. "I really like this one. The . . . Excelsior."

He stares at me for a second and then his expression softens.

"You do?" he asks.

His delight at this fact fills me with guilt. He squints in the light, then joins me at the desk, leaning in to look at it. Subtly, he moves another paper on top of the Securities and Exchange Commission letter.

"Yeah," I say, wondering what invitation I've just agreed to. I regard the clean, polished, classic font. Okay, that'll work just fine. "I do."

"I thought you might," he boasts, looking "chuffed" as he might say. "That's why I took it out of the folder." His pleased smile turns into a yawn though, and he rubs his eyes. "But come back to bed, would you? It's three in the bloody morning."

"Yes," I say, carefully placing the invitation next to the swollen binder of samples. I hobble out of the office.

He turns off the lights and watches me leave.

CHAPTER THIRTY-TWO

NOW

Esther and I sit at the kitchen table, waiting for Noah to get his phone from upstairs.

I feel like I'm in a time warp, stuck on a movie set from the '70s, with the avocado-green countertops and burnt-orange backsplash tile, both chipped and faded.

I've eaten three dry ladyfinger cookies (also from the 1970s?), the pasty residue still stuck on my tongue. I sip her bitter black coffee to wash it down, the chipped ceramic hot in my hand. My elbows rest on the flowery rubber tablecloth, but I quickly remove them at her corrective stare.

Steam rises out of my mug, serpentine.

"You should never have gone to that lodge," she says, not looking at me. I can smell the subtle scent of her night cream. "It's an evil, evil place."

I drink the undrinkable coffee without saying anything. Not engaging seems the best approach while waiting for the damn phone. It's already been about forty minutes since I got here, which is about forty minutes too long.

"She should have known better too, that *Nicole.*" She injects her name with venom. "Serves her right."

"Serves her right?" I ask, shocked into speech.

Esther sneers. "I know what she was after, going to that lodge so late at night. She was the same way with Noah, pretending to tutor him." Her face darkens. "*Tutor* him, right. More like trying to seduce him, pushing her titties out."

I can't help but gasp.

"What?" Esther asks, with a smirk that mocks my prudishness. "You think I didn't notice?" She throws back her black-oil coffee. "Oh, I noticed all right. Hussy, she was. A real Jezebel. Pretending she just wanted to be his friend."

"Who was?" Noah asks, coming down the stairs as if she summoned him.

"No one," she answers.

He shoots her a look, then pulls a smartphone from his pocket, turning to me. "Here. It should have a couple bars at least."

But in an astonishingly fast motion, Esther grabs the phone right out of his hand. "What did I say about those phones at the dinner table?" she asks, fire in her eyes. She pulls the window up with a creak and tosses the phone into the snow.

I let out an embarrassing shriek, and Noah looks on with horror.

Esther answers both with a satisfied nod. "If you need to talk to other people so badly, or text or whatever you do, go find it, then." She shuts the window with a slam, but the blast of cold air still hovers in the room. "The devil's in those phones of yours. You know I've told you that."

"Mom," Noah yells, indignant. "Jesus fucking Christ."

She stands up. "Don't you take the Lord's name in vain, Noah. I'll tell your father." She nods with vehemence. "He'll take the belt to you yet."

"Mom," he mutters, standing up as well, though a few inches shorter than her. "Dad's dead. We've been fucking through this."

"Language," she shouts, as he marches over to the mudroom, suiting himself up with his boots and winter gear and grumbling to himself. "That'll teach him." Esther sits back down with a triumphant smile. "Having those phones at the table."

I fight the panic coursing through me.

"My friends might be hurt," I say, in a slow, measured voice. "Bleeding." Maybe she would take pity, and that would pierce through her paranoia. "Do you understand? I need to call the police."

She gives me a blank look.

"Okay." Now I shoot up to a stand, gazing around the kitchen and into the family room. I need to get to a phone and get out of here ASAP. "Do you have a phone anywhere? The phone with the big buttons . . . or maybe a landline—"

"Landline?" she asks, with irritation. "What the hell is a landline?"

"Just," I say. "A phone. Any phone. You must have one. In your bedroom? Listen, I'll use it really fast, then I can go."

She puts her hands on the table. "You're not going into my bedroom," she informs me, then gives me an icy smile. "Why don't you ask Noah? Since you've taken such a liking to him."

CHAPTER THIRTY-THREE

JULY

It's been a week of dead ends.

I've left several unanswered messages for the stepfather, filed a Freedom of Information Act request for him and Ryan Johnson, and tried Leigh Jones again. At least Ryan Johnson finally answered my call, so I'm on my way to see him.

But I still can't stop thinking about the letter. Is that what Eli was so upset about on the boat? Bad investments? *Illegal* investments?

I asked my friend Troy from college about it, another hedge fund guy that Jay doesn't know. Troy scoffed at the whole thing and said SEC letters aren't a huge deal, that it could be totally innocent. He went a little quiet when I mentioned crypto though.

Crypto. Literally code, and one that I can't solve. I've read everything I can get my hands on about crypto but still can't quite get my head around it. I've asked multiple people to explain it to me like I'm five, and what I've gathered is that no one else understands crypto either.

Wiley said, "I know enough not to buy it." Troy tried to explain it but didn't really explain it. My mom said, "Honey, I can give you money if you need it." Melody helpfully mentioned that she's reading the "best script" with crypto in it, and Lainey gave me the most honest answer yet, saying, "I have no fucking clue."

If anyone could explain it to me, it's Jay, but obviously I can't ask him.

Seeing the turn ahead, I decide to put the crypto question out of my head for a while.

Troy is right, I ought to give Jay the benefit of the doubt. The SEC letter is probably routine, signifying nothing nefarious. But Eli's words keep flashing in my head. THIS IS YOUR MESS. CLEAN IT UP.

I turn onto Ryan Johnson's street.

"So, I'll be on the news, then?" Ryan asks, excitement buzzing in his voice.

We're sitting in his rundown family room in his mobile home. The decorating theme appears to be "right-wing chic," with a plethora of American flags, "Don't Tread On Me" logos, and a stitched pillow next to me reading "Liberals can suck my D*CK." (The asterisk seems a bit fussy to me, given the sentiment.) I am drinking instant coffee from a mug of "Liberal Tears."

"They're redoing it, like?" he asks.

Ryan has probably put on fifty pounds since the trial. In the *Crimeline* episode, he was shown only as a typical smiling teenager in swimming trunks, holding a beer, his face partly blurred out.

"Because I wanted to be on the first episode, but my lawyer wouldn't let me."

"Is that so?" I ask, putting my undrinkable coffee aside.

I'm already regretting this wasted trip. Ryan Johnson seems more concerned with being on TV than being reinvestigated for murder. I don't see Ryan Johnson killing anything but a six-pack.

I adjust myself on the couch, which smells like wet dog. Then, as if beckoned by the observation, a sad-eyed mutt with a gray muzzle wanders out of the kitchen. The dog makes a slow, arthritic path to me, then nudges my knee for a pet.

"Oh, don't worry about Reagan," Ryan says, giving him an absent-minded stroke behind his ears. "He's a pussycat."

I half wonder if he's named after the former president but decide not to ask.

"It *might* be turned in to a show," I say. I'm not lying. I *might* be invited to lunch with Diane Sawyer one of these days. Anything's possible.

A buoyant smile appears, and he straightens his polo shirt. Then he seems to think of something. "There's no camera though."

"This is the scouting portion," I say, also not completely a lie.

"Oh." His expression clouds with uncertainty. But then he smiles again, enticed by the slimmest possibility of a

Crimeline appearance. Might as well shoot his shot. "What do you want to know, then?" he asks, putting his hands on his knees.

I wipe some dog drool off my pants. "Who do you think killed Nicole White?"

He scrunches his eyes. "What do you mean? Her boyfriend. That psycho guy, obviously. The 666 guy."

"Okay," I say, noting not a jot of doubt or uneasiness in his manner. If he actually did kill his girlfriend, he ought to take up poker. "But I heard *you* were her boyfriend."

He shrugs, seeming uncomfortable with the characterization. "I don't know if I'd say all *that*. I mean, we dated a couple of times. But . . . she was still kind of young."

I write down the word. "How old were you back then?"

"Eighteen," he says, glancing at my pad to make sure I wrote the number down. "So, it wasn't like, weird, or anything. It's just . . . I was starting to work, and she was still in high school. It felt . . . I don't know. Like we were at different stages of life, you know?"

"Uh-huh." The words sound oddly mature coming from his mouth, though he is twenty-eight now. Different stages of life. As in, a few years out of college or divorced with a child.

"I was really more dating Clare at the time," he says. Reagan has shifted over to him for as a more reliable source of petting. "But then I dumped her." He shrugs. "She was kinda needy."

The dog slumps down from a sit to lie down, and a pungent scent arises in the room.

"Reagan," Ryan complains, waving the smell away. Reagan opens one eye, then snuggles back down. "Sorry about that."

"That's okay," I say, though breathe out of my mouth. The smell really is overpowering. "You and Clare were watching Netflix at the time of the murder, they said?"

He swallows. "Is that what we said?"

My pen pauses. "Is that not what really happened?"

Ryan clears his throat. "Well, if that's what we said . . ." He toys with a stray thread on the couch.

I stare at him, deciding the best way to get to the truth is to threaten what he prizes most. "You need to tell me the truth, Ryan. Otherwise, there's no way this is getting on *Crimeline.*"

He bites his lip, apparently debating. Becoming a suspect versus being on *Crimeline* . . . "That might not be exactly what happened," he says. The allure of Hollywood wins out.

"Okay." I ready my pen again.

"Clare fell asleep, right? She just got off a double. But . . ." He loops the loose thread around his finger, and I fear the whole couch might unravel. "But, well, I had just started seeing a new girl. Ryan."

I pause. "Her name was Ryan?"

"Yeah." He laughs. "Weird, right? Ryan and Ryan. But she was free, so I sort of . . ."

I'm writing Ryan with a female sign next to it. "Went for a booty call?"

This is answered with relieved laughter. "I guess you could say that." He turns pensive then. "Though that relationship didn't last long either."

The dog farts audibly this time, the result even more noxious.

"Could she confirm that, do you think?" I ask, wondering how quickly I can get out of this room.

"Yeah, I think so." He pulls on the bottom of his polo. "I can look up her info, but I'll probably have to email it to you. Fair warning though, she's not my biggest fan."

"Oh yeah? And why's that?" I stand up.

"Um," he hems, standing up as well. "You might want to just ask her. Oh, and talk with Clare too. She knew Nicole from church. She was like a year above her. But she's also not my biggest fan." His face takes on a guilty cast. "She went a little psycho on me when she found out I cheated with Nicole."

I pause. "Are you saying you met Nicole through Clare?"

He looks even guiltier. "Yeah, I was picking Clare up from her Bible class. Me and Nicole started talking."

"Bible class?" I pause. This can't be a coincidence. "Does Revelation 13:18 mean anything to you?" I ask. "Or . . . the name Adam?"

He stares off for a second. "Well, Revelation's in the Bible. And . . . Adam's in the Bible too, right." He grins, tickled to have made the connection. "Along with Eve?"

"Right," I say, leaving my mug of liberal tears behind. "Thanks for your time, Mr. Johnson."

"Yeah, sure, okay." He follows me out the door. "Just let me know when they're coming with the cameras, okay?" he asks, with stars in his eyes.

CHAPTER THIRTY-FOUR

NOW

Ten minutes later, Noah comes back into the house, slamming the door. He grunts, taking off his boots and coat. Cold air trails him into the kitchen. By his gloomy expression, I'm guessing he didn't find the phone. "Sorry," he mumbles. "No phone."

A half cup of my coffee remains in my mug. Cold.

I check Esther's face, but it reveals nothing, no hint of triumph or gloating. I am not sure she even remembers causing the ruckus.

"So," I say, changing tacks. "Maybe we could just run into town so I can make a call. Or we can get to a police station."

"No one's driving in this weather at this time of night," Esther returns, her tone allowing no discussion on the matter.

"Or I could just drive," I offer. "I grew up in Vermont, so I know how to drive in the snow."

Esther lets out a derisive laugh. "Not this kind of snow."

"Yes, this kind of—" I say, then stop. Stooping to her level is not going to help.

Maybe I can convince Noah to drive me once she falls asleep. On the way in, I saw his SUV parked outside, which should be able to handle the snow. But then again, it looked snowed in. It would take some effort. And we could shovel the snow off, but we still might get stuck.

"You'll sleep in the guest room," she says, the statement sounding more like a demand.

I'm surprised at the offer; maybe manners would be the last to go in dementia. Still, I'm wary of this plan. I'd rather just take the SUV. I've been here almost an hour now, and the minutes keep ticking off, subtracting from my remaining forty-eight hours. I gaze out the kitchen window at the snow blowing haphazardly.

"I should just—"

"No, she's right. You should stay here," Noah says, in an overly solicitous voice. As his mom stands up to clear her coffee cup, he mimes a phone with his hand, tilting his head upstairs.

"Oh," I say, heartened by the thought. Perhaps he has another cell phone up there? "Thanks. I would appreciate that. Absolutely."

"Come on," he says. "I'll get you some towels and stuff."

Esther's suspicious gaze, which we blithely ignore, follows us up the stairs. Once upstairs, he makes a demonstrative racket picking up towels and sheets in the linen closet.

"Okay," he announces, performatively. "And there should be soap in the bathroom."

"Do you have another cell phone?" I whisper.

"Not exactly," he whispers back, leading me into the guest room, small, with lemon-yellow walls. A yellow square quilt hangs over a rocking chair in the corner, with baby feet prints in some of the squares. Above the rocking chair hangs a picture of a baby swaddled in a pink blanket

"You have a sister?" I ask, before even thinking to ask more about the phone. She wasn't mentioned in any of the research.

He follows my gaze. "Had," he says, laying towels on the bed. "She died."

"Oh," I say, embarrassed. "I'm sorry."

"Thanks, that's okay." He moves a pillow. "It was crib death. I was only six so . . . I can barely even remember it. Now, to the phone." He walks to the nightstand and yanks open a drawer. But then his eyebrows pull downward. "Shit. There used to be a phone in here."

I peer into the empty drawer, as if he needed confirmation. "I don't get it. You had a cell phone in here?"

He shakes his head. "No. We do have a landline. I just told her we didn't. I had to hide the phones because she kept calling 911." He leans on the bed to check the other night-stand, his T-shirt riding up, revealing a slice of skin. "I keep meaning to cancel it but . . ." He pulls open the other drawer. "Damn it."

"So . . . no phone." I stagger back a step, the blow of this news almost physical.

"Noah," Esther calls up. "You know the rule. No boys and girls in the same room."

He shuts his eyes in frustration. "Okay, Mom," he says. "Maybe I hid it somewhere else. I don't know." He glances around the dimly lit room. "The closet, maybe. I don't know."

"Noah," she shouts up again.

"Coming," he says, and starts to leave, but I grab his shirt. I touch muscle and warm skin, and he turns to me with surprise.

Embarrassed, I release his shirt, not even sure why I touched him. "Sorry," I say. "I'm just . . . I'm afraid."

A bellowing emerges from downstairs. "Noah!"

He grits his teeth, his jaw muscle flaring. "I'm sorry," he says, in a low voice. "I'll try to help you once she falls asleep."

Dust bunnies flitter up as I search under the bed, coughing from the musty air. I try the nightstand drawer again, in case it has magically materialized, but find only a worn Bible.

Footsteps creak by the room, slow and hobbling. "You doing okay in there?" Esther asks.

"Oh yes," I call back. "Fine, thanks. This is perfect."

I jog over to the bathroom and turn the tap on for a few seconds, then off, to feign washing up before bed. Rust rings the drain.

As soon as her footsteps fade, I look under the sink to find old cleaning supplies and a stack of toilet paper. I rummage around in the dark, touching grime and plumbing, but no phone.

I check the closet again, though I've already looked in there. A few wire hangers clink around among the scent of moth balls. No phone.

Dejected, I sit back on the bed.

Esther probably threw the phone away, which means I shouldn't waste any more time here. It would be easy enough to sneak out again. They wouldn't force me to stay. Esther would be thrilled to see the back of me. And Noah wants to help but can't with his mother around. I could slip a note under his door telling him I've gone. Hopefully he'll find the phone soon and call the police himself.

I gaze outside into the snow, where his phone remains buried. The wind whips against the windowsill, creaking the casing. I can already feel the bitter cold wind stinging my face, my fingers numb and stinging. I really, really do not want to go back out there.

Maybe I could just stay here for an hour. Getting some "kip," as Jay would say, wouldn't be the worst thing. I could get my energy back, then face the elements again.

But even as the temptation tugs at me, my inner voice rails against it. Much as I would love to close my eyes for an hour, it would be another hour lost.

So . . . here we go again. Time to pack up my backpack and head out. At least I dried my clothes and got some caffeine. I stand up and stare out the window, dreading the cold.

As a last-ditch effort, I decide to try the closet one more time. The top shelf is empty, but maybe she's pushed the phone back too far back to see. She's certainly tall enough to do it. I back up to get a glimpse of it, but still can't. So I move forward again and jump, managing to just hit the shelf with my hands but not get anywhere near the back. This is where Lainey would come in handy. She was always the go-to tall person to reach anything in our college dorm (Melody was hopeless in this department). But I don't have Lainey or Melody to help me.

My throat tightens.

No, I scold myself. *That will not help right now.*

Looking around, I see the rocking chair. That might work. Hobbling footsteps sound in the hallway again, and I pause. Then I make plenty of noise moving the blanket and fluffing the pillow, and the footsteps retreat again.

After waiting a beat, I grab the heavy chair and, lifting to avoid the racket of dragging it, maneuver the chair in front of the closet. I pause again, listening for footsteps, but silence remains. Stepping up on the creaky chair, I wobble on my tube-socked feet. I lean forward, balancing with my arms like a surfer, when I catch a glimpse of something. I grab a precarious hold of the shelf with both hands, going on my tiptoes and lifting my gaze up a couple more inches.

Then I see it, the most beautiful sight ever.

A phone.

A crotchety voice calls out from the hallway, nearly toppling me off the chair.

"You need anything, Alex? Or are you gonna turn the lights off?" Esther complains. "Some of us are trying to sleep here."

"Oh," I say, righting myself and simultaneously grabbing the phone. "Yes, I'm all set, thank you." I tiptoe off the chair, settling its rocking, and flick the lights off.

The footsteps return back to her bedroom.

CHAPTER THIRTY-FIVE

AUGUST

Sitting in the deli with my mom, I run over remaining items from the profile. The stepfather still hasn't called me back, nor did I reach the female Ryan, who the male Ryan claims as an alibi during the time of the murder. Although, the female Ryan could just be covering for the male Ryan, since a sleeping Clare couldn't provide one. So, we got the stepfather and two Ryans as possible suspects (none of whom have a 666 tattooed on their wrists, incidentally.) A motley crew, as far as suspects go. I doubt Toby would find any of them terribly convincing as alternative killers. At least not enough to put the profile on the air.

"Whatcha thinking about?" my mom asks, taking a sip from her near empty coffee cup.

"Oh, nothing," I say, doubting she wants to hear complaints about my serial killer project.

When she turns to the window, I see myself in her profile. She is a palimpsest of me (or me of her), a thinner, frailer version, while I got the thick genes from my father. *Juicy, you mean,* Jay would say.

My mom steals a glance at her huge purse on the chair next to us. She keeps it within eye view at all times. In the "city," someone might dash off the street and into the restaurant to grab it.

"So, Melody and Lainey will be there?" The names blend into one word, Melody-and-Lainey, complementary goods like peanut butter and jelly.

"Yup," I say, swallowing the last of my turkey sandwich. "Hopefully. Sometimes auditions go late or practice goes late or whatever."

"Sure," she says, then glances at her purse, which, despite all odds, remains on the chair. "Jay?" she asks.

"Nope," I say. "Bad luck."

She spoons her soup with a smile. "I wasn't sure if you millennials still hold with that."

"I'm Gen Z."

"Ah, of course," she says. Then she assesses me, and takes a breath, and I know what's coming. "You're sure about this, right?" she asks, her face scrunched with worry. "Because this is a big step, you know. A huge step. And you're still so young. You don't have to marry the first guy who you—"

"Mom," I snap. "I'm not marrying the first guy that I've met. I've dated plenty of guys."

"But this one is not even six months," she argues, pulling closer to the table. "How well do you even know him?"

Did you take care of her?

This is your mess. Clean it up.

"I know him," I say, ignoring the voices.

She fiddles with her napkin. "You're young is all I'm saying."

"Mom," I say, the word rounded with frustration. "How old were you when you married Dad?" I ask, already knowing the answer. "Twenty-three, right? I'm twenty-six."

"And we know how well that went," she says, with a sardonic smile, which looks out of place on her face.

I take a sip of coffee. "Okay, well, maybe that's a bad example but . . . I'm sure, okay? I love him."

"Okay, okay." She puts her hands up in surrender. "I just want you to be sure." The waiter fills my mom's cup for the hundredth time, and she nods a thank you. "I just . . . worry, you know?" She reaches over and rubs my knuckle. "That's our job. You'll find that out. Moms worry."

I guess I'll find that out pretty soon. Though I don't think I'll ever really feel like a mom to Greg. The thought spikes my blood pressure.

"Hey," I say, to change the subject. "You're good at puzzles, right?"

She allows a smile. "I suppose so."

She and my father used to race at crossword puzzles, which she always won. I half wonder if he still does them.

"What do you think Revelation 13:18, followed by the name Adam, means?"

My mom crinkles her eyes. "Revelation is the quote about the beast, of course."

"Yes," I say, though I wouldn't have known that without researching it.

She frowns, sipping her coffee. "Sounds like a band name or something . . ." Her expression perks up. "A code word maybe?" She pauses. "Though I don't know what it would be a code word for." She titters, raising her eyebrows. "I'm a big help, huh?"

"No, it's okay," I say.

"What's it for, anyway?" she asks, putting her empty cup down again.

"Oh," I say, lifting my hand for the check as the waiter approaches. She could afford lunch, having just retired with a nice pension from her school library job. But she's frugal and would be aghast at the final tally. "Just for the case."

"Ah," she says, her expression icing over. She knows which case and doesn't want to go there. Nor do I. I don't want to describe a blood-stained piece of paper extracted from a pocket of a dead girl.

A girl like Lissa, who never got to live her life.

"What do you think?" I ask, twirling. I feel silly, like I'm auditioning for the part of Cinderella. Though with my broken toe, my foot would be too swollen to fit into the glass slipper.

"It's nice," my mom says, which means she doesn't like it. She seems intimidated by the store, as am I, to be honest. This is the third dress. The first two barely fit, and the saleswoman, Chandra, barely hid her disdain at that fact. I head back into the small fitting room, which smells of peach potpourri, and start putting on the next one, but then peek out as I hear bells jangle.

Melody races in, with Lainey loping beside her. Melody wears a babydoll dress with an oversized jean jacket and black combat boots, Lainey her usual New York Liberty sweats.

"I'm so sorry," Melody says, breathless. "It's all my fault. Rehearsal went long." Lainey widens her eyes in agreement.

My mom gives a quick hug hello to them both. She might not love Jay unconditionally, but my roommates, she definitely does.

"Where were we?" Melody asks, swooping in on the empty sofa, the scent of her rose perfume swooping in with her. Lainey sits next to her, leaning back and stretching out her long legs.

"Three dresses in," I say, frowning at the sleeve cut on the current dress that accentuates my arm fat. "What do you think of this one?"

Lainey tilts her head side to side, which, like my mom's "nice," means *Take it off as soon as humanly possible,* and Melody gives a more straightforward throat-cutting motion. I go back into the fitting room and get into another dress while my mom and roommates chat. I exit the fitting room to the full-length three-part mirror.

"I think he might ask me, you know," Melody muses. "He slowed down by the Tiffany's window the other day."

"Who?" Lainey asks, still looking at her phone. "Mason the Med Student?"

"Would you stop calling him that?" she complains. Then she puts her chin in her hand. "Although, I *did* give him my blood."

Lainey's face pinches in disgust. "What does that mean?"

Melody demurs. "Just a few vials. He was practicing phlebotomy."

"Ahem," I interrupt. "Anyone have an opinion? Or should I just stand here like an idiot all day?"

"Mmm," Melody says, focusing on me. "I like the jewel neck on that one . . . Lainey?" she asks, pointing to the dress.

"Um. Sure, sure, looks great," Lainey says, but barely looks up from her phone.

My mom hems. "I'm not sure about the cream color. Sort of washes you out."

She's right, as usual. I'm ushered into the changing room yet again, the door kept slightly ajar. After carefully twisting and unbuttoning, the new dress comes on.

"This one is a Carolina Herrera," Chandra announces, in a possibly fabricated European-type accent. "Gorgeous."

I nod, pretending I've heard of Dongre as I exit the room to the mirror. I move around, pretending I'm dancing, gingerly with my toe.

"Do the YMCA," Melody quips, putting her arms into a Y. Lainey yawns.

I lean toward the mirror, which divides me into thousands. "Makes me look a little hippy, no?"

"I think it's nice," Lainey says, with a shrug.

"It absolutely makes you look hippy," Melody confirms.

Lainey shrugs again. "I thought it wasn't so bad."

"You've got a beautiful body," my mom says, in her mom way. "But that one doesn't completely flatter it." In other words, hippy.

A chink of frustration breaks through the saleswoman's ever-smiling countenance, and I go into the dressing room, where another dress gets shuffled on. I do another tryout hobbling jig and am informed by Chandra that Claire Pettibone has designed this one.

"It's a pretty dress," my mom says, her tone inviting a "but . . ."

"But not on you," Melody offers.

By the next dress, I've lost count of the total, and am getting sweaty and dejected, my toe throbbing. Melody is practically lounging on the couch. And Lainey is texting someone, probably Ruby, by the way she's smiling. But this time, when I leave the dressing room, I hear gasps circling the room.

"What?" I say, looking all around to see what happened.

Melody has her hands up to her mouth. "That's it," she squeaks out. "That's the one."

"Wow," my mom says, blinking back tears.

Lainey looks up from her phone, her expression floored.

I examine myself, but my audience has called it. I can't explain why it works, but it does. The dress transforms me from someone trying on dresses into a bride.

"I love it," I say.

"Who's the designer on this one?" Melody asks.

"Vera Wang," Chandra says.

Even I have heard this name, which means it must be expensive. It may be gauche to ask, but my mom wanted to buy it for me, and she definitely won't ask. "How . . . how much is it?"

"The dress?" Chandra asks, seeming affronted.

I nod. It seems asking the price was indeed against the rules.

"It's thirty-eight," she says.

"Ah," I say. Thirty-eight hundred is more than I've ever spent on a dress, obviously, but not as bad as I thought. My mom could definitely afford that.

Melody sits forward on the couch. "As in, thirty-eight hundred or thousand?"

Chandra offers a cold smile at the apparently asinine question. "Thousand."

Now, I'm the one who gasps. "Oh, there's no way I can—"

My mom looks shocked—struck-by-lightning shocked.

"Yeah," I say, starting to undo it without Chandra's help. "I think I'm done for now. We'll have to make an appointment for another time."

My mom bites her lip, not speaking. I'm furious at myself for putting her in this position.

"I can FaceTime you for the next one, okay?" I ask her. At another store, where mortgages are not required to buy a dress.

"Um . . ." my mom says, fanning herself with a bridal brochure. "I could come up again, I'm sure." I go back into the dressing room and put on my "civvies" with the relief of putting on sweats after a long day at the office. "We ready?"

My mom nods, appearing dazed, as if she's been through a battle.

Melody "mm-hmms" with a ladyfinger cookie from the store in her mouth, and Lainey zips up her coat, her mini flip-flop key ring in hand.

I'm adjusting my purse when Chandra reappears. Her smiling façade reveals a genuine, almost joyful grin. "Happy news," she says, with a hand clap.

We all look at her in bewilderment.

"I just spoke to Caitlyn, and the dress is a go," she says, practically squealing with pleasure.

We gaze at each other in confusion. "No," I say, with full ire. "The dress is most certainly not a go."

Chandra shrugs. "You'll have to speak with Caitlyn, then," she says, with a confident lilt, clearly unwilling to lose her monstrous commission.

"Because your fiancé has already purchased it."

CHAPTER THIRTY-SIX

NOW

She has a real rotary phone.

Not even an ironic one from a catalog or curio store; an actual old rotary phone. I search in the dim moonlight for a jack, afraid to attract attention by turning on the lights again. I slip my hand behind the nightstand but find nothing. I crawl over the bed to the other nightstand and come up empty there too. Every room has a jack, doesn't it?

On my knees now, I shove my hand as far as I can behind the headboard, and finally, my fingers touch the jack. But then, I hear something. Murmuring.

Slowly, I stand from my crouch position and tiptoe over to the door, putting my ear against the fake wood veneer. It sounds like Esther's voice, the words angry but inaudible. After each utterance, I hear a pause, followed by her heated responses, but no deeper voice answering. So, she's not talking to Noah.

Is she on a phone that she supposedly doesn't own?

Or maybe she's hearing voices and talking to herself? I don't have time to worry about it. I just have to try to get some help and get the hell out of here. Racing back to the bed, I snake the line behind the headboard. Fingers crossed, I plug the landline in and bring the receiver up to listen.

The glorious sound of a dial tone sings in my ear.

But now I've got to dial this rotary thing in the darkness without making any noise.

I dial 911, the cranking and whirring booming in the room. Muffling the dialing with a pillow, I hold up the receiver again. But I must have done something wrong. The dial tone remains absent, as if I haven't finished the call.

Before trying it again, I decide to call Jay, turning the dial slowly and letting it settle after each number. I usually just call from my contacts, but I think I got the number right.

And sure enough, it rings.

I wait out the ringing, over and over. "Pick up, pick up, pick up," I whisper, gripping the receiver. My heart clenches with every ring, praying for him to answer. "Come on," I plead.

His voicemail doesn't even come on. I could see him not answering with Greg there, but his voicemail should come on at least. It doesn't, just keeps relentlessly ringing.

I hang up. Maybe I got the number wrong, since I can barely see the damn dial. I decide to try Lainey and Melody this time, before 911 again. If they're out there, maybe I can help them at least. I carefully dial Lainey's number, and it goes through. After four rings, her voicemail picks up.

Hey, Lainey here. Leave a message.

That's Lainey, straight to the point. "Hi, it's me. I'm trying to reach you." I realize then that this is a blindingly obvious statement. But I don't really have anything to say. *I hope you're not dead?* I don't even have a phone for her to call me back. "I hope you're okay. I . . . I don't know what happened, but I'm trying to find you. I'm in the old Thompson farmhouse. I'm trying to find you." I pause but can't think of anything more. "Okay, bye."

Hanging up, I hear rumbling from the next room. I put a pillow over the phone, waiting and listening. The noises stop. I wait out a long minute and call Melody's number, the pillow still on the phone to muffle the ratchety noises. It takes me two slow dialing attempts.

Hi! It's Melody! I'm crestfallen that I missed your call. But leave me your message, and I will call you anon! Au revoir!

I leave a similar unhelpful message.

Then I pause, strategizing my next steps.

I could call my mom but don't want to needlessly frighten her. I won't bother with my father, who only answers half the time. So I decide to try 911 again, and if it doesn't go through, call Jay again. After dialing the three numbers with great care, this time the call goes through.

They answer after one ring.

My heart rate shoots up, the receiver sweating in my palm.

"Hello, this is 911, what's your emergency?" The voice sounds oddly casual, almost bored.

I cup my hand around the mouthpiece to muffle my voice. "I need help," I whisper. "My friends went missing. They were hurt, and I don't know where they are." Panic rushes through the words. "And it's a blizzard out here and—"

"Ma'am," the voice interrupts. "Let's start with your name and address."

"Oh, yes. Okay. My name is Alex Conley. I'm not sure of the address here, but the street is—" But before I can finish, the call drops.

"Hello?" I push the button up and down. "Hello?" I keep pushing and releasing the button, but no dial tone sounds. "What the hell?" Leaning over, I take the jack out and plug it back in. Still no dial tone.

Then a slice of light appears under the door.

"Alex," Esther whispers, her voice taunting. "Were you trying to call someone?"

CHAPTER THIRTY-SEVEN

AUGUST

The subway screeches to a stop.

"Is it weird?" I ask, as the voice announces the station. We're all standing next to each other after the dress fiasco, as passengers disembark. I'm on my way back to the apartment to finish my day remotely.

Lainey loosens her grip on the grab hold. "Maybe he was just being nice."

"Yeah," Melody agrees, moving away for some final stragglers jumping on the train. "You're probably overthinking it."

"I don't know," I say, as the train jerks to a start. I monitor my toe to avoid any nearby foot traffic. Lainey grabs the grip, and Melody has her arm looped around the pole since she can't reach the hooks. "It just seemed kind of . . . *Pretty Woman* to me."

"Kinda," Melody admits.

"Like he's being a savior, but I don't need a savior." Or showing off his money. *She doesn't know anything.* "I'm sure it was nothing but . . ."

Lainey ducks her head as the train hits a curve. "You could just return it. Get a dress your mom can afford."

"What did your mom say?" Melody asks, adjusting the strap of her satchel.

"You know her," I say, moving my feet to keep my balance. "She didn't want to cause any trouble."

No one speaks for a moment. A little girl down the row whispers to her father, pointing to us, probably amazed at Lainey's height. The father smiles.

"Do you think it's a little . . . controlling?" Melody asks, swinging on the pole to face me.

As usual, Melody plumbs right down to the heart of the issue. *Is* it controlling? Or just loving? Like the time when I called the Stanford loan office, asking why the automatic payments had stopped. Yes, they had stopped, because someone had paid off my debt. My *one-hundred-thousand-dollar* debt.

"I don't know," I answer, truthfully.

After a pause, Melody speaks again, digging in her satchel for some gum. "Do you ever feel like you're in the first scene of *Music Man* when you're standing on a train like this?"

"No," we answer, in unison.

The little girl approaches us, holding something. She glances back at her father for support, who motions her ahead. Then she stops about a foot away from us. "Are . . . you . . . Lainey Trevor?"

"Um," Lainey says, in a low voice. "Yeah."

The girl beams and thrusts out a piece of paper and a pen. "Can I have your autograph?"

Lainey blushes three shades and stammers, "Yeah, sure, of course."

The train jerks to a stop, and the little girl stumbles as Lainey grabs the neck of her coat, keeping her upright. Now, the little girl blushes. "Thanks," she says.

Lainey hands her back her signed paper and pen. "No problem."

Limping back to the apartment, I tell Wiley about the phone call with Eli and the crypto letter. I just can't hold it in anymore. The day has turned sweltering, the hot scent of garbage arising from the sidewalk vents.

"Just ask him," Wiley says. "I'm sure there's a perfectly logical explanation."

"I know, I should," I say, waiting at a corner as a taxi whizzes by, horn bleating in its wake. "But it's like the longer it goes, the harder it is to ask."

The sound of crunching chips comes over the phone. "All I know is this. If you're going to get married, you probably shouldn't have any secrets."

"Right," I say, crossing the street with the masses. "And have you told Josie about how you slept with her cousin?"

"Once," they say, sounding defensive. "Before we were really serious. And he's not even really a cousin, more like a second cousin twice removed or something."

"I'm sure that will make all the difference."

"You're deflecting."

"I'm not de—"

"You so are. Here's the thing. Either you trust him, so you tell him and try to figure this out. Or you're afraid that maybe he's hiding some awful secret . . . like . . . bestiality or something."

"Bestiality?" I pull my head back. This gets a few stares from my fellow pedestrians. It seems bestiality is a bridge too far even for New Yorkers.

"Or something," Wiley emphasizes. "Oh shit. Sorry. I gotta go. Got a meeting in like two seconds. But . . . tell Smokeshow what's going on. Please."

"Okay, okay," I grumble. "I will."

I see our block coming up as we hang up when the phone vibrates with a text in my hand.

I can meet with you, but near me in Hudson Valley

Okay, thank you, I type back. *When? Where?*

How about this Saturday?

Works for me.

Okay, 1 pm. Meet me at the Cooper

1414 Genesee Street

See you there, I write back.

It's Adam Redmond's number. The stepfather.

I feel myself smiling. Finally, one thing is going my way.

"I didn't mean to embarrass you. Or your mom. Honestly, I didn't."

Jay and I sit next to each other on the couch, while Babushka perches on an ivory-tassled pillow. Jay combs his hair with his fingers.

"But you have to understand how it was presented to me. Caitlyn said you really wanted that dress and were super upset that you couldn't get it."

This sets my teeth on edge. "Does that sound at all like me?"

He shrugs, his expression abashed. "No, not really."

"Then I think Caitlyn misled you."

"Yeah, maybe," he agrees. "Or the saleswoman misled her."

"Maybe," I admit, as Babushka leaps into my lap. "Anyway, I'm not getting it. I'll go somewhere else with my mom." *Somewhere Caitlyn hasn't recommended,* I add, in my head. "But I do appreciate the thought."

He nods, then after a pause, slaps his knees.

The cat startles.

"Okay. That's settled, then," he says, with an air of relief and pops up to a stand. "So now the real question is . . . what should we do for dinner? A curry, I'm thinking?"

But that's not the real question. The words tickle my lips. *Did you take care of her?* It's now or never.

"Or Chinese, maybe?" he asks, misinterpreting my silence.

"Jay," I say. "I have to ask you about something."

"Okay," he says, looking alerted by my tone. Slowly, he sits back down.

My mouth gets sticky dry.

"What?" he asks, with some alarm. "What is it?"

"At the tasting," I say, taking a deep breath. "I saw a text from Eli. I didn't mean to pry, but your phone was face up, and I saw it. It said "Did you take care of her?""

His face turns ashen, beads of sweat popping up on his forehead. "Okay?"

"And then I heard you talking about something with him, when I came home a little early the other day." I don't say anything about sneaking around his office. "You said she doesn't know anything. Again, I didn't mean to be eavesdropping, but I heard it."

Jay looks down at his interlaced hands but doesn't say anything.

"So I guess my question is . . . who is she?" I ask.

Frowning, he shakes his head. "No one," he says. "It's . . . it's not what you think."

"It's just," I say, strangling on the words. If I don't get them out now, I may never. "Are you involved in something . . . illegal? With Eli? Like a Ponzi scheme or something?"

He rears his head back. "No, God no. Of course not. Why would you think that?"

I shrug. "Or maybe not that. Maybe something with crypto?" I ask, giving him the chance to confess.

He looks puzzled for a second, but then he pauses and his mouth stiffens. "This is from the letter, isn't it?" he says, simply. He doesn't even sound angry, just disappointed. "In my office. You weren't looking at invitations. You were snooping."

A wave of shame washes over me. "Is it true though?" I ask, in a small voice. "Is there something wrong?"

He pauses a moment, as if trying to collect himself, his face taking on an unhappy cast. "Listen, we both know Eli's a bit much. And I get why you might not trust him. But no, we're not doing anything illegal." He sighs. "The crypto market took a hit, you probably know that."

"Yes," I say. "I guess I did."

"And we were invested in it . . . to some degree," he amends. "So we have to report that to the Feds. That's all. Nothing else. It's a comment letter. That's just . . . part of doing business, Alex. Everyone gets comment letters."

I busy myself petting Babushka. "So, who's she, then? Who was he asking about?"

"A woman from our board. She's . . . making noises." He grips his knees. "As she should. That's her job. But it's making Eli nervous."

I consider his explanation. It makes sense. Maybe that's all it is, a meddling board member. But why be so sneaky about it?

"Alex, if this is going to work, we need a level of trust between us." He motions between us with his hand. "Right? You agree with that?"

I nod. "Yes, I agree."

He gives me a long, hard look. "And if you're not ready to get married, it's okay. But . . . just be straight with me, okay? I know I love you. I know I want to spend my life with you. But if you're not ready to make that step, I get it. You are just starting your career, and I know you're worried about Greg and—"

"I'm ready," I say, interrupting him.

He's right. I need to trust him. He isn't just a Chris rebound. My mom's wrong. I do love him. I know that I do.

"I'm ready," I say again.

CHAPTER THIRTY-EIGHT

AUGUST

The next morning, we kiss each other goodbye, but an air of mistrust lingers between us. Jay's rightfully upset at me for sneaking around his office. And I feel rightfully guilty about that.

But I still feel unsettled inside, like he's not telling me the whole truth. I try to put it out of my mind, to put my full focus on my meeting with Adam Redmond, the stepfather.

He's living in Hudson Valley about an hour away from his old house, teaching high school English now. As I walk into the Cooper bar from the sunny day, my eyes take a moment to adjust to the darkness of the room.

The place looks lifeless and depressing. Dead, like a mall after closing time. A pool table stands unused in one corner, a jukebox in another. The long-bearded bartender stands there cleaning glasses, like a stock "bartender" character from a movie. A lone man sits at the bar with a drink. A country song plays over the speakers to no one but them.

"Mr. Redmond?" I ask, sitting down next to him. "Alex Conley," I say to his nod.

Adam Redmond is a good-looking man, no denying that. He's tall, with broad shoulders, blond hair with streaks of gray, and silver-blue eyes. He would look more appropriate strutting around Wall Street than sitting at this dank bar.

"You want something?" he asks, spinning to face the bar again.

"A Coke," I tell the bartender.

Adam throws back his drink, the ice cubes clacking. He taps the table for another, and the bartender obliges. He seems like a regular.

"So," he says, a puff of alcohol coming out with the word.

"So," I answer, with a sturdy smile. I place my notebook on the bar.

"I understand you have questions," he says, with a hint of a slur to the words. "Go ahead. Ask them. I have nothing to hide."

"I spoke with Eric Myers," I say, as my drink is deposited next to me.

His face sours at the name. "Is that so?"

"Yes, I'm doing an anniversary profile, like I said."

Adam sneers at this. "What an anniversary that is."

I nod, patiently. "I know . . . he's not the most trustworthy. And he has reason to lie. But . . . he said you had issues with your stepdaughter."

He shrugs, staring at his drink. After a long moment, he says, "I suppose we did."

The straightforward answer surprises me. "Because?" I ask.

Adam cradles his glass but doesn't drink from it. "Here's the truth, Alex Conley. When you marry someone with kids, you're marrying them too, like it or not. And I loved her mom. Hopelessly, in fact. But, and this sounds awful to say, I couldn't bring myself to love her daughter."

His soliloquy is sounding uncomfortably familiar.

"So, I'll tell you the God's honest truth. She didn't like me. And I didn't like her. But obviously, I didn't kill her." He gives me a sad smile, showing me his wrists. "Look, ma . . . no tattoos."

"But . . . why? Why didn't you like her?" I ask, astonished with this broad admission.

"Listen," he says, pushing his sweating drink to the side. "Her mother thought she walked on water. But I could see something else." He leans over the bar, his eyes narrowing. "She had darkness in her. A real darkness."

I take a sip of my soda. Is he saying she had the beast in her? Some 666 in her? "What do you mean by that?"

"Impulses," he says, after a long drink. "She liked to drink, do drugs. Have sex. Impulses. Impure impulses." Slowly, he spins his drink on the table. "I wanted to help her. I tried to help her. I gave her a ring, explained how she should respect herself. Keep herself pure, unsullied." He frowns into his drink. "But I was too late. She couldn't be deterred. The devil took his due in the end." He stares ahead at the liquor bottles and sighs. "He always does."

I don't have an appropriate response. We could have a long philosophical discussion on the devil, but Mr. Redmond's suppositions would come down to some basic religious misogyny.

"Why did she have your name written in her pocket?" I ask instead.

He looks defensive at the question. "It wasn't my name," he says, then takes a shaky drink. "There was blood covering up the word. It was like MADAME, or maybe DAMNED or something." He shakes his head. "It wasn't my name. I told them that."

"Okay," I say, writing this down. "And where were you the night she was killed?"

He half smirks. "What, are you the police now?" He adjusts himself on his barstool. "I was at a meeting that night. They ruled me out. I took a polygraph and all that," he says, waving his hand in dismissal.

I dash this down in the notebook too. I'll have to check his story, hopefully when the police records come back from my FOIA request. The conversation hasn't established any new leads, other than the surprising fact that they didn't like each other. Still, his God complex doesn't sit well with me. Maybe he was showing her the light, and it didn't take.

I don't think that theory would be enough to get Toby to bite though.

"Does Revelation 13:18 mean anything to you?" I ask.

He smiles, nodding. "Let the person who has insight calculate the number of the beast, for it is the number of a man." He takes another drink. "Yes, it means something to me."

"Six, six, six," I say, "would be that number."

"Right," he says, gripping his glass. "So it seems that Eric Myers knew that passage too."

"Uh-huh," I say, sensing a dead end. I decide to pivot off religion. "Do you know Leigh Jones?" I ask. "The other woman who was attacked?"

"All I know is they finally believed me that I wasn't involved when she stepped up with her story. Thank Christ," he says, shaking his head. "But otherwise, I don't know her from Adam." Then he lets out a sloppy snort-laugh. "Look at that. I just punned myself."

I answer with an uncomfortable smile. "Or Amelia Adams or Angela Atwood? Do you know them at all?"

"No, my dear," he says. "Not them either."

We both sit for a while in a heavy silence, me sipping my Coke and him his brandy. Then out of nowhere, he turns to me. "Do you believe in God, Alex Conley?"

"Um," I stammer, put on the spot. "I guess I would say that . . . I don't know."

He nods, hunching over the bar. "I suppose that's an honest answer at least."

I close my notebook. "How about you?" I ask. "Do you believe in God?"

"I used to," he says, and takes another drink.

CHAPTER THIRTY-NINE

NOW

I stare at the silent receiver in my hand.

Did she actually cut the line?

"I was just calling 911," I say. "I'm not trying to get anyone in trouble. I'm just trying to help my friends."

"Is that so?" Esther asks, her voice faded behind the door. "Or are you trying to make plans with Noah?"

Trying to make plans with Noah? I hang up the phone then, striding to the door to confront her. "No, I'm not trying to . . ." I say, opening the door. But the handle won't budge. "Esther, you let me out right now. You hear me?"

"I told him you were trouble," Esther says, with a querulous note. "I told him from the very moment I set eyes on you. Just like that Nicole girl."

"Okay, listen," I say to the door, adjusting my tone to convince her. "I promise you. This has nothing to do with your son. I'm not trying to date Noah. At all. I'm engaged already in fact. Remember?"

This is answered with an unconvinced snort.

"Esther," I say, still trying to reason with her. "I was having a *bachelorette* party."

"So you say," she answers.

Again, I turn the knob without success. "I'm not lying about my friends. They might be hurt." I wait to see if she might take mercy on my plight, then hear something metallic knock against the door.

"Noah," I scream, pounding on the door now. Obviously, she will not be swayed, and I can't waste any more time trying to convince her. "Noah!"

"You shush right now," she commands, just above a whisper. "You wake him up and you'll be in some real trouble here."

"Noah," I yell louder, then body-slam the door, creaking the door frame. "Noah, help me please!" I kick the door now and notice the hinges loosening. Maybe I don't need anyone to let me out. I give the door another karate kick. Lainey could probably have kicked this open in two seconds. But Lainey's not here.

"I'm warning you," she growls.

I keep kicking and kicking, my chest sweating.

Hurried footsteps sound down the hall. "What the hell is going on?"

"She locked me in here," I scream, bashing the door.

"Jesus," he grumbles. "Not again."

Not again?

"Come on, Mom. Put that thing away. We've been through this before. It's dangerous." A tumbling sounds in the hallway. "Mom, seriously," he snaps. "You're going to hurt someone."

"She's the seed of the devil, son," she says, her voice strained with effort of fighting him off. "We can't let her out of here."

"Mom, Jesus Christ. Stop. Please." A scuffle emerges on the other side, the knob twisting back and forth. "You need to stop this. Right now."

"It's for your own good," she returns, her body knocking against the door in the invisible skirmish.

"I'm going to call Dr. Singh again," he warns. "Is that what you want? This time, he'll start the medication. I promise you."

"I won't let her hurt you," she cries. "You'll start up again. I know it. And you've worked so hard to be clean, son."

I scoop up my backpack and step back a few paces. Then, with everything in me, I rush my body against the door. The hinges pop off and the door flies open, putting into full view the surprised, sleep-ridden face of Noah and the enraged face of his mother. And in her arms, a shotgun.

She aims it at me.

"No, Mom, no!" he yells, pushing her and the shotgun toward the wall and away from me. "Hurry. Get out of here," he says, holding his mother back.

I barely slip by her and run down the stairs, my backpack thumping against me. Tripping on the last step, I twist my ankle and grunt with the sharp pain. Grabbing my hat, coat, and mittens from the fire, I throw them on as I'm running toward the door, the clothes still damp but warmer now.

"Mom," Noah yells. "Stop!"

Glancing back, I see Esther coming down the stairs, faster than her bad hips should allow, with Noah trailing after her. Her shotgun bobs up and down with each step. I throw on my boots, wet and cold on my new socks, then push the door open and leap outside, wincing at the shot of pain in my ankle, only half in my boots.

I try to run, but it's hardly a run, my ankle and hip killing and snow weighing down every step. I want to look back but can't waste a single second. I just keep jogging in long, lurching steps. A muted voice sounds out behind me.

"It's for your own good, son."

"Mom, please . . ."

I keep pushing forward, as fast as I can. A voice wails inside my head. *Run, Alex.*

Run.

The crack of a shotgun breaks the sky.

CHAPTER FORTY

AUGUST

Later that week, I'm still waiting for my FOIA paperwork on Adam Redmond and Ryan Johnson, when the female Ryan finally answers her phone.

"Sorry," she says, with a strong Long Island accent. "I wasn't trying to avoid you. I just . . . don't have the fondest memories of that time."

"I get that," I say, tapping my pen on my desk. "Ryan said you might not be his biggest fan. That was his exact quote actually."

"Damn right I'm not his biggest fan," she says. "He gave me a fucking STD."

Wiley guffaws, and I take the phone off speaker.

"I see," I say, writing down Ryan-female sign-STD. "But he was there, that night? You're sure?"

Wiley motions drinking coffee with a questioning eyebrow raise, and I shake my head no.

"I'm abso-fucking-lutely sure," she brays. "That's not something you forget."

I guess that would make me bray too.

"And he stayed all night?" I ask, though with a touch of imposter syndrome. I'm asking questions from cop shows since the real-life police never bothered to dig past the superficial layer of male Ryan's story. And if I want to uncover new angles here, then I need to do so. "All night?" I repeat.

"Yes," she answers. "All fucking night." I hear typing noises over the phone, sounding as if she's stabbing the keyboard. "Of course, he wasn't there when I woke up. He said he had to work early. But I bet he went back to see Clare. I was just his side piece back then."

I write this down. The fact is, he could have left at any time after she fell asleep. So the alibi isn't a full alibi after all. This still puts him in the window for the murder.

A loud slurping sound comes over the phone. "I kicked his ass to the curb. But not before he gave me gono-fucking-rhea."

"Uh-huh," I say, giving her some credit for the most creative use of the f-word I've ever encountered.

"But if you're asking if I think he killed that girl, Nicole White?" she says. "The answer is no. No fucking way."

The certitude of her statement surprises me. "And you say that because . . ."

"Because he's an idiot," she says, irked. "I mean, seriously. Ryan was too fucking dumb to get away with that." I hear another slurping sip, and then the keyboard being pounced again. "Plus, he's an asshole, right? But that doesn't mean he's a killer."

"Okay," I say, as Wiley returns with a coffee in hand. "That's good to know." So again, not the nicest guy ever, but not a killer. But also, without an alibi. "Hey, while I have you," I say. "Do you have any idea what Revelation 13:18 means? Followed by the word Adam?"

"What?" she asks, sounding annoyed and done with the interview. "Sounds Biblical. Ryan might remember. He was in that Bible class with her."

I pause. "Ryan was in the class? I thought Clare was."

"They both were," she says, "as far as I remember." She slurps another drink. "Explains why Nicole was a bit of a wild child anyway."

I flip to a new page in the notebook. "I know she was in the class too. But . . . why would that make her a wild child?"

"Because obviously she was rebelling against the teacher," she says, with some annoyance. "I don't remember his name, but . . . you know . . . her stepfather."

***

"Yes, but the investigators must have known that too," Toby says, unimpressed.

She spins from side to side in her chair, her feet barely reaching the ground, looking like a child playing at her parent's office.

"I didn't see it mentioned anywhere," I return, gripping the arms of my chair across from her. "Any of this. It's like they just gave up on any investigation of the note when they got word on Eric Myers."

She shrugs, the movement barely visible under her oversized blazer. "Can you blame them?"

"No," I say, rubbing my arms in the overly air-conditioned room. "And I'm not saying he didn't do it. Just that it deserves another look. No one has adequately explained the Revelation note. No one has—"

"That just points to the 666 thing again, doesn't it?" she asks, sounding dubious.

"Maybe," I admit. "But it also might have to do with this Bible group. Nicole and Ryan Johnson were in it. So was Clare, his ex. And Nicole's father led the class. That just seems too coincidental."

Toby squints in thought. "I don't understand this. Ryan was dating who? Another Ryan?"

I exhale. "Okay," I say, leaning forward with my elbows on my knees. "Boy Ryan met Clare in Bible class, and they started dating. He then met Clare's friend Nicole, the victim, in the same Bible class and cheated on Clare with Nicole. But he was still sleeping with Clare, and the night of the murder, he went creeping to cheat on Clare with Girl Ryan. But he left Girl Ryan's house before morning, maybe to go to work. Maybe to go back to Clare. Maybe to kill Nicole. And in the midst of this all, Nicole's stepfather was leading the Bible class."

Toby lifts one eyebrow. "This Boy Ryan has gumption."

"I suppose," I say, though this is not the moral of the story I would have come away with.

"So, let's say the father did it. Or . . . Boy Ryan did it. Either one."

"Yes," I say, cheered that she's even considering it.

"Then why did they attack Leigh Jones first? Before Nicole? What's the connection there?" She tucks a pencil behind her ear. "And why kill the other girls?"

A long pause follows the question. I have ruminated on this too, without an adequate answer.

"I can see the stepfather or boyfriend being in the frame for Nicole's murder," Toby says, pursing her lips. "But then they suddenly become serial killers?"

I rub my ice-cold hands together. "But they've never actually proved that Eric Myers killed the other girls. It might be someone else altogether. It's possible that this isn't a serial killer after all. Maybe the A-girls are totally separate. And we just need to find a connection between Nicole White and Leigh Jones."

The pencil slips out from behind her ear and onto the floor. She dips down to retrieve it, then pops back up, looking like Ariel arising from the water. "And have you?" she asks. "Found any connection?"

I shake my head. "But it's a small town where they live. There still might be."

Toby tilts her head side to side in debate. "But we have one more problem. How do you explain the tattoo?" She starts half spinning in the chair again. "Neither Ryan nor the stepfather have it."

"No," I admit. "They don't."

Toby stares off, her eyes scrunching together. "What does Leigh Jones have to say about your theory?"

I clear my throat. "I haven't exactly reached her yet."

This is met by a look of consternation. She lets out an exorbitant sigh. "We're not putting any more resources into this profile until you at least speak with the main witness. You got a couple months left. Get it together, Alex."

CHAPTER FORTY-ONE

NOW

Another shot rings out, hurting my ears.

I'm sucking the cold air, running too slowly, like a dream where you're slogging through molasses, snail slow despite using every muscle as a mad murderer chases you.

But this time, it's for real.

Another shot. A scream.

It takes me a second to realize I am the one screaming. Something smacks beside me, sending a cloud of snow into the air.

A bullet.

I keep going, my boots nearly getting ripped off in the deep snow. Zigzagging to make myself a harder target, I am cringing against incoming bullets, imagining the hot piercing of skin, a scattershot of pellets tunneling into my back, my thighs, my ribs. Blood filling my chest cavity.

Maybe I deserve this. If I had the knife and I hurt my friends, then getting shot would be one form of justice. My life for their lives, still not an even trade.

But I don't stop running.

Bullets hit the snow, powder bursting all around me. I keep up a maddeningly slow pace, but every additional foot makes me a harder target. I don't hear more gunfire, but I don't dare turn around. Maybe Noah held her off, but she could still strike. I'm not that far out. A bullet could still hit me. Maybe not with a shotgun though? I don't know enough about shotguns to test my theory, so I keep up my jog-running.

Soon enough, I find myself sidestepping into the driveway again. My boot prints remain from my previous trek, half filled with fresh snow. Moving back into the driveway, I step in my old footprints to ease my way, making the journey marginally faster.

It hits me, literally walking in my own footsteps, how futile this whole interlude has been. I haven't accomplished anything except nearly get myself shot by some demented farmer's wife.

This time, I do take a chance and glance backward. The house stands on the hill in the moonlight, forlorn and desolate, Noah and his mother gone. I slow my pace just a bit, my breath slowing too. The immediate danger has passed, and I'll need to reserve my energy now to find Melody and Lainey.

As I look up at the moon weaving in and out of a cloud, icy wind slices my neck above my collar in the vulnerable inch of skin.

I flip open my trusty compass again. Maybe I should head back to the lodge. They could be back there waiting for me, for all I know. Or the killer could be there.

Unless . . .

No. I put the thought out of my mind. I really don't think I could have done this.

I look behind me again at the depressing house and ahead at the depressingly long driveway, and let out a disconsolate sigh, smoking the freezing air. I don't have any great options here. I just have to get back to the street.

Maybe a car will come by.

I trudge along the monotonous street.

The epinephrine from my brush with death has worn off. But I have renewed energy from the rest and warmth of the farmhouse at least, my clothes are no longer sopped, my hunger has been abated by the cookies, and a jolt of caffeine is running through my system.

My improved physical state has only worsened my mental state, however. Instead of spending every ounce of energy on focusing on staying upright, my brain can stray from its leash into dangerous territory. Visions keep popping up, and I keep trying to shut them out, like some sick game of Whac-A-Mole.

Blood soaking the sheepskin rug, dotting the pillows.

The scrunchie matted with Lainey's hair.

The long knife blade, slick with blood.

The handle warm in my hand.

My arm lifting up and . . .

"Stop!" I yell at myself. *Stop. Stop. Stop.*

I blink my eyes to stop the visions, squeezing them shut. Then I open them again to everlasting white. Snow, snow, and more snow.

But then I see something—a little black dot in a halo of light, barely visible through the vast snow. The dot swells. Then I hear it, the buzz of an engine. I almost don't want to wave in case I jinx it, like acknowledging this mirage might make it disappear. The black dot expands into a car.

I step toward the street, carefully this time. I was lucky to have woken up from the last fall. That concussion could have turned into an eternal sleep. As the car crawls closer and closer, I hear the rumble of the tires, the engine hum, and the squeak of the wipers. Closer and closer, until the car reveals itself to be a pickup truck, definitely not a silver sedan this time.

I give the driver an uncertain wave, and the black truck slows down and stops, the smell of hot fuel smoking the air. My heart soars. The car is stopping, actually stopping for me. I can't believe my luck.

The window lowers, revealing a man's face. He leans across on empty seat.

"Need a lift?" he asks.

CHAPTER FORTY-TWO

SEPTEMBER

"Lilies?" my mom asks, as if she just said a bad word.

"I don't know," I grumble. I'm trying to "get it together," as Toby put it, and don't have time to worry about the wedding right now. I called Ryan back to double-check with him on the Bible class but didn't hear back. I called Leigh Jones yet again without any success, and I'm planning to confront Adam Redmond on the Bible class, but surprise, surprise, he's not answering my calls either.

And I still haven't made any further headway on the Revelation 13:18 ADAM question. The whole thing seems like a fool's errand. If it even *is* a password (which isn't certain either), I still don't know the matching username, email, or website.

"I thought you said you wanted roses," my mom says, with a plaintive edge that grates.

"It's not a big deal, Mom," I say, examining the close-up of ADAM in the book. Maybe Adam Redmond is right about blood blocking a letter? Could it be MADAME? That makes no sense either though. "I guess Caitlyn thought they would look nice with the Rainbow Room décor. Jay did too."

My mom doesn't say anything, but I know what she's thinking. *And what does Alex want?* But Alex doesn't care that much.

"I'm just saying it's not a huge deal." I search TikTok for Eric Myers and come up with thirteen different profiles, none of which belong to him. Though they wouldn't have had TikTok ten years ago.

"Okay, if you want lilies, then," she says, disappointment flooding the words.

"Mom," I say, her name a sigh. "You can look into roses. Roses would be pretty. I would *love* for you to research roses."

"Oh okay, good," my mom says, her tone suddenly cheery. Then she pauses. "Hold on, that's the florist on the other line as we speak. Gotta go."

She hangs up and I go back to work, investigating other email servers, Yahoo, WhatsApp, even AOL. They searched his Apple email at the trial, finding nothing incriminating. I doubt he has an extra email anyway. He isn't exactly a computer mastermind. He wouldn't have been changing VPNs or using an encrypted site. I'm trying out another username when Wiley takes a seat next to me.

"'Sup?" Wiley asks.

"Nada," I answer. "Arguing with my mother over lilies versus roses."

"I hope you decided on lilies," Wiley says, taking a slurp of coffee. "Roses are so passé."

"Your opinion is noted and duly ignored," I say, pulling up the segment on the *Crimeline* episode about the note. Though I recall the piece being useless. All they did was insinuate and hypothesize, and add a dollop of overzealous intrigue, à la Fletcher Fox.

"Hey." Wiley turns to me, pulling a rubber band through their hair. "What did Smokeshow have to say about the texting? And don't tell me you 'forgot' to ask."

"No, I asked him," I say, taking a sip from my Babushka mug. "I'm an idiot. It's just a normal SEC letter, not a Ponzi scheme or something. I just have an active imagination."

They adjust their ponytail. "Occupational hazard, I suppose," they say, checking their computer. Wiley's researching a case of a wife killing her husband for a change of pace.

After some time, I finally hit upon the Revelation 13:18 ADAM portion in the *Crimeline* episode. The piece reads as I recalled, information-free. They just zoom in and out on the image, a camera technique both dated and nauseating. "Ugh," I say. "This is useless."

Take a break," Wiley says, then pauses. They spread their arms out with a flourish and sing "Take a Break" from the *Hamilton* musical. Wiley never misses an opportunity to launch into a *Hamilton* song.

They're still going when luckily we are by interrupted by Benji, the shy and skinny mail clerk, dropping off stacks of mail. Benji moves down intern row, and Wiley stops singing to check their mail. I, too, peruse my small pile, immediately tossing the Hawaiian cruise brochure (Caitlyn said she was sending cruise ideas, I told Jay that would lead to an immediate divorce), along with a clothes catalog.

Then I see an envelope with the address handwritten. My mind goes back to a few months ago, when Eric Myers first wrote me. But this envelope shows no return address, so it couldn't be from him.

As my journalism professor used to say, sometimes the best tips come from unexpected places, so I tear it open, taking out the trifolded paper.

The message looks like it was written in finger paint, with large, smudged letters in a rudimentary print.

666

YOU'RE NEXT BITCH

It takes a second to realize that it's not finger paint though. It's blood.

"We'll send it for DNA," Juanita says, holding the letter with gloves. "But it's gonna take a bit. Two weeks at least."

"Okay," I say, sitting by her desk, my heart finally slowing down. "You think it's the same person who sent the first note? With the roses?"

"Maybe. We'll take another look at that one, but probably won't get much further than we did before."

I consider who could have sent it. It wouldn't get through the prison. It could be Adam Redmond, though he would probably view such an act as beneath him. Ryan Johnson might have done it. He seems too benign, too lightweight for such a deed. But then again, he lied to me about the Bible class. And he doesn't have an alibi for the whole night.

Of course, it could be any old Twitter bro or some sicko following the Armchair Sleuths. "What do you think?" I ask her. "Maybe I'm stirring up a hornet's nest?"

Juanita shrugs, taping the bag shut. "Could be a false flag op too." She offers me a water bottle, which I take.

"What do you mean by that?" I ask, unscrewing the cap and taking a shaky sip.

"Pretty classic, actually. The prisoner gets a friend to send a scary message, then it looks someone else is threatened by your investigation, so the original suspect . . ."

"Eric Myers," I say.

"Yes," she answers. "Then he himself must be innocent."

I consider it, though I don't know how many "friends" Eric Myers has on the outside. The underdressed executive producer's son lopes by the office, giving us an ironic salute, and we both pretend not to see him.

"Anyway," Juanita says. "We'll run it for fingerprints too. Get our handwriting folks involved if we need to as well." She yawns into her fist. "Let me know if you get anything else."

"Okay," I say, standing up. I guess that's about all they can do. If it's a false flag operation, then it just points to Eric Myers again. But maybe that's not it. Maybe I'm getting close to the truth and someone doesn't like that.

And that just might convince Toby to give the profile a closer look.

CHAPTER FORTY-THREE

NOW

I nod, too dumbstruck to speak.

I don't want to spoil this dream, to pervert it somehow. It seems too good to be true. A car came and actually stopped. I will not freeze out here. I will find my friends. Someone will finally lead us all back to safety.

"Come on in, then," he says. The man looks about forty, with a military-style buzz cut, black hair mixed with gray. His face is stubbly, with a prominent cleft chin. "You might as well get out of this weather."

I make a lightning-quick assessment, deciding he might or might not try to kill me, but it's still the best option I've got. With a sharp click, the door unlocks, and I hobble toward it. But my ankle gives, and I nearly slip on the footrail.

"Whoa," he says, holding out a hand for me to grab.

The gesture feels unexpectedly intimate, his hand warm and thick, even through the mitten. "Steve," he says, to our pseudohandshake.

"Alex," I answer, catching my breath.

My body quivers with cold, but the heat in the cab instantly envelops me. When the window whirs back up, the pine air freshener overwhelms the little space, and I cough, my lungs transitioning from bitter cold to warm chemical air. The blue digital clock reads 3:10 AM

"You okay?" he asks, pointing to my face. "Looks like your lip is swollen."

"Yeah," I say, holding in a cough. "I fell."

"Hmm," he says. The car rumbles off. "So where are you headed?" he asks. His tight black shirt covers intimidating muscles. Dog tags swing from the rearview mirror. He reminds me of an actor from some corny SEAL movie.

"I . . ." I don't have a ready answer for this. I could go back to the lodge, but where does that get me? And what if he's back? "I'm actually in a bit of trouble," I admit, still trembling with cold. "I was hoping maybe you could take me to a police station."

"A police station?" he repeats, sounding spooked. His large hands squeeze the steering wheel, a large boxy ring with a blue stone on his pinkie finger. Words encircle the stone. *United States Army.* So not a SEAL, but close enough. "Why, what's going on?" he asks.

I pause. I don't know if I can trust this guy, but I don't really have a choice right now. "Someone hurt my friends," I say.

His eyebrows shoot up. "What do you mean, hurt your friends?"

"We . . . we were staying in a Vrbo and someone came," I say, but then start coughing. "I don't know exactly what happened but . . . they took my friends." The words come out between fits of coughing. "And I went to this farmhouse and . . ."

"Wait a second," he says, putting his hand up in a stop motion. "Calm down. Take a breath." He mimics deep breathing for me, in the most patronizing way possible. "Why don't we start at the beginning here?"

"Okay," I say, slowing the words down. The heat pours out of the vents, turning from luxuriating to sweltering, and I unzip my coat. "My friends and I were staying in this hunting lodge. And we had too much to drink." I don't tell him about the White Widow, unsure if he would approve, given his Army background. "It's my bachelorette party," I explain.

"Congratulations," he says, with a nod.

"Thank you," I answer, getting the perfunctory polite exchange out of the way. "And I woke up in the bedroom shower. I don't even know how I got there. Maybe . . . sleep-walking or something." I also don't tell him about the REM Behavior Disorder—too much detail. "And when I went back into the main room, there was blood all over." The hot air dries out my nostrils, stinging my sinuses. "And my friends were missing."

His eyes widen. "You say there was blood?"

I nod.

His thumb thumps on the steering wheel. "How many people were at this party?" he asks, in a straightforward military logistical mode.

"Just two. Lainey and Melody. My best friends."

"Okay." His hands rest on the steering wheel in a perfect two o'clock, reminding me bizarrely of driving lessons with my father. My throat tickles with another cough. "And they were gone," he verifies. "And you saw blood on the premises."

"Lots of blood on the premises," I say, repeating the word, which conjures up a bad cop show. "We're staying at the Hobbes Lodge."

He frowns with disdain. "The 666 Lodge? You one of those crime junkie tourists or something?"

The heater blasts my cheek. "It was just . . . for the party. They thought it would be funny."

"Young girl gets slaughtered," he says, leaning over the steering wheel. "Hilarious."

I pull at the collar of my sweater, my neck sweating. "No, it isn't funny. You're right. But . . . nevertheless, they might need help. That's why I wanted to go to the police station."

He nods but doesn't answer. I have no idea whether he's driving in that direction or not. He taps his fingers on the wheel, his ring clacking.

"Or if you have a phone, maybe I could just call 911?" I ask.

Again, he doesn't answer, just stares straight ahead, his expression undecided.

It strikes me then that I don't know this guy at all. Maybe he has a reason to avoid the police.

"Listen," I say, swallowing with a dry throat. "Forget about the police station. All I need is a phone. I can make the call. You don't even have to get involved."

His gaze shifts from the road to me. "It's coming from my phone number though."

"We'll put it on private," I say. "And you can just drop me off at a corner somewhere around here. I'll tell them where to pick me up."

He bites his lip, seeming to consider this. "How do I even know you're telling the truth?" He turns to me again, the streetlights glaring off his brown eyes. "You don't have a spot of blood on you."

"Yeah, I washed it off." I can barely even remember doing this, but I can see the blood ringing the drain of the sink, soaping my hands in a sort of delirium. Still, it brings up a good point, which gives me minimal comfort. If I had done this, it should be over more than my hands. I should be covered in it, with cuts on my fingers from the knife. My mind flips back to interviews with Eric Myers, which seem from a different lifetime. *There would have been something on me. Blood, sweat. Some DNA.* But again, I feel the knife handle in my hands, see it flying down.

"All you have to do is let me borrow the phone."

He looks at me for another long second, then sighs. With further hesitation, he takes the phone out of his pocket. But before he can hand it over, the popping sound of static interrupts us.

Yeah, we got a report of a 10-22. I repeat a 10-22.

The message comes from a box on the dashboard, the disembodied voice filling up the cab. I point to the box. "What . . . is that a—"

"Police scanner, yeah," he answers, with a serious nod. "I like to keep abreast of things."

And *I'm* the crime junkie tourist, I think, but don't say anything. The phone lingers in his hand. I think back to my interview courses in college and decide to try flattery. "Interesting," I say, adding a feminine lilt to my voice. "Do you know all the codes, then?"

"Yup," he says, and puts the phone beside him in his seat, tempting me. I could just reach out and grab it. But I don't trust Steve. He might not like that. "You know what a 10-22 is, for example?" he asks, with a hint of braggadocio.

"Um . . ." I stare at the phone. "No, I don't. What's a 10-22?"

The box squawks again.

Static . . . static . . . believed to be armed and dangerous. White male static . . . static . . .

"Prisoner escape," he says, then taps on his temple. "All in here. Every single code."

A sick feeling slithers through me. "I'm sorry . . . did you say . . ."

"Yup, 10-22. Prison break."

CHAPTER FORTY-FOUR

SEPTEMBER

"I still think we should look into it," Jay says, sitting up on his elbows. "First the roses, then this letter. It seems like the guy's escalating."

We're in bed, half reading and half conversing, lying on top of the covers on this hot summer night. He sleeps shirtless, so I'm basically sleeping with an underwear model.

"I don't need security," I say, turning the page of my newest thriller.

He sighs. "At least think about it," he says, swiping the page of some financial magazine on his tablet. "For my sake."

I smile at him and turn back to my book. "Okay, for your sake." The mattress conforms to my body, some expensive foam mattress that doesn't have bedsprings to creak. "It's weird though, right?"

"Getting a letter written in blood? Yeah, I'd say that was weird," he says, tapping on his tablet.

"No, the stepfather thing," I say, which we were discussing earlier. "That he was the Bible class teacher."

On my nightstand, a text chimes from my phone. Leaning over, I check out the screen, which shows roses in two subtly different pink colors. *Bridal Akito or La Perla?* my mom asks. *Or we could do the lilies if you really want.* I show Jay the screen.

"Bridal Akito for sure," he says, with utter confidence.

He says everything with utter confidence. He could land a plane with utter confidence. But then again, he actually *does* know how to fly a plane.

"By the way," he says. "My mom likes roses more than lilies too."

I smile. I know he's trying to appease me. His mom pretty much hates me but is too well-bred to admit it. Her smile was icy when we met over FaceTime, naturally melting when she spoke of Jay's ex, Emily, of course. But then again, my mom doesn't love Jay either.

I pause for a minute then, thinking of something. "Moms," I say. I've been so focused on her stepfather, I barely even thought about the mom.

"Yeah," he answers, absentmindedly. "They're the best, huh?" He turns off the tablet and puts it on his nightstand.

"No," I say. "Maybe the mom knows about it."

He turns to me. "Knows about what?"

"The Revelation thing."

It could have come up in the unedited interview. She could have some glimmer of insight, a clue they didn't catch.

"Ah," he answers, in an "I should have known" tone. "You could maybe research that tomorrow?" he asks, drawing his wrist toward him to check his watch. "It is midnight."

"Yeah," I say, putting my thriller on the nightstand. "Good thought. Tomorrow."

I'm about to turn off my light and go to sleep when I remember there's an underwear model lying next to me. I give him a little smile, which he returns, then I reach out to him, running my finger down the ridges on his stomach.

"Mmm," Jay murmurs, shifting over to my side. He starts kissing my neck, soft kisses trailing up to my face, the finest prickle of his beard tickling my skin.

"Mmm," I purr back, tugging his boxers down. I slide my hand across the carved-out muscle of his thigh, and I'm stealing breaths between kisses as he nudges my legs open with his knee.

"No!" I yell, shoving him away.

A man in a balaclava is trying to stab Babushka. I try to pull him off her, but he just keeps stabbing so I punch him as hard as I can. I hit bone, my knuckle splintering. Blood spurts out of his face, but he keeps lunging for my cat so I keep punching him, smashing his lip open, cracking his eye socket.

I wake up when I punch the wall.

My pajama shirt soaked, I sit up, catching my breath. Jay sleeps an inch away from where I was punching. Babushka opens one eye, and drifts back off, unaware of my attempts to save her in my dreams. In a daze, I look at my knuckles, the middle one pink and swollen already.

Unnerved, I get out of bed, rubbing my hand. I know from experience that there's no use trying to fall back to sleep.

Either I'll stay up all night in bed, my body anxious and wired, or worse, I'll fall back asleep and into a dream where I'm fighting again.

I sneak quietly out of the room and check my phone, the bright light burning my eyes, extinguishing any hope of sleeping again anyway. The Akito rose picture is still on the screen, which brings to mind my train of thought before I got distracted by Jay's six-pack beckoning me. My mom. His mom.

Nicole White's mom.

Revelation 13:18 ADAM.

Since no sleep is on the horizon, I figure I might as well do some research and head to the guest room to find my laptop on the table still. The computer hums as I turn it on, the light turning the room a ghostly white. With a yawn, I get to the unedited *Crimeline* episode, searching and finally finding the interview with Nicole White's family. Picking up my notebook from the table, I turn the volume down on the player, so as not to wake up Jay, then press PLAY.

CHAPTER FORTY-FIVE

NOW

S teve flicks off the scanner.

I almost fall over, leaning with my ear right up to the box. "Can you turn it back on? So we can get the prisoner's name?" I ask, a shrill note to the question. "Or the prison at least?"

"Don't worry about it," he says.

"Yeah, but . . . do we know if the escape was from around here?" I ask, inches away from turning the box back on myself.

Steve scratches his chin, his hand rasping against the stubble. "Nah, it could be from anywhere. Scanner picks up lots of stuff. Pennsylvania, New Jersey . . ." He puts one of his hands across the back of the seat, uncomfortably close to me, and I shift over.

"Listen," I say, deciding to lay it all on the line. "I work at *Crimeline*. As an intern. And I'm interviewing a prisoner for a profile. And the prisoner that I'm interviewing is Eric Myers." I pause for him to register this.

He switches lanes. "Am I supposed to know him or something?"

"He's the 666 Killer," I say, my patience thinning. "And I've interviewed him. A lot. So that prisoner escape on the scanner, that could be him. And if it is, he might have returned to the murder site. And he might be taking this very personally."

This provokes laughter. "Which means what . . . he sped off to the Hobbes Lodge to attack your friends and kidnap them?"

"Yes," I answer, weakly. Put that way, it does sound far-fetched. But is it any more far-fetched than the alternative? That I committed this atrocity? Or Chris did?

Or Adam Redmond or Ryan Johnson?

"You know what I think?" he asks, but doesn't wait for me to answer. "I think you're seriously disturbed."

I take a breath. "And I appreciate that opinion, but—"

"You know what else I think?" He sizes me up, then seems to make a decision. "I think this is what we're gonna do." Out of nowhere, he makes a skidding U-turn, and I grimace as my hip slams into the console. The car righted, he turns back to me with a chilly smile. "We're going to drive back to the lodge. And see if you're telling the truth."

He tucks his phone back in his pocket, and my heart falls to the floor. But at least we're going to the lodge. Maybe he'll finally help me then. And if the killer is there, at least I'll be with someone with military training.

"Because if you're lying to me," he says, an edge to his voice. "I'm going to be very, very angry."

We seem to be going in slow motion though, with Steve in no hurry to get back to the lodge.

"Hey, listen . . ." I move my arm, hitting my elbow against the console with an electric shock of pain. "Maybe we should call the police in the meantime. They can meet us there."

"No. I want to see this place first," he says. "Then we'll call the cops. I'm not getting the police out in a blizzard if it's not worth it."

I don't say anything in answer, and we continue to crawl ahead. He puts on the radio to a Classic Rock station, and Lynyrd Skynyrd sings out, while I impatiently drum my fingers on the console. After a few minutes, he looks at them and scowls.

The minutes keep ticking away. But I can't easily grab his phone out of his pocket. At least we'll be there soon enough. Maybe it's the best I can do for the moment.

I stay on guard, watching outside for landmarks. I don't know the area at all but vaguely remember an old tractor by the side of the road, snow piling on the seat. I remember a huge white cross with a carefully written "Jesus loves you and I do too." The snow blanks out everything. We might not even be going in the right direction for all I know, but I'm afraid to take out my compass in case he takes it. Despondent, I stare out at the snow, while Steve Miller urges us to take the money and run. Then we pass the old peeling vodka billboard, and I sit up straighter. I definitely remember that one. We are probably only a mile away from the lodge right now. The turnoff is just ahead.

For the first time since getting in the car, my body relaxes a millimeter.

But then we pass the turnoff to the driveway.

"I . . . I think we missed the lodge, actually," I say, trying to keep the panic out of my voice.

Steve glances in the rearview mirror. "Yeah, I wanted to take care of something else first."

My heart thumps hard in my chest. "Listen," I say. "You know what? I'm good. I don't even need the phone. You do your thing. I'll get going. I know my way from here."

He doesn't slow down though. "It won't take long," he says. "I have some friends nearby. Figure we can pay them a visit before we go to the lodge."

This does not sound promising. "Yeah, but I really need to help my friends out," I insist.

"We will," he says. "Eventually." He shifts lanes to find dry pavement. "You got drunk. You smell like weed . . . so obviously you like to party. My friends like to party too. I think you'll get along with everyone really well."

My stomach dips.

He chucks me on the chin. "Relax. It'll be fun."

But right then, the wheels hit a patch of ice. He yanks on the steering wheel, hitting the brakes, as we skid several several feet ahead. Then we finally stop, the wheels thudding into a snow bank.

"Fuck," he says.

Without a second thought, I whip myself over and open the door. A frigid wind blasts inside the cab area.

"Hey," he barks. "What do you think you're doing?" He lunges toward me, and I kick out, hitting his testicles as hard as I possibly can. The effect is immediate. "Argh," he cries, sounding like a wounded animal. His face shrivels in pain.

"Thanks for the ride," I yell, while he's otherwise occupied, grabbing my mittens and tumbling out of the truck. My knee hits the footrail, sliding off, and my coccyx slams against the pavement. I scramble myself up.

"Fucking bitch," he wails, climbing out of the car. "Get back here right now."

I start running.

"You get back here," he screams.

The words echo into the night.

CHAPTER FORTY-SIX

SEPTEMBER

"**S**he was a joy," Donna White says, with a pained smile. "A joy from the first day she was born."

I don't bother putting that in my notes, the statement said often enough in these interviews to be a cliché. The fallen family member was always a "joy from the day she was born." But maybe I'm just getting jaded.

"She was popular?" Fletcher Fox asks, in his annoying gravelly voice.

"Oh yes. Very," Donna White says. "She was the most outgoing of all of my kids. Everyone just gravitated to her."

Fletcher Fox nods, sympathy still plastered on his face. "And she did well in school?"

"Very," Donna White says.

"She was really, really smart," her sister, Kelsey White, confirms. Kelsey sits next to her mother, nodding along with most points. Kelsey looks like Nicole, as the not-quite-as-pretty sister. "She used to tutor kids, you know, but . . . for free."

"She did, yes," her mother agrees. "She did do that." She gives a distant smile. "That was her though. Always helping everyone. That was just . . . her way."

These "mom" interviews seem almost scripted at this point. The murder of a child fractures families. The victim becomes sainted in death, and all the remaining family members less than perfect by default. Kelsey becomes a bit player, a supporting role in the interview, and in the family, in her life. She has the rotten luck of still existing in a world where Nicole does not.

I know this because it happened to my mom too. Her sister lived on for years in a shrine on the mantel, and my mom could never compete. My grandfather stopped trying. He just checked out and moved across the country. And my mom married someone who would eventually do the same.

These serial killers don't just kill daughters, they kill families too, their bloody fingerprints not just on the murder weapon but embedded in the family for generations.

"What were things she liked to do?" asks Fletcher Fox, rubbing his silver-flecked goatee.

"Oh." Mrs. White smiles at the question. "You name it. She played volleyball. She loved reading. Tennis. She was good at pretty much anything she did." She appears in a reverie for a moment. "Video games," she says, with a laugh.

"Really?" He gives her a wide, bemused smile.

"Yes. I know it was funny." She nods at the memory. "But she really did like them. Even the ones that were kind of . . . violent . . ."

The word palls the moment, and I can see why they cut it now. It doesn't fit the groove of the usual saccharine family interviews.

"It wasn't easy to be . . . what do they call it . . . *gaming*, as a girl. People disrespected her." Donna White appears cross at the thought.

I consider the Twitter bros, and how this has changed depressingly little in the last decade. But I don't think someone would kill her over it.

"Oh, and butterflies," Kelsey says, jumping in her seat.

This part was in the television version. Butterflies will always make the final cut.

"Oh my God, butterflies," Donna White says, laughing, then wipes a tear. "She did love those butterflies. She knew all the names, all the types. It was almost . . ."

"An obsession," Kelsey finishes the sentence, laughing.

Donna White joins in the good-natured laughter, wiping her eyes again. "An obsession is right. Everything butterflies. Her jewelry, her journals, her room."

Here they cut to a purple room with a huge purple butterfly tapestry. Butterfly decorations hang from the ceiling, floating and flitting with every door and window opening. On the bed lie butterfly pillows atop a butterfly duvet. I wonder if her room was preserved, as families sometimes do, like a morbid museum or time capsule. The fake butterflies still flying, though their owner has left, never to return.

"She had something else that was a butterfly too, did she not?" Fletcher Fox adds, his eyes crinkling.

"Yes," Donna White says, followed by an awkward pause. "She had a butterfly tattoo . . . on her ankle."

I'm half surprised they allowed this in the interview, but then again, even a sugary interview needs a dash of spice.

"Mom, you were so mad," Kelsey says, saving the tense interaction.

The moment becomes a lark instead of a blot on her otherwise sainted memory.

"Yes, I was kind of mad," Donna White admits, with a sheepish grin. "She snuck off with her friends and got that one. She was . . . testing boundaries."

I pay closer attention here. Testing boundaries. In other words, she wasn't the perfect scholar-athlete, butterfly-loving child with a side of violent video games. There was cannabis in her blood stream. She got drunk with her friends. She got a tattoo on the sly. (Not that any of this deserved to get her killed, mind you.)

A picture of the tattoo flashes up on the screen, with knifed slash marks through it.

Eric Myers didn't like the tattoo, it seems.

"I told her I'd pay for her next one," Donna White says, with a rueful smile. "If she'd wait until she was twenty-one to get it."

Crying again, she wipes her nose, and Kelsey leans over to hug her.

"Unfortunately, she never . . ." Fletcher Fox says, liberally rubbing salt into the wound.

Donna White sniffles, then straightens up. "Got that chance," she says, finishing his sentence, with a touch of coldness at his insensitive prodding. But that's *Crimeline*, rife with gently insensitive prodding. "No, she never got that chance."

The voice-over comes on then.

The 666 Killer didn't just break Nicole's heart necklace. He broke her mother's heart.

I'm about to turn it off after that smarmy cut. The interview added nothing of merit, no clues to the password anyway, when something hits me. I rewind a few seconds and play the outro again.

The 666 Killer didn't just break Nicole's heart necklace. He broke her mother's heart.

Her mother's broken heart. Heart necklace.

I grab the book on my desk, flipping over to the autopsy photos, and gasp. Jay murmurs something in his sleep, then quiets down, his soft snoring starting up again. In shock, I stare at the autopsy photos.

How the hell did I miss that?

CHAPTER FORTY-SEVEN

NOW

The car door bangs shut.

"Hey," Steve bellows, the word exploding with fury. "Where do you think you're going?" His footsteps creak in the snow behind me.

My limp slows me down, my hip jolting with every step. The frigid air stings my lungs, but I keep running as best as I can, not daring to look back.

A hand swipes my backpack, and I shake it off and keep running.

I have no idea where I am or where I'm going. All I know is that I need to escape him. My backpack bobs against me, sending riveting pain into my hip, and my elbow feels loose, hyperextended. I ignore the pain, just focusing on outrunning him. And he remains right on my tail, his footsteps inches behind me. My footing slips, but I catch myself.

Run, run as fast as you can, you can't catch me, I'm the Gingerbread Man!

The nursery rhyme worms into my head. I have no idea why. But I feel like I'm trapped in some warped fairy tale. The people who should be helping me are not helping me. The farmer's wife wanted to cut off my tail with a carving knife, and I just got into a truck with the Big Bad Wolf. But I've gotten no closer to finding Lainey and Melody.

All I've done all night is run away from crazy people.

"Get back here," he screams in frustration. But he's huffing. Maybe Mr. Army Man hasn't kept up with his training. "It'll only be worse for you when I catch you."

That may be true, but I'd rather not test the theory, so I do not stop. We keep running, his breathing growing as ragged as mine.

At some point, I can feel distance expanding between us. A half foot. A foot. Three feet. His footsteps thump in the snow, but then grow fainter before slowing down.

"Come back here," he yells, catching his breath. The command sounds halfhearted, and his voice fades behind me. Hopefully, he's deciding I'm not worth the trek.

I don't dare slow down or look back. Sucking in the freezing air, I keep moving ahead until I don't hear his breathing anymore, or his slogging in the snow.

You can slow down now, my brain says. But I can't chance it. He could still catch up with me. I focus on my feet, ignoring the throbbing, burning air in my chest, the aching stitch in my side. I run until I hear the faintest sound of a door slamming behind me.

Only then do I dare to look back.

Steve has disappeared.

The truck engine revs, and an odd thought strikes that the truck has somehow swallowed him up and saved me from him.

When the truck takes off, the wheels squealing, I finally relax.

I keep half running in case he returns.

After a while, I take a chance, slowing my pace, slower and slower until I am walking more than running. Finally, I stop. He's not coming back. Bent over, I put my hands on my thighs, catching my breath, my backpack strap digging into my shoulder. Out of escape mode now, I look around me.

I am in the middle of a field.

White. All around me, shadowy white.

The sky has turned from inky black to gray black, a dark slate. Pine trees are capped with snow. Fields and fields of snow surround me.

With no better plan, I decide to go back to the street. I can barely see it now, with his truck gone. I'm turned around, not even sure I'm walking the right way. I flip out my compass, but the moonlight isn't strong enough to see the face. And I don't have the energy to rifle around my backpack for the flashlight and the map.

Then it's obvious. Another fairy tale. Hansel and Gretel. Just follow the breadcrumbs, or in this case, my footsteps. So I turn back around, going to the street yet again. As I walk, questions bounce in my head in rhythm with my feet.

Could it be Eric Myers?

Could he have escaped? He talked about it. But they all talk about it.

I never took him seriously. Eric Myers was full of bravado. They all brag about escaping one day, but how many prisoners actually manage that feat? I answer myself. Not even 1 percent (a tidbit from my research on a prison break called "The Great Escape," another episode of Fletcher Fox overacting.) And even if he did manage to escape, why would he try to hurt me, the only one who could help him? On top of that, how would he even know I was there?

Unless he was revisiting the site of his former glory and we just had the bad luck of hosting a surprise bachelorette party there. Talk about being in the wrong place at the wrong time. But even then, why would he come back to the 666 House, and not just lay low? Why on earth would he risk doing something that would surely get him caught this time?

The questions keep multiplying.

Why, why, why? A scene from my past floats into my head. I was ruminating over a slight from a childhood frenemy. "But why would she *do* that?" I sobbed to my mom. Why? Why? She shrugged and said that's like asking a snake why he's a snake. If Eric Myers is a snake, no use asking him why he's a snake. (She referenced that phrase a lot. Even at a young age, I realized it was an oblique reference to my father.)

My sore ankle twists again on an icy patch of snow, and I suck my breath in pain, nearly tripping. I pause a moment, letting the rolling pain even out, before starting up again.

So, there was a prisoner escape. But as Steve said, his radio picks up a lot. That doesn't mean that was Eric Myers's prison. If Eric Myers didn't escape, could it be the *real* 666 Killer?

It's possible. Maybe the real killer came back, and Eric Myers has been innocent all along. The real killer would certainly know all about the 666 House. Maybe the timing is just coincidental. He just happened to be away for ten years, jailed and released, or off killing somewhere else. We've seen it on *Crimeline* before, both plausible scenarios. Alternatively, there could be some random psychopath out there with no connection to the case.

I keep walking, the wind scorching my ears, snow soaking my jeans again.

Or, maybe it was me.

I have to accept this possibility. Maybe I was dreaming it.

Maybe the White Widow pushed me over the edge. I don't remember dreaming, but then again, I don't always remember the exact details when I act them out. I could have easily dreamed that Chris was attacking me and grabbed a knife. My shocked roommates could have tried to stop me and then run away, hurt. But honestly, I don't think I could have done that. It just seems too extreme. They would have woken me up, not fled.

So, I'm not going to waste any more time thinking about it. I can't afford to.

I have to find them.

Once on the street, I backtrack to the old vodka billboard.

The chalky gray sky lightens. It's got to be close to four or later. I watch for another car, but one never comes, and after my run-in with Steve, I'm gun-shy about hitchhiking anyway. So, I am left with Plan B—get back to the lodge. I keep following my footsteps, and after some time retracing my steps, I'm already halfway up the driveway. But my energy has dipped dangerously low.

I catch a tantalizing glimpse of the lodge ahead, still deceptively far off.

Maybe Noah will find me in the meantime.

Ironic that the boy from the photo could be my only chance at survival. Noah was just a side character in a profile that I treated more like a film, a fictional account. A dramatization, as they say in the subtitles, using C-list (okay, maybe D-list) actors, better looking than the real-life characters but not so much that you are distracted by them, disbelieving of them.

But this is not a film. And in any case, he probably won't come, not for a while at least. He'd have to dig out the SUV. And who knows, his mom is crazy enough to have hidden the keys. I think back to our moment in the guest room, so close I could smell his clothes. In another life, I could see dating him maybe. Or what the hell, just sleeping with him. In another life, I would have that gap, that space, where that option might still exist. I half regret shutting down that space, perhaps prematurely. But then again, that may be cold (literally) feet talking. Marriage always means closing those doors and opening up other ones.

I quicken my pace on the driveway, skipping to keep up with my old footprints. Focusing on each one, it almost becomes a game, hopscotching over each one. The metal cans bounce in my backpack, mocking me. Because if I've come this far only to return to the lodge, I could have left the damn soup cans there in the first place.

Out of nowhere, a giggle escapes.

It isn't funny. None of this is funny. But I keep laughing. I can't even control it, the laughter rolling through me. Rollicking through me. Even the word makes me laugh.

Rollicking. Rollicking.

I keep walking and laughing until tears come, laughing and crying at the same time. My emotions rollercoaster up and down until they finally collide.

I can definitely see the lodge in the distance now, not just a glimpse, a true view, but still maddeningly far away. So close and yet . . . so far. The cliché sounds like a Fletcher Fox line in a *Crimeline* segment, with his over-the-top theatrical flair. I say it out loud to test it. "So close and yet . . . so far." I'll have to work on the delivery.

I am losing my mind.

My thoughts dash all over the place. Rollicking. My thoughts are rollicking.

This sends me into another spasm of laughter, and I keep going, desperately laughing until that fades off too and I'm left with a football field to walk. How many yards are in a football field? Rollicking, rollicking.

I move forward, automatically, lurching like a windup toy. My eyes keep closing, and I smack my face to stay awake. I can't even feel my Novocain-numb face. With every step, I fight the temptation to just fall down, collapse into the snow and rest and wait for help. Or maybe just get my strength up. Then I could try again. My knees bend with relief at the alluring thought. Just a quick rest.

No! a voice in me screams.

I force my knees straight, not stopping. The cold, logical part of my brain cuts through the trickery, the beguiling chorus telling me to lie down. The rational voice reminds me of mountain-climbing survival stories. The ill-fated decision to take a rest in the snow is hypothermia talking, certain death.

Keep going, Alex, the voice berates me.

I keep walking, trying to imagine the warmth on my face, the sweet cedar smell of the wood from the fire in the family room.

You can do it. Keep going.

But the steps add up.

Too many steps.

I can't keep compounding them, amassing them. My legs won't do it. My energy falters, exhaustion sapping everything. I am walking through thigh-high water. Breathing is a chore, an extra burden. My arms stop swinging, weighing me down, chewing up more energy. I am walking in slow motion, my legs wilting with every step. I will not make it.

You must make it.

So close and yet so far away. Rollicking. Rollicking.

Time slows and quickens. Time morphs into something else. My brain tells me to give in. Lie down. Rest, just for a moment.

"No," I moan out loud, barely making a sound. No breath left for a sound. I can't even cry. I'm too exhausted, too dehydrated, for tears.

This close, and I will not make it. *You must make it. I can't make it.*

I don't make the decision, my body does. My bones cannot stay upright any longer, and I fall onto my knees, the snow cradling them. I hear my raspy, uneven breathing.

I can't get up again.

My muscle fibers are tapped out, every last chemical reserve in my body spent. It is just not possible. I almost feel relief at this fact. I am not a failure. I am not giving up. I am just accepting the reality that I can go no more. Blame my body, my legs. Blame the physical fact of me. The lodge is too, too far away.

As I slump down, sitting, wet seeping into my heavy, soaked jeans, a smile crawls onto my face. Sleep. I can sleep. A sigh falls out of my mouth, fog in the air. My last breath.

My eyes close. I will snuggle in the snowy blanket. I will take a rest.

I open my eyes one more time.

But then, I blink. I blink again, and again, and still see it. It doesn't go away. Is it a mirage? I blink again. No, not a mirage. It is real.

In the distance, I see it, in the lodge.

A light turns on.

CHAPTER FORTY-EIGHT
SEPTEMBER

Before going to work, I read through the confession again.

> She laughed at me like it was a big joke and I got angry. I
> should not have got so mad but I did and then things got
> out of hand. I grabbed onto her heart necklace and broke
> it. She got upset and slapped me and that really set me off.
> There was a knife on the kitchen table and I grabbed it.

But it wasn't a heart necklace.

It was a butterfly necklace.

The list on the autopsy report clearly lists that in the victim's effects.

> Car keys with metal keychain reading "Hawaii Forever"
> and pink nail file. Near the victim's head was found a torn
> gold necklace with butterfly pendant.

Words, descriptions are one thing. The photographic evidence does not lie. Tagged and numbered in the evidence is a necklace with a small bloodstained gold butterfly. Maybe, at a certain angle, it could look like a heart, the way it hung on the chain. But the coroner did not mistake it. And a mother knew her child's jewelry. Nicole was obsessed with butterflies. This was a butterfly, not a heart.

So, why did he say it was a heart in his confession? Was he making it up?

"Hello," Jay says, his feet thumping down the stairs in his usual rhythm.

It's his day off from running, so he's dressed in his usual work clothes, a button-down and blue chino pants, gratuitously handsome. I think about that body lying on mine last night. Babushka looks up at him from my feet.

"Have you been up for a while?" he asks.

"Had a bad dream," I say, sipping my coffee at the kitchen table. "I stayed in the guest room. Didn't want to bother you." I did fall back asleep after all on the couch. But I dreamed of Eric Myers pinning live butterflies to a wall, blood dripping down their brightly colored wings. I tried to cup one with my hands before he could reach it, and I leaped off the couch, waking up on my knees, my hands cradling air.

"Did you do anything?" he asks, walking to the cabinet for a mug. He takes out the Number One Dad mug with Greg's gap-toothed first grade picture on it.

"A little," I say. "But I didn't hurt anything."

He nods, pouring coffee, which burbles into the mug.

"Do me a favor," I say, holding up the book. "Look at something for me." So he comes over, mug in hand. "Do you think this looks like a heart?" I ask, showing him the page.

Jay leans in close to see, his hair still damp and smelling of shampoo. "No," he says, then leans back and sips his coffee. "Definitely a butterfly."

"So, it wouldn't be easy to mistake it for a heart, correct?" I ask, reexamining the page myself.

Jay shrugs, sitting next to me. "I mean, if you're actively stabbing someone, you might not pay close attention."

"True," I say. "But why would you add that detail to the confession statement? It seems like . . . superfluous. I mean, you already said you stabbed her and threw the knife away."

Jay takes a long sip of his coffee. "Maybe he was in shock. Maybe it was dark and he didn't see it very clearly."

"Yeah, I suppose." He's right. It doesn't have to be the big deal I'm making it out to be. There are a hundred valid reasons to get that wrong. But something is nagging at me.

"Wait a second," I say to myself, while Jay finishes his coffee, then stands up. I flip through the pages, searching for the police statement from the scene.

ONONDAGA CRIME SCENE REPORT
Reporting Officer: Delwyn Davies
Date: October 18, 2010
Call Time: 9:46 AM
Location of Call: Hobbes Lodge 2145 Scott Street
Bureau: Homicide
Tools used: magnetic powder, fluid swab, DNA sample
swab, crystal violet, shoe print stone cast Narrative:

Weather: Daylight and Cloudy

Reporting Officer Delwyn Davies made the scene at the house located at 2145 Scott Street and met with Sgt. Baker of the Homicide Bureau. Sgt Baker states that he is working a homicide and requested that photographs be taken of the scene and evidence collection. Reporting officers observed a White female lying on the floor with multiple stab wounds and lacerations. Victim was found on her left side with her face on the concrete subfloor, arms extended in front of her with red substance that appeared to be blood. Reporting officer made a sketch of the scene with measurements and collected and tagged all evidence into property.

The car keys are mentioned. The purse. The tampons. The cell phone. And the necklace.

"Torn, gold heart pendant."

"There we go." I slap the book shut.

Jay puts his mug in the sink with a thunk. "There we go where?"

"It came from the police statement," I say, feeling suddenly wide awake despite my crappy night of sleep.

"Which means?" Jay grabs his house keys from the entryway dish.

"Which means," I explain, "they fed it to him for his confession. He was just regurgitating the detail. Basically, repeating the error from the police report."

Jay stands there with keys in hand. "Which means?" he asks again.

"Which means . . ." I say, with a triumphant smile. "Eric Myers might be innocent after all."

CHAPTER FORTY-NINE

NOW

I don't know how long I stay there, staring at the light.

Did I really just see that? Or did I imagine it? Are my eyes playing tricks on me? But my brain says no. Someone is in there. *Get up. Get up.*

Finally I do, my legs burning and shaking. "Come on," I say to myself, my voice hoarse and soft. "Come on."

I don't know how I do it, but I do it. I slog through the snow, my feet past numb, my vision slits from iced-over eyelashes.

Did I leave the light on?

The question ricochets in my head. Maybe I did? But I could swear I saw it turn on. And anyway, I would have turned it off before I left. That's how I'm conditioned, turning the lights off every time I leave the house. But did I leave that one on this time?

If I left it on, then no one is there.

But I didn't leave it on.

Two football fields become one football field as the gruesome march toward the lodge continues. Step after step, yard after yard.

Did I leave the light on?

No. Someone must be there now. But who? Maybe Lainey and Melody came back. Maybe they got away from him and are hiding out there. Or they are hiding from me. It could be some stranger seeking shelter from the storm.

Or it could be the killer.

A football field becomes ten feet becomes me standing outside the lodge.

Energy spikes through me.

I sneak up to a side window, taking small quiet steps. On the racks, the coats still hang along with the *Bougie Bachelorette* crown. Nothing has changed. Putting my ear as close as I can, I listen. But I don't hear anything. No voices, no movement, just the hiss of the wind through the trees. Still, the wind may be masking any noises inside. So, maybe someone is in there waiting for me.

Or hiding from me.

Slowly, I walk away from the window over to the front windows. I have to stand on my sore, numb tiptoes to peek in. I catch glimpses of the fire, the sleeping bags, the rug. The blood has congealed on the floor. Nothing has been moved or cleaned up.

Again, I tilt my ear toward the window and hear nothing inside. I climb the stairs to the front door, nearly losing my footing on a patch of ice.

Should I go in?

I don't have much choice. I came this far for a reason. I have to take the chance. It won't help anything to sit out here all night in the cold. I could try to get back to the street, but I simply don't have the physical strength. I'll die trying.

I stand there, shivering in front of the door.

What if the killer is in there?

I have no choice. Lainey and Melody could be in there too. *Did I turn the light off?* I reach my hand out to knock, then pull it back. No, that would be idiotic, giving away any element of surprise. If the killer's waiting, I need to either fight him or escape him. Unless Lainey and Melody are back.

I stand there and take a deep breath, slowing my heart down. I know I'm just delaying the inevitable, wasting time I don't have to waste. The killer might be in there. I don't want to confront him. I don't want to do this. But I don't really have a choice.

I try the handle, quietly, slowly, and it turns. Opening the door by inches, I hide behind it to cover myself. I can see into the kitchen, drawers still open that I searched through, extra soup cans on the table. I open the door wider, trying not to let the hinges squeak. I don't see anyone, anything. I don't hear anything except for my own heartbeat. I take a chance and walk into the doorway.

Someone is there. I feel their presence before seeing them.

I step back, but too late, as a blurry arm swoops down. Metal smashes my skull, which turns into a bolt of pain, sparks of light shooting into my eyes.

And then blackness.

CHAPTER FIFTY

SEPTEMBER

Wokebro: Who cares about a fucking necklace?

Alex33: It doesn't make sense though.

BreannaT: She's right. It's not a small detail.

TNT: Hard disagree. I mean, come on.

Daddy-oh: Exactly. Leigh Jones saw his tattoo. She put the nail in the coffin. Guy's guilty as sin.

Alex33: It fits too well though, his confession. Especially with the heart detail.

Wokebro: The confession doesn't even matter though. Leigh Jones is all that matters.

Alex33: She's a key witness, I'm not arguing that.

TNT: She's *the* witness. That's the point.

BreannaT: And if the police had listened to her in the first place, the guy would have been caught before killing more people.

Daddy-oh: Who knows how many people this guy's killed.

Hannahbanana: Nobody listens to women. That's why serial killers get away with it.

TNT: JFC. Can we make this not about feminazi-ism for once?

BreannaT: She has a point.

Hannahbanana: It's called femicide. Educate yourself.

TNT: It's called you're a cunt. Educate yourself.

Hannahbanana: Wow, dude. You a little fragile? Your mommy hurt you or something?

Alex33: Why would you say it's a heart necklace? Why specify that if it's not?

Wokebro: Memo to Alex. No one gives a shit.

"What's wrong?" Wiley asks, to my frown.

"Misogynist pricks on Twitter," I answer.

Wiley lets out a scornful laugh. "Try being a *they* on Twitter. That's a barrel of laughs."

"Yeah," I say, feeling guilty for complaining. "I'm sure that sucks worse."

Wiley fact-checks something while I leaf through the confession, the autopsy, and the police report again. I find no other connections or insights.

"Do you think I'm overthinking the heart thing?" I ask, having blurted out my discovery right when I came into the office.

"Meh." Wiley opens their desk drawer, searching for Nicorette gum, then pops out a piece from the foil. "I think it won't push the needle for Toby, if that's what you're thinking."

"That's for sure," I say, with a groan. "I'd have to have an actual video of someone else killing Nicole White to get any traction with her."

They chomp the nicotine gum. "What did she say about the newest 666 letter?"

"Not much," I answer. "Sent me an email apologizing for the lapse in workplace safety that was basically cut and pasted from an HR manual."

Wiley harrumphs at this.

Tidying my desk, I notice a thick manila envelope that had been covered by a book. With a beat of excitement, I recognize it as the FOIA packet and, picking it up, uncover yet another FOIA packet for Ryan Johnson. "Ah," I declare. "Two FOIA packets. My cup runneth over."

"Yippee," Wiley says.

Ignoring them, I make haste with my packets. I open the
first one with some hesitation, given the contents of the last
letter, but find nothing but normal, boring official-looking
photocopies. Flipping through, I see Adam Redmond's fingerprints, along with DNA results from a freely given saliva
swab. He was very cooperative, in fact. A detective's report
full of typos fills another page, along with handwritten notes.
The handwriting looks large and sloppy but is actually fairly
legible. *States alibi was an AA meeting. Wife confirms. AA meeting
was scheduled that night at St. Mary's Baptist Church.*

"AA meeting," I say to myself.

It seems their wise counsel hasn't stuck, unfortunately. But
as for the meeting, I can only hope the police verified that.
Ten years later, I would have no way of doing so, short of
asking the church for any records, which I doubt they kept.
And the group's confidentiality would be another strike
against me. Further down the page, I spot another line, typewritten this time.

POLYGRAPH: PASSED.

I skip over pages with less legible handwriting, deciding to
move onto Ryan Johnson before tackling that. This time, DNA
was not freely given, and neither were fingerprints. It appears
his parents spent money they didn't have on a lawyer. He coop-
erated only inasmuch as absolutely required. He gave his Clare
Dibold alibi, which was minimally checked. His noncompliance
with police efforts seemed to start after one key development
early in the investigation. This was also typewritten.

POLYGRAPH: FAILED

CHAPTER FIFTY-ONE

NOW

The blurred face looms over me.

"Oh my God . . . did I kill you?" a voice cries out.

For a confused second, I think it's possible. Maybe I am dead.

Then my muddled, sluggish thoughts start connecting into logical lines. I wouldn't hear words if I were dead. Though maybe dead people still hear words?

I move my head toward the voice, and my vision swims. Feeling water dripping into my eyes, I realize it's blood. Slowly I lift my heavy, aching head. When my eyes steady, her face comes into focus.

And I'm stunned.

"You're alive," I say, with amazement.

Melody stands above me with the tennis racket in her hand, her eyebrows torqued in worry. "Are you okay?" she asks, bending down to my level. "I'm so sorry. I didn't know it was you."

Trying to sit up, I groan without even meaning to. "Where's Lainey?" My words come out slurred, the sound of my own voice blasting my head with pain.

"You don't know?" Melody squats beside me. Her face appears upside down, her features in a disarray, her chin becoming her forehead, her mouth above her eyes, like some kind of Picasso painting. "I was hoping that you might have found her."

"No," I say. I try to sit up again, but my head goes woozy and I slowly lie back down. "Why? What happened?"

Her eyes narrow. "What do you mean, what happened? You don't remember?"

"I . . . don't know." I lick my dry lips. "All I remember is waking up in the shower."

"In the shower?" she repeats, with confusion.

"Yes. And when I came back to the lodge, there was . . . blood." The word comes out hoarse. "And I saw the knife in the basement." I try to sit up again, but my head spins. So I lie back down, staring at the ceiling in misery. "Did I do it?" I ask, the words trembling. Tears mix with the blood in my eyes now, stinging them. With effort, I turn to look at her exhausted face. "Did I hurt you guys? I had the knife. I could feel it."

The confusion on her face turns to horror. "No," she says, the word charging out. "No. It wasn't you. It was *him*." She grips my arm. "That's why I hit you. I thought you were him. I thought he was coming back."

"Oh," I say. Unexpected relief floors me, leaving me almost giddy. It wasn't me. I didn't do this. I knew it. I knew I couldn't have done this. "But . . . who's him?"

Melody leans her chin in her hands, her elbows on her knees like a tripod. "I don't know. He was wearing one of those"—she makes a circular motion toward her face—"mask thingies . . . you really don't remember?"

"No." I wipe the corners of my eyes as the heat kicks on, dry air filling my nostrils.

"Where did you go, then?" she asks, looking me up and down. I know I look a sight. But she doesn't look much better, her hair straggly, the neck of her T-shirt ripped, and a nasty, bloody gash ripped through the calf of her jeans. "I can't believe you don't remember anything," she muses, almost to herself.

"I must have gone into shock or something," I say, sitting up slowly onto my elbows. I lean onto the uninjured one. "It's a long story. But after I woke up in the shower, I went out trying to find you guys. And ran into some . . . trouble along the way. How about you?"

"I was just running away from him." She motions toward the door. "But after a while, I didn't see any of you, so I came back to see if you were back. And . . ." Her eyes shine with desperation. "I think he took her, Alex. I think he took Lainey."

"Who, though?" I ask again. "Did you recognize him at all? Did it look like Chris? Or Eric Myers?"

"I'm telling you, I don't know," she answers, brusquely. "He was wearing that thing, that ski mask thing, I don't know what you call it."

"A balaclava," I say, dejected, laying my aching head back onto the floor.

"Yes, that's right," she says, nodding. "A balaclava. How did you know?"

CHAPTER FIFTY-TWO

SEPTEMBER

"What does Ryan Johnson have to say about the polygraph?" Toby asks.

I picture her ensconced in her office chair, while I'm in my car on my way to see Donna White. It turns out, Nicole's mother lives only an hour away from me. She has a new last name, so it took some time to track her down, and more than a few messages left for her to agree to meet with me. But she finally did.

"He didn't say anything," I answer. "I've called multiple times now. About this and the Bible class. He's stonewalling me." It seems he has relinquished his dreams of stardom.

"Worth another trip out there?" she asks, then quickly adds, "Of course, *Crimeline* can't reimburse you, but it might be the best way to reach him."

I'm switching lanes when my blind-side light comes on, and I swerve back into my lane. "I might have to," I say, watching for Donna White's exit. "But I'm meeting with her mother first."

"Good," Toby says, one of the first positive things she's said since she hired me. A monosyllable of praise. "Let me know what you find out."

"Will do," I say, switching into a free lane to get to the exit.

"It's not enough to put our resources into reinvestigating," she informs me, in case I get the wrong idea here. "But keep at it."

With the teeny amount of encouragement, I make my way toward Donna White's house.

As we walk together in the park, I muse on how her life looks quite different in the ten years since her daughter's murder. She's twenty pounds thinner than on the *Crimeline* episode (maybe thirty pounds—the camera really does put ten pounds on you.) Her dyed-brown hair has been reborn as a silver pixie cut. And she's remarried, living in a McMansion in Tarrytown. She's a website designer, which is fine work but doesn't buy you a five-bedroom house with a pool in this town. So, I'm thinking she married well.

We're strolling on this warm September day, the lovely weather an uneasy reminder of global warming. It'll be Halloween next month. I remember puffy coats over my witch's garb, my mittened hand gripping a broom in one hand and a bag in the other. The kids won't even need sweaters in this weather.

Since we're walking, I'm recording with my phone instead of taking notes. Donna White wanted to "get her steps in." And maybe she wanted to walk through her sadness instead of sitting right in it.

"I didn't think much about the heart on the necklace, to be honest," she says, unzipping an unneeded fall jacket. "I knew it was a butterfly. I figured they just didn't see that well with the . . ."

Blood. I don't finish the sentence.

A gust of warm wind blows up crinkled red leaves. "So you don't think it has any bearing on the . . . case?" The word comes out awkward. The *case* is her daughter's life. Or her death, more accurately.

"How would it?" She takes her jacket off now, looping it over her arm.

"It's just that . . . the mistake was directly repeated," I say, walking faster to keep up with her. "From the police statement. And I just wondered if . . ." I pause, wanting to phrase this correctly. "Is it possible that Eric Myers was fed this misinformation? And *that's* why the mistake was repeated?"

Her fashionable brown boots clomp at a clipped pace, as if trying to outrun the question. "What are you trying to say?"

"Just that," I say, again hurrying to keep up, "if he just said what he was told by the police, then maybe it supports his claim. That it was a false confession after all."

She purses her lips, appearing to consider the idea. Then she shakes her head. "I don't see it," she says, sounding both skeptical and irked. "I know he says the confession was forced, but he's lying, just like he is about everything else. He gave every detail. The knife. The fight with her." She shrugs. "So what if he got one detail wrong?"

I don't mention the obvious, that he could have been fed all of these details too. "They never found the murder weapon, you know."

We pass a seesaw, the wooden slab creaking. A bigger boy keeps trying to shove himself up while a smaller girl dangles on top, both appearing perplexed by the conundrum.

"Not surprised," Donna says. "They'd have to dredge up that whole lake." She walks a few more steps. "Although, with this weather"—she points in the air in reference—"the lake's been receding. Maybe they will find it eventually."

I pause. "So you don't think that—"

"No," she interrupts me, walking even faster, as if trying to escape me. "I don't. I think that we have more than enough evidence. Evidence inked directly on him, in fact."

"Yeah," I acknowledge, "I know. That's true."

With this admission, she slows down a notch, and we walk without talking for some time, taking in the fall colors, tangerine leaves on a sugar maple tree, a burning bush in full flame.

I decide to give up on the pendant questioning. She'll shut me off entirely if I broach it again. "Do you have any idea what that note in her pocket meant?" I ask instead. "Revelation 13:18 with the word ADAM?"

She looks unpleasantly surprised by the change in questioning. "No," she says, "I assume it's something to do with the Bible study. Or maybe something from school. I have no idea what Adam is supposed to mean though."

I jump at the opening. "Your ex-husband led that, correct? The Bible study class?"

"For a while there, yes." She lets out a bitter laugh. "They were trying to pin it on him." She speeds up her pace again. "Which I get. You have to look at the family and all. But Adam doesn't have a violent bone in his body." She looks down at the ground. "I thought it was her boyfriend, to be honest with you. That Ryan Johnson boy. Until we found out about Eric Myers."

My spidey senses alert. "Why . . . was Ryan Johnson ever violent?" I ask. "Or abusive or anything?"

"Not exactly," she admits, her boots clacking on the pavement. "Just . . . I don't know. Something about him didn't sit right with me."

After walking a few more paces, I ask, "Did you know he failed the polygraph?"

She stops so suddenly that I nearly crash into her. "He what?" She stares at me, a hot flush rising in her neck. "That can't be true."

"I'm . . ." I take a step back. "It is. It was in the police reports."

Her expression hardens. "Are you sure about that?" she asks, the question short.

Cowed by her reaction, I nod. "I can show you if you want. It really was in the police reports."

Her jaw clenches, but then she shakes her head and starts walking again. "I don't know why you're starting all this up again." She turns, regarding me with a cool fury. "That wouldn't even stand up in court. Maybe he was nervous or something. He had an alibi. The police told me." She speeds up again with a frown. "Leigh Jones saw the tattoo. Eric Myers has the tattoo."

"True but," I insert.

She spins her head to face me. "It really isn't that complicated, Alex. He has a 666 tattoo on his skin."

"Yes. I know. You're right about that." I don't say anything else. Her forbidding tone doesn't invite more questions.

Donna White slows to a stop, so I do as well. In the ensuing pause, I expect some great reveal or revelation. But she peers into the distance. "You see that?" she asks.

I follow her gaze.

"There," she says, pointing to a hydrangea bush, the flower petals in papery maroon clusters. It takes a second, but I see it then. A butterfly. It flutters briefly, a flash of orange with leopard spots. "The monarch," she says.

"Hmm," I say. I'm about to walk again, but she doesn't so I stand there with her.

"They're dying out, you know," she says, her tone more matter-of-fact than sad. "They can't survive hibernation if it's too warm out."

"Interesting," I say, which sounds stupid and pointless. It's not interesting, it's awful. She gives me a look that says as much. I swallow. "I remember how you said that she liked butterflies," I say, to make up for the dumb comment.

She looks back at the tree with a pensive smile. "It comforts me, just a little," she says. "That maybe her spirit is in there with the butterflies. Like every time I see one, maybe she's talking to me."

We both watch the looping butterfly until it disappears.

And Donna White starts walking again.

CHAPTER FIFTY-THREE

NOW

M y head pounds.

Not just normal headache pounding. An almost unbearable pounding, like something might be seriously wrong, brain hemorrhage pounding. Melody found some Tylenol, but it barely touches the pain.

I hold an ice pack up to my head, fashioned by Melody from snow in a plastic zip-up bag from the kitchen. It's ironic to be icing my head while trying to warm the rest of my body by the fire. My feet have some tingly feeling back, but I still can't feel my toes. At least my teeth have stopped chattering, and my lips have regained some movement. But my face still moves slowly, oddly. I feel like a robot pretending to be a human, forcing my facial muscles to make normal expressions. And I can't stop my body from shivering.

"I'm sorry, really," Melody says.

This is approximately her hundredth time apologizing for hitting me. Neither of us mention the grotesque setting, the blood spatter all over the room next to us.

"It's okay," I say, yet again.

Melody tinkers with her phone, and I move the ice pack and glance over there, my eyes hurting with the movement. "Anything?" I ask.

She shakes her head with a grimace. "Tried 911 again. Nothing is going through."

But at least we have a phone.

And hopefully Lainey has one too.

"Can we go over it again, what exactly happened?" I ask, adjusting the ice, which drips into my sleeve. "Just one more time?"

"Okay," she says, with a note of irritation, maybe tired of telling me this story.

She's gone through it several times, but my brain can't seem to absorb it. She jabs a log with a poker, making a clang that burrows right into my head.

"Like I said, we were asleep. I don't know how he got in, because we locked up before we went to bed." She looks pointedly at me. "Right?"

"We were stoned out of our minds," I say. "So who even knows?"

"I think we did," she says, without conviction. "So maybe he had a key or something."

"Could be." The skin from my goose egg stretches on my forehead, throbbing. "Maybe it was hidden on the windowsill or under a flowerpot somewhere." Neither of us point out that both would have been buried under a foot of snow.

"Maybe," she says, chewing her lip. "Either way. He seemed . . . I don't know . . . calm. Preternaturally calm. Like, not even angry." She says this with some befuddlement. "He didn't say a word."

"That's weird."

"Yeah. It was. He was absolutely silent. So I can't even tell you what he sounds like. But he just started moving his arm around almost, like, gracefully. Like he was in a duel or something."

I try to picture it, but the vision seems odd. Why make a spectacle? Why not just come in and start stabbing?

"I was lucky though." She motions to her shoulder and calf muscle. "He only got me a little."

The cuts look fairly gruesome though, for only getting her "a little," each gash about a few inches long, with congealed blood and raised edges. The sight nauseates me. Though that could also be a concussion.

"And you said he was tall, with blue eyes? You know that for certain?"

"Yes," she says, resting her chin on her elbow, her face pale. "Tall, with blue eyes. Very blue eyes."

I think of the eyes looming on my computer screen, session after session. Blue, yes, despite his declaration that they are green. But "very" blue? I don't know.

"Did he have any tattoos or anything? 666?"

She shakes her head. "I didn't see any tattoos. But he was wearing all black. And gloves. But it could definitely be Eric Myers, if that's what they said on the scanner . . ."

I had told her about my unfortunate run-in with Steve, as well as my unfortunate run-in with Esther Thompson.

"They didn't say which prison but . . . it seems like quite a coincidence." I adjust the ice pack. "And you don't think it was Chris," I confirm.

"Not really?" she answers in a question. "But I don't know. It's possible. He's tall with blue eyes too." She jabs the fire again. "But do you really think he would do that? He's psycho and all, but not *that* psycho."

"Yeah, I would agree." The water from the bag drips rhythmically onto the hearth. *Drip, drip, drip.* Like ancient water torture. "Plus, how would he even know we were here? I didn't see his car following us or anything."

"Good point," she says, with a yawn. "Who else knew we'd be here?"

"No one, really," I answer, thinking about it.

Melody winces as she moves her injured leg. "I mean, we told Jay. Just in case of an emergency." We don't comment on the irony of this. This would certainly qualify as an emergency.

"Anyway," I say. "As you were saying. The guy, maybe Eric Myers, maybe not, came in with a knife and started waving it."

"Yes," she says, taking up the story again. "Then, like I said, we ran to the basement to hide," she continues, which explains my footprints down there, as the victim, not the assailant. "And Lainey tried to keep the door closed." Melody rubs her hands together."But she was losing blood. Otherwise, I know he wouldn't have been able to overpower her to get into the basement."

"She's strong," I agree, wishing I could remember any of this.

"But she still grabbed him when he got in. And held him back long enough for us to . . ." Here, she takes a long breath. "Run."

I pause then. "Wait a second. Did you already tell me this part?"

Staring into the fire, she shakes her head, her eyes brimming with tears.

"Are you saying that we just ran?" A chill shivers through me. "And she . . . she stayed back with him?"

She answers with a rueful nod.

"You mean, we just left her there?" I ask, sickened. "We abandoned her?"

Her lips tighten in a grimace. "I don't know, okay? I don't know for sure. She might have escaped too. All I remember is that I ran outside." She rubs her arms, as if chilled. "You were running too, Alex. I didn't know where you went. But you must have hidden in the shower."

She's right. That makes sense. Even if I was in shock or half-asleep, I must have been hiding from him. I certainly wasn't brave enough to fight him off.

"But then I didn't see you or Lainey, and I just kept running," she says, the words rushing out. "I was going to get help. That's what I was trying to do. But then it was cold and I got lost and I couldn't find anyone." She squeezes her hands on her arms, cradling herself.

"It's okay," I say, rubbing her back.

"I came back to get her though," she insists. "I came back to get her, but she was gone." Melody looks up at me, tears rolling down her cheeks. "I was coming back for her. I promise."

I keep gently rubbing her back. "It's not your fault, Melody."

She shakes her head, not wiping the tears. Black mascara streaks down her face. "I should never have left her there. I just ran away. I ran away like a coward."

"Hey," I say, squeezing her shoulder. "Of course you ran away. You were hurt. And scared." I stroke her hair, which feels rough instead of the usual silky texture. "What else were you supposed to do? I ran away too."

She nods, crying softly now, hugging her knees and rocking back and forth.

"We just have to make it up to her now," I say, still touching her back.

Melody wipes her mascara-smeared eyes. "Yeah, but . . . how?"

CHAPTER FIFTY-FOUR

OCTOBER

"**S**o, if the mom doesn't think the heart thing is a big deal, it's probably not. Don't you think?" Lainey asks.

She's come to Jay's apartment (*our* apartment, Jay would remind me) after a love spat with Ruby, which, in true Lainey fashion, she doesn't want to discuss. But after all the drama with Chris and now the wedding, I'm happy to offer moral support in whatever manner possible. Lainey lounges on the couch with Babushka in her lap, licking her paw and accepting pets. Lainey's more of a dog person, so naturally my cat decides to lay all her loving on her.

"But the mom may not be objective here, obviously."

I push my research books, essentially coffee-table murder reading, to the side to make room for my legs. Jay hates it when I do that. He doesn't say anything, though he will to his son. *Oi*, Jay will say, and Greg grumblingly complies. Greg, who looks so much like his father, with the same shade of blue eyes and black hair, but awkward and gangly. He seems to be on a nonstop growth spurt these days, taller than most twelve-year-olds, that's for sure.

"She might be wrong about it."

"That's true," she says, yawning. She has a right to be exhausted, after back-to-back games this week. Lainey stands up with a groan, sending a mewling Babushka off her lap. Gingerly, she rotates her shoulder, which she pulled in the last game. "Got anything to eat?" she asks, heading for the kitchen.

"Probably." I get up to join her there.

We open the refrigerator and stare into the dim light, a soft hum sounding out.

"Your fridge is kind of empty," Lainey comments, stooped over to search.

"Yeah, I know," I admit. "We don't cook much."

Which is ironic, given our state-of-the-art kitchen. I have a couple go-to dishes, a vegetable lasagna and a roasted chicken, but nothing that warrants two Gaggenau ovens. And yes, we have a Sub-Zero fridge with nothing in it.

"Hey, look," I say, pointing. "There's something right there. Pickles. Spicy pickles."

"Spicy pickles? Why would you make a pickle spicy?" she asks, grabbing the half-empty jar. She evaluates it with wariness, then opens it. "Oh well, desperate measures."

"Yeah," I agree, as she closes the door. "This fridge really is a cry for help."

Lainey leans against the veined gray counter, which matches the glossy gray subway tile backsplash and gray paint, along with the gray everything else in his apartment. Melody once voiced surprise that we can find our gray cat, who camouflages right into the walls. Lainey positions herself to avoid the brass drop light fixtures. As she crunches into a pickle, her face draws into a prune.

"Oh my God, this is awful." She offers me the jar.

"Wow, you sure know how to sell it." But I take one out collegially. I bite into it, and my face probably looks the same as hers did. They are as awful as advertised.

"Hmm," Lainey says, with a side-to-side head shake, taking another. "They kind of grow on you." She swallows, fanning her mouth. "What about Leigh Jones?" she asks, between fans. "It seems like she's kind of been forgotten in this whole thing."

"Not exactly," I say. "I've called her several times now. She won't get back to me. I can't just harass the poor woman."

Lainey screws the top back on the jar with one pickle left. "Did you offer her anything?"

"Can't," I say. "*Crimeline* won't pay for intern profiles."

Lainey raises her eyebrows and makes a sweeping motion all around us.

"Yeah," I admit, catching her point. "Maybe I could still give her something."

The idea bolsters me. She could have some insight on the heart or the note. I can pivot my research back to Leigh Jones, starting with the podcast search again. Deciding there's no time like the present, I text Leigh Jones.

Hi, Alex Conley from Crimeline here again. Spoke with executives. How about $1,000 for the interview?

I'm pulling the phone away when a text flies back.

5K. 2.5K upfront and 2.5K after the interview.

"Holy shit," I say, shocked at how quickly she got back to me. Lainey gives me an I-told-you-so smile.

Deal, I write back, not looking forward to talking to Jay about this.

CHAPTER FIFTY-FIVE

NOW

"We can't go outside again," Melody says.

"We're the ones who left her," I argue, taking the ice pack off my stinging skin. "We have to find her."

Melody throws up her hands. "But we don't even know where to look."

I don't answer, but she's got a point. It's already past four in the morning. By the time we get help, *if* we can get help, it will have taken a few hours anyway. We might as well stay warm inside for those few hours. Hopefully by morning, the streets will be plowed and we'll have signal back.

Then again, the attacker could come back too.

"It would be one thing if we had the keys for her car," Melody reasons. "But I couldn't find them. He must have taken them."

I turn to her, my eyebrows raised. "He didn't take them. I took them. They were in her coat pocket."

"Oh," she says, looking baffled. She turns suddenly animated then, standing up from the hearth. "In that case, of course we should go look for her."

"Can't. Car's dead." I rub my hands by the fire. "Sorry. I figured you had already tried."

With resignation, she sits back down. "No," she says. "But I guess that's not shocking that it's dead," she says in a tired voice.

We don't speak for a moment, listening to the fire crackle.

"Can I try to text Jay again?" I ask, holding out my hand for the phone.

"Yeah, sure. But I doubt it will go through." She gives me the phone, which still has no bars. And the screen is cracked from her falling on her trek.

Gripping the phone, I call the number and wait breathlessly. Sure enough, it doesn't go through. Frustrated, I hand the phone back and put the ice pack on the hearth. The ice melts in the bag, reminding me of a goldfish prize from a fair but sans goldfish.

I take my coat from the hearth and shake off any clinging snow in case we do venture out again, when something falls out of the pocket, a scrap of paper wafting down to the floor.

"What's that?" Melody asks, reaching over to pick it up.

"I don't know," I say, perplexed.

We huddle over the slip of torn paper, reading the sloppy blue handwriting.

Sorry about my mom. Will come to lodge when I can. Stuff to tell you about Eric Myers.

A phone number is scratched out under the message as well.

"Noah must have slipped it into my coat," I say, trying to think when he could have done it. Maybe when he went digging for his phone. The *Crimeline* reporter in me turns on, a light bulb icon appearing above my head. Maybe he knows something new, never reported before. But then I shake the thought away. Who the hell cares? None of this matters if we can't find Lainey. I stash the paper back in my pocket.

"Maybe he'll be driving on the road, then," Melody says. "Watching out for us."

"Maybe," I say, to appease her. I don't want to dampen her spirits, but it seems unlikely. He would have to elude his mother, dig out his SUV, and make it down an unplowed road. "I could try to call him at least."

She hands me the phone again with a sigh. "It's gonna be the same deal though. We don't have any signal."

She's right, I know. But I also don't know what else to do. Just sitting here is killing me. And it isn't helping Lainey. I pull the damp piece of paper out of my pocket, squinting to see the phone number against the dim, flickering light of the fire, then call the number. Nothing goes through. "I'll try a text just in case."

I type with stiff, shaky fingers. *Got your note. We're back at the lodge. Please come when you can.* I hit send, and it looks like it got sent. Heartened, I sit up, gripping the phone. I stare at the screen, waiting for a response back.

"Did it go through?" Melody asks, with surprise, crowding in to see.

"I think," I answer, willing his response to come to the screen already. But then a red exclamation point swoops on the screen. *Not delivered.* "Fuck."

Melody leans back, scooting back to her spot. "I was hoping there for a second."

"Yeah," I say, wanting to throw the phone into the fire. Instead, I hand it back to her.

We go back to silence and tending the fire. I try not to think of the minutes ticking off while we sit here, useless, every second wasted lessening the chance we'll see her alive. For a minute, I think about Melody and me in a *Crimeline* interview. Fletcher Fox with his cheesy delivery asking, "She was a good friend, wasn't she?" And us answering, "Oh yes. Yes, she was."

Standing up, I shake the morose thought from my head. "I just feel like we should be doing something," I grumble, and start pacing. "Not just sitting here."

Melody rubs her hands by the fire. "But . . . what?"

"I don't know," I say, still pacing, the wooden floor creaking beneath me. "If we leave, we're just gonna freeze to death, and probably won't find Lainey anyway. But if we stay, we're sitting ducks if he comes back here again."

She rubs her hands, as if washing them. "True." Then her hands stop. "The gun. We should get the gun."

I stare at her. "What gun?"

"Downstairs," she says, eyeing me with some confusion. "You didn't see it?"

CHAPTER FIFTY-SIX

NOW

Shardai: But seriously, Tray. There's something else
we need to discuss here. (Sound of drinking water.)
How he should have been caught, *before* he killed
Nicole, and before he killed the *A*-girls.

Trayvon: *If* he did it, yeah, for sure.

Shardai: And no one listened to her because . . .
drumroll, please . . .

Trayvon: She's Black.

Shardai: Ding, ding, ding. Same old, same old. Blah.
Blah. Blah. She was probably hanging out with
thugs. She was probably drunk or high or something. She was probably in a bad neighborhood,

where we incidentally don't want to go. She survived anyway, so what are we gonna do about it? Etc. Etc.

Trayvon: Essentially, she wasn't worth their time.

Shardai: One hundred percent. Oh, let's start hearing about budget cuts, and being stretched to the limits, and no money for rape kits and—

Trayvon: Yeah, but she wasn't raped.

Shardai: No, I know that. I'm just saying it's endemic of the same issue. Women aren't worth it. Black women especially.

Trayvon: I hear you.

Shardai: And in this case, not only did they not listen to her. They didn't even *remember her testimony.* The cops would have remained clueless, but she came back to them, like, oh, hey guys, remember me? I know you barely gave a shit when this guy nearly killed me, but I heard about a *White* girl now?

Trayvon: (Laughs.) I'm laughing and I'm not laughing.

Shardai: Right? You might be interested in this one little piece of evidence, namely a freaking 666 tattoo, that I already told you all about! (Puts on a male voice.) "Oh, it wasn't because she was Black that we didn't listen to her. Nicole White lived in another county a half mile away."

Trayvon: Unless . . . he didn't do it.

Shardai: Come on, Tray. The tattoo, okay? The tattoo. The tattoo. The tattoo.

Trayvon: Okay, you're right. I get it. But, listen. Okay? If you didn't have that, everything else falls apart . . . right? Let's talk about some of the other evidence.

Shardai (Loudly sighs.) Okay, go ahead.

Trayvon: So you have a cast made of a boot print.

Shardai: Yes, and I know where you're going with this.

Trayvon: It doesn't belong to Eric Myers.

Shardai: True but . . .

Trayvon: It's not even his size!

Shardai: Okay, so it wasn't his boot print. But there are a lot of people who've been at that lodge. Kids drinking there, getting high, etc. etc.

Trayvon: And?

Shardai: And . . . so it's not that weird that it wasn't his boot print. It was a messed-up crime scene.

Trayvon: You're making my argument for me!

Shardai: Okay, okay. (Laughs.)

Trayvon: Let's hear what else they found there. Four cigarette butts. One used condom. One bag with pot residue. Sixteen different boot prints, some partial. Two crushed beer cans. One broken bottle. And . . .

Shardai: A partridge in a pear tree?

Trayvon: Very funny.

Shardai: Okay, for real. What else did they find . . .

Trayvon: Nothing. Absolutely nothing. That's the point. None of it, I repeat none of it, not one little piece, had any connection to Eric Myers. Not a fingerprint, not a speck of saliva on the beer or the cigarettes, not semen from the condom. Not a boot print. No DNA. Nada. Nothing.

Shardai: You're right about all that. I'll admit it. You're right.

Trayvon: So how the fuck . . . do you . . . explain . . . that?

Shardai: I just led you right back to the obvious, Tray. Whatever else you have is secondary, icing on the cake. To the big kahuna of all evidence. And what would have saved Nicole White and two other girls if the police had, for once in their damn lives, listened to a Black woman.

Trayvon: Yeah, yeah, yeah.

Shardai: The tattoo.

CHAPTER FIFTY-SEVEN

OCTOBER

J ay wasn't thrilled, but he agreed to fund Leigh Jones's request for 5K.

I thanked him up and down and told him how much it would help me. He grumbled and said, "I'm doing it for her more than you." Which is . . . yeah . . . fair play.

So now I'm reviewing everything I have on Leigh Jones, including the police files that *Crimeline* had stored on a hard drive somewhere. Juanita dug them up for me.

The doorbell rings, and Jay and I both stare at the door a second, wondering who would be visiting us at night. Then we remember.

"Oh, crap. Where did we put the candy?" Jay asks, jumping from the couch.

I motion to the kitchen. "Big bowl on the island." I wasn't sure if kids trick-or-treated on Halloween in apartment complexes, but it seems they do.

Since I'm doing research, he jogs over and comes back with the bowl as the doorbell rings again. "Coming," he calls out. Babushka leaps off the couch to apprise herself of the goings-on.

I scan through photos taken of all Leigh Jones's lacerations and puncture wounds during her hospital stay. Luckily, she didn't end up with a black slash across her eyes in a crime scene photo or a list of wounds in an autopsy report. But she was sure close.

"Trick or treat" is yelled out. Then I hear candy being distributed.

"You're dice? That's a great one," Jay says.

He sounds sincerely *chuffed*, as he would say, not faking. Not for the first time, I think how he would make a great dad. I then remember, not for the first time, that he already is a dad. He comes back to the couch, landing next to me. Babushka stays midway between the door and the couch, hedging her bets.

Half-dead, Leigh still described the attack, including the crucial information, the 666 tattoo on his wrist, in exquisite detail. The detectives wrote up a nice report about all of this, then promptly ignored it until six months later, when Leigh Jones found out about Nicole White's murder and two more girls had gone missing.

"Trick or treat."

Candy is shuffled.

"A mermaid?" Jay asks. "Are you Ariel, then?"

I'm half reading and half listening to the Halloween patter, thinking I'll have to bone up on my Disney movies. Do twelve-year-olds even watch Disney movies? Yet another thing I don't know about Greg, or kids in general. Ignoring the agita this gives me, I delve deeper into the police files when the doorbell rings again.

I read through the embarrassingly brief write-ups of multiple follow-up visits from Leigh Jones and her sister about any progress on the case. Again and again, the answer was no. The attacker had worn gloves, so no fingerprints were left. And if there was any DNA from the attacker, the police didn't try terribly hard to find it. Giving them the benefit of the doubt, it could be not due to the color of her skin but because Leigh Jones had the audacity to survive the attack, and police bother with women only after they've been murdered, not on the way there. At least, they didn't with Chris. But maybe I'm taking this too personally.

"A fireman and a snowman," he says, with a chuckle in his voice. "Am I right?"

I wonder if Jay wishes he were with Greg tonight. I didn't even think to ask what he's going as. Do twelve-year-olds still trick or treat? Another unnerving question about parenthood.

Flipping through the files, I don't find much more than is mentioned in the true crime books, where Nicole White is the lead character with Leigh Jones in a supporting actor role. We all know why that is.

Jay comes back to the couch with a sigh. "That should be it for a while. We don't usually even have this many." Babushka noses a mini candy bar. "Not for you," Jay scolds, as if the cat were his actual child. When the doorbell rings again, Jay gives a good-natured groan and grabs the candy bowl again.

I get to another page that somehow got misfiled with the Leigh Jones notes. The page runs off a DNA profile of the

Hobbes Lodge crime scene. Most of the items tested say "no match found," including a beer bottle, a cigarette butt, and a used condom. Nicole White's DNA was plentiful, and the owner's, of course. But Trayvon is right, as is Eric Myers. None of his DNA was anywhere to be found. But there was another match found on a piece of broken glass, in all capitals.

CLARE DIBOLD

"What the hell?" I say, dumbfounded.

Jay wanders back my way. "What?" he asks. "What is it?"

"No way," I say, but think back to what Ryan Johnson said, how she supposedly went "psycho" on him over Nicole. I've been focusing more on the boyfriend, which playing the odds would be the right move. She was reportedly alone in her room, sleeping. But he left to go see the other Ryan. So not only does he not have an alibi, neither does she. And she would have a motive.

Why would she move on to kill more women? My *Crimeline* brain runs the numbers. Though exceedingly rare, female serial killers do exist. But they don't usually mutilate bodies. Unless, as I've been wondering, the other girls are just a red herring. And this was all about Nicole White. But it wouldn't explain Leigh Jones.

"Did she do it?"

"Who?" Jay asks, but then duty calls again as the doorbell rings. "Hold that thought," he says, and turns back around.

A sweet chorus sings out from the front door.

"Trick or treat."

CHAPTER FIFTY-EIGHT

NOW

We walk into the darkness of the basement, the room growing perceptively colder. When we hit the concrete floor, I wave my hands around, trying to catch the drawstring from before. My fingers slice through the air, then finally catch it. I yank it down with a ratchety sound, followed by a thunk, lighting the room up a dull gray.

The room hasn't changed, the pool of blood on the floor now nearly dry, as well as the footprints. It doesn't look like anyone's been here in our absence. The knife lies where it was, the scrunchie stiff with blood.

Melody gasps, jumping backward. "That's . . . Lainey's," she says, in a half-whisper, pointing to it.

"Yeah, I know," I say, sadly. "You haven't come down here since . . ."

Her eyes lowered, she shakes her head with a grimace.

"Here," she says. "The gun is this way." She walks down a few yards, and there it is, hanging askew on the wall.

I'm not surprised I didn't see it now. Once I saw the scrunchie, I panicked and tore back upstairs.

"Let's look around for anything else," I say.

She agrees, and we start casing the room. We creep around, examining every last crevice, including the circuit box, the sump-pump, and the pocket of space behind the furnace. Then we back out of the space.

"I don't think there's much more to see," I say.

"No," she says. "I guess not."

And we make our way back to the gun. We both stare at it, seemingly afraid to touch it.

"Odd, isn't it?" she says, moving closer. "That he didn't take it?"

I think about this. "Not his weapon of choice, I suppose."

She reaches up for the gun, going on her tippy-toes. Then she falls back with a moan. Her wounds look worse since she tried to clean them in the bathroom, the blood weeping now.

"Here." I grab the gun off the hook, handing it to her like an offering.

"Thanks." Melody gives me a pained smile. "It's better than a tennis racket at least."

―――

Back in the family room, Melody cocks the gun, tilting the barrel down to reveal two bullets nested side by side in the chambers.

"Yup," she says. "It's loaded."

Her hunting cap is appearing less and less ironic.

She puts the gun rest on her shoulder and squints down the barrel, her stance natural, as if she's done this a million times before.

"You seem scarily at ease with a shotgun," I comment.

She smiles, still staring down the barrel. "Remember that pilot we shot?" she asks. "That never got on the air?"

"Maybe?"

I vaguely remember this from a few years ago. Unfortunately, Lainey and I have been witness to a fair number of false starts and coulda-beens in Melody's professional life. Her latest get was a commercial against narcotics, with a still of her shooting up in a bathroom. *Hey, Mom, guess what? I got a part of someone OD-ing in a bathroom!*

"I played Sister Number Two," she says. "I shot an intruder." She lowers the gun in her hands. "We used blanks, of course, but I had to have a whole session on shooting and gun safety. And I took a few extra lessons on my own, since it was supposed to look like I knew what I was doing." She eyes me. "Want me to teach you?"

"Um," I say. I know the statistics on guns too well from *Crimeline.* A gun in the house means you're twice as likely to die. And that goes up to seven times more likely for women, who usually get shot by people who supposedly love them. "I think I might pass."

"Come on," she says, raising the gun up again. "If he comes back, you need to know how to shoot."

I consider this. I may not want a gun at home, but with a mad killer on the loose, I should learn how to shoot. "Yeah, okay."

"All right," she says, "come over here." Waiting for me, she says, "Now, copy my stance." And I do so. Again, she squints down the barrel, her eyes trained on an imaginary target. "Once he's in your sights, you pull the trigger." She turns to me, her expression earnest. "It takes more force than you would think."

"Okay." I stand there like an idiot, stiff and unnatural, with an imaginary gun in my hands.

"You take aim. You pull the trigger . . ." She mimes this. "And . . ." She lifts the gun as if it's gone off. "Pow."

Her "pow" echoes in the room.

"Now you try," she says, extending the gun out to me.

I take it with reluctance, still semishocked that Happy the Dwarf knows how to handle a shotgun. The gun feels foreign in my hands.

"Is there a safety or something?" I ask, nerves in my voice.

She points to a small rusted lever on the handle. "I made sure it was off."

Made sure the safety was off? Who is this woman? I rest the gun on my shoulder, and she shadows over me. I mime pulling the trigger too, then vocalize a halfhearted pow.

"Good," she says, in a teacherly manner, and I take the gun off my shoulder with relief. "Careful," she scolds me, grabbing it from me and leaning it against the wall. "You have to be very careful with these guns."

I give her a look. "Okay, Annie Oakley—"

We both hear it then. A delightful, splendiferous sound. A text message.

"The phone," I squeal, and we both run over to see.

CHAPTER FIFTY-NINE

OCTOBER

Lainey: Bored.

Alex: Another hotel?

Lainey: Yup.

Melody: Where's Ruby?

Lainey: Asleep. In Seattle.

Alex: With you? J

Lainey: I wish L. I'm sleepless. In Toledo.

Melody: Sucks.

Alex: Sucks.

Lainey: Sucks. What are you all doing? Alex . . . boring wedding stuff?

Alex: Nah. After much fierce debate, we decided on the Excelsior Font.

Melody: Phew. So relieved.

Alex: Indeed. What about you, Melody? How's Mason the Med Student?

Melody: Ugh. The asshole broke up with me.

Lainey: WHAT???

Alex: No way!!! What an asshole!!

Melody: And to think, I let him practice phlebotomy on me. Honestly, I think he was just using me for my blood.

Alex: Uber-asshole.

Lainey: You're way too good for him anyway.

Alex: Absolutely. Truthfully, I thought he was kind of boring.

Lainey: Yeah, totally. He never got your jokes.

Melody: Le sigh. This is true.

Lainey: Big game tomorrow, gonna get some sleep.

Melody: Yeah, I have rehearsal early.

Alex: Guess I'll go back to researching my fave psychopath.

Lainey: Ah, your 666 obsession.

Alex: Not an obsession . . . well . . . okay maybe J

Melody: Good night y'all.

Lainey: Good night.

Alex: Sweet dreams.

CHAPTER SIXTY

NOVEMBER

"I was asleep that night," Clare complains. "It's Ryan you should be talking to."

Over the Skype screen, she toys with her diamond stud earring, twisting it. Her thick glasses magnify her blue eyes, making her look like a carnival-drawn caricature, her eyes taking up half of her face, with her nose and chin smushed down to make room for them.

I could kick myself for not talking with her earlier. My own bias stopped me from even considering a female serial killer. But luckily, not only was her number easy to find, she was willing to talk.

"I did talk to Ryan," I assure her. "He has an alibi." Not strictly true, but she doesn't have to know that.

She outright laughs at this. "Who, that other Ryan chick? She'd do anything for him. I wouldn't trust a word she says."

After the gonorrhea discussion, I would debate this point but decide to let it go. "The police spoke to you?" I ask.

"Yeah, they did," she says, defensively. "They talked to a lot of people." She twists the earring again, puckering the skin of her earlobe. "They ruled me out."

"Yes," I say, though I don't know that to be true. I only saw her DNA results by luck, since they happened to be in the *Crimeline* files. But hopefully, I can review her FOIA soon. "You were in a Bible class with Nicole?"

"CCD." She chuckles with an eye roll. "Massive waste of time that was."

I turn a page in my notebook as Wiley strides by the fish-bowl office in black jeans and a flouncy white blouse.

"How well did you know her?" I ask.

"Not that well apparently," she says, with a scornful sniff. "I thought we were friends. Then she goes and steals my man." She lets out an extra scornful sniff. "Not that he was worth stealing."

"Was Ryan in the class too?" I ask, recalling that's what female Ryan said.

"Duh," she says. "That's how he met Nicole."

So he did lie about being in the class. But was it a lie of omission? Or is he hiding something?

"And her father taught the class," I confirm.

She nods. "I see him time to time." She reaches for a coffee and sips it. "I work at Hudson Valley Bank nearby. But . . . he was really weird. Even before she died, he was."

"Weird, how?" I ask.

"You know," she says, sipping her coffee again. "Going on and on about the devil. And darkness and light. Revelation and—"

"Wait," I interrupt, surprised at her blithe recall of the passage. "Revelation? Why do you say that one in particular?"

Unexpectedly, she chuckles. "Because he wouldn't shut up about it. It was almost like a joke in the classroom. Would he talk about Revelation today or not."

This throws me from my planned line of questioning. But then again, if she knew about the note, she might want to play it up to blame the father. I decide to stay the course and ask her about the DNA. Pausing, I brace myself for the question. I need to ask it in such a way as to shock her enough to provoke an unguarded response but not shut the interview down. I decide not to ask a question at all. "Your DNA was at the murder scene."

Her hand flies up to twist her earring again. "How do you know that?"

"I saw it in the police report. Your DNA was discovered there. Hobbes Lodge."

The twisting accelerates, her earlobe turning pink. "I never said I wasn't there. Lots of kids went there. To get drunk or whatever."

Toby walks by the office now, her eyes scrunched to peer inside. Seeing me, she subconsciously frowns and moves on.

"Ryan's DNA should be in there too," she protests. "Since we had sex in there a few times. It probably just wasn't in the system. I bet if you checked it would be now. He had a DUI, so his DNA should be in the database."

I consider this. He refused to give his DNA. I assumed that was because he was a suspect. But maybe he knew it might be there for less nefarious reasons and didn't want to be in the frame for a crime he didn't commit. I could ask if Juanita can get the police to re-run the DNA evidence and see if his pops up in the system now. But I doubt it, if they even have it still. Clare could just be trying to throw me off track. The DNA would take weeks anyway, and I only have a month left to sort all this out. *Get it together, Alex.*

"The only reason they even had my DNA is because of a stupid shoplifting prank." Her hand starts twisting her earring again.

"A prank?" I ask.

"Yeah, we had this dare club senior year and she . . ." Clare stops, her hand freezing.

"You know what, this is stupid. Why am I telling you anything?" She chews on her lip. "And even if I did kill Nicole for being such a lying bitch . . ." She pauses just a beat to say "May she rest in peace" before speaking again. "Why would I attack that Leigh Jones girl?"

She has a point. That's the connection I seem to be missing in everyone but Eric Myers. But as soon as someone says, "Even if I did . . . why would I . . ." my ears perk up. If they can imagine it, you can imagine it.

"Did you know Leigh Jones?" I ask.

"No," she shoots back. "That's what I'm saying. I don't know her and I'm not a freaking serial killer. Jesus Christ," she rails.

But no one has proved that the *A*-girls were the work of the same person, though it's been assumed. And Clare had no love lost for Nicole.

"Would you be willing to take a polygraph?" I ask, thinking of her boyfriend, who still hasn't returned my calls. I know *Crimeline* has a polygraph machine, though it doesn't have any legal bearings. I also don't know if I'm even allowed to use it.

"Absolutely not, you psycho," she answers, in a nasal voice. "We are done with this interview. Next time you call, you'll be talking to my lawyer."

"Hey, listen," I say, pulling back. "I'm sorry. I didn't mean to—"

"Oh, one more thing," she adds. "If you hadn't noticed, I don't have a 666 tattoo."

"I know, I know. Let me just—" The connection drops.

Toby walks by again, peering in and out, and I review my notes. So far, I have Ryan, who's been lying, failed the polygraph, and doesn't have a true alibi; Clare, whose DNA is at the scene and doesn't have a true alibi; and Adam Redmond, whose name is on the note, had an obsession with the devil and that particular Revelation passage, and led their Bible class. And yet none of them really seem like serial killers. None of them have a connection to Leigh Jones. And none of them have a 666 tattoo.

And none of them will convince Toby to green-light another show on the murders. With a sigh, I start gathering my stuff to go when my cell phone starts ringing.

"Hello?"

Silence comes over the phone, and I check the number, figuring it's probably spam.

"Hello?" I repeat.

This time, a voice does come on the line.

"I can't wait to cut you open," a voice says. "And write 666 all over the walls."

I see my reflection on the computer monitor, my face stricken.

"Who is this?" I demand, looking away from myself.

And the caller hangs up.

"Most likely a burner," Juanita says, handing me my phone back. "That's why no one's answering. They probably already dumped it." She leans back, her dimpling elbows resting on the arms of the office chair. "And you didn't recognize the voice?"

"No," I answer, gripping my phone, my heart rate still elevated. "They had one of those voice changer things."

"Looks like you hit a nerve somewhere," Toby says, leaning against Juanita's desk, highlighting the juxtaposition of the two-hundred-ish-pound Juanita and ninety-ish-pound Toby.

"So you can't trace it?" I ask, staring at the number on the phone as if it might reveal something more.

"Not easily," Juanita says. "You can maybe trace a serial number to a store and a credit card. But if he or she has half a brain, they would have paid cash." She leans back in her chair. "It could still be someone connected to Eric Myers. The false flag thing. They want it to seem like some outsider threatening you, just so it looks like he's not guilty."

Toby nods knowingly. "We've seen it before."

"Maybe," I say, though that seems like a backward way of accomplishing this.

"Did we get DNA results back on the 666 letter?" Toby asks, now boosting herself up on the desk to a dirty look from Juanita.

"Still waiting," Juanita says. "I pushed them. If he's in the system, it'll come up."

Toby starts swinging her legs. "But as you said, none of these folks have a connection to Leigh Jones. Or 666 tattoos."

Juanita shuts a drawer loudly, with the intended result of having Toby hop off the desk. "As for the connection to the others," Juanita says, "hard to know. But if it's a serial killer, you gotta start somewhere."

"I suppose," I say, but it doesn't sit right.

"What about Leigh Jones?" Toby asks. "Where do we stand with her?"

"Gonna meet with her tomorrow."

"Oh," Toby says, looking surprised and pleased. "You convinced her?"

"Yup," I say, not mentioning the 5K it took to do so.

"And something else came in the mail," Juanita says, handing a typed letter to Toby, who flashes it to me. I catch the name of a legal firm up top.

"What's that?" I ask, as Toby gives it back to Juanita.

"A cease-and-desist letter," Juanita says. "From Ryan Johnson's lawyer."

CHAPTER SIXTY-ONE

NOVEMBER

The moisture disappears into the air, leaving an odd, unpleasant berry scent. "It's a stupid habit," Leigh Jones says, putting her vape pen in her pocket.

After I deposited twenty-five-hundred dollars into her account, she kept up her end of the bargain, meeting me today as planned. We make our way to the food court in the mall in Allentown, Pennsylvania, where Leigh Jones *came for a guy, stayed for a kid.*

Unlike Donna White, it's amazing how little Leigh Jones has changed over the years. Maybe gained five or ten pounds, switched her hairdo from braids to an Afro. Her scars have healed now from raw gashes into long, thin lines, some criss-crossing her arms, one tracking from her clavicle to her chin.

"You want to get something?" I ask, gazing around at the meager selection. Panda Express. Sbarro. Jamba Juice. Cinnabon. The Cinnabon smells over-the-top good (they pipe in smells, a factoid from an economics class). But that would definitely not help my dress fitting.

"You paying?" she asks.

"Of course," I say, opening my purse.

"Then I'll get pizza," she says, and we head toward that line. Pizza would not do my dress fitting any favors, so perhaps a diet soda will suffice. With more workers than customers, we get through the line pretty quick. We pick a table with the fewest crumbs, sitting down in the uncomfortable metal seats. The scent of Cinnabon hangs heavy in the air.

After her pizza arrives, I put my phone on the table and hit RECORD. "If you don't mind," I say, since we already agreed to it. She answers with another shrug. "So, you knew Eric Myers?"

She chews for a while before answering. "I wouldn't say I *knew* him, knew him," she responds, brushing a crumb from the Formica table. "Met him at a party. He stuck out."

"Stuck out, how?"

"Only White guy there," she says, swallowing. "Think he was dating someone. Somebody's cousin. Mighta said two words to him." She takes a loud drink through her straw.

"Did you realize who he was when he attacked you, then?" I ask, shifting in the uncomfortable seat.

"No. Only found that out afterward. One of my friends pointed it out." She dabs pizza sauce off her chin. "He barely registered at the party. And then he was wearing the balaclava so . . ." She puffs out a bitter laugh. "That came out at the trial though. How come I didn't identify him right away, since I'd already seen him? I mean, I saw the guy once, at a loud party, in a dark room, and I was wasted. And I didn't see his tattoo." She shakes her head. "That's not on me. That's on them. The police didn't listen to me. My side of the street is clean on that one."

I nod in agreement. "If you don't mind . . . can you go over what happened with me again?"

She breathes in deeply, her fingers taking up a nervous rapping on the scarred plastic table. "I was walking home from work. Walgreens," she clarifies. "It was late, but not that late, ten o'clock maybe? It ended up being near Tully's, the auto repair shop where he worked. But I didn't think anything of that. I didn't even know he worked there. Just walking by a gate on a dirt road." She shifts in her chair. The loud buzz of beans grinding emerges from the Cinnabon, and we both look toward the sound, then away as it stops. "I heard footsteps."

I do an inconspicuous check on the phone, which is still recording.

"But again, I wasn't too worried. I mean, I'm a woman. I'm always worried. But they seemed . . . I don't know . . . slow. Not threatening."

"Uh-huh." I wait a long time for her to continue.

"The rest is," she says, with a visible shiver, "a bit hazy. He jumped on me, and I hit my head on the rocks. I remember having gravel embedded in my forehead."

I sip my drink to hide a wince.

"And I got the wind knocked out of me, so I was struggling just to breathe." Her lips quiver in remembering this. "He spun me on my back, and he was wearing a balaclava, like I told them. But I could see his eyes. I will never forget those rat eyes. When I saw Eric Myers again, I saw those eyes, right away." She starts shredding her napkin. "He was tall, strong. It didn't take much to overpower me. And . . . he just started cutting me. Like . . . like he enjoyed it. Like he was . . . making art or something."

My expression must show my disgust.

"Twisted, right?" she asks, her voice tight. "I thought he was going to rape me, but he didn't. That wasn't his *thing*, I guess," she says, with a sort of eye roll. "Anyway. That's it. He just cut me up. Bad." She twists her arms in demonstration. "You see these, obviously. But he got my legs pretty bad too. And even weirder, I have a couple of tattoos. A Chinese symbol for life on my left ankle, and my niece's name on my right." We both look down, though she's wearing pants and socks. "But it's like he took offense to them. I mean, he cut me all over, right? But he just really dug into those with the knife," she says, with a shaky breath. "He x-ed them out, till the skin was shredded there, to bone."

The vision sickens me.

"I ended up needing a skin transplant there," she says, examining one of her scars. "It was like he didn't think a woman should have tattoos or something. Or maybe he just didn't like mine." A smile emerges on her face. "Ironic, huh? Since his tattoo is what got him caught."

I think of Nicole White, her butterfly tattoo defaced as well. "Yeah, it is." But then I pause, thinking back to what Eric Myers said. Everything hinges on this tattoo. Without it, he might never have been convicted, or even caught. "Could it be . . . that it wasn't a real tattoo?" I ask.

Her expression turns wary. "What do you mean?"

"Like, just drawn on, to make you *think* it was Eric Myers." I toy with my straw. "That's what Eric Myers says. That someone wrote it on them just to frame him."

"Well, of course he's gonna say that. Please." She guffaws. "I know exactly what I saw. Every little detail etched into my brain. That was *not* somebody's Sharpie, okay? No one drew that shit on."

"Okay," I say, not pushing it. After all, she's probably right.

"There was something weird though," she adds, staring into the distance. "That he just . . . stopped," she says, sounding perplexed. "I hate to say this. But I was dead. I mean joining the eternal choir dead. And he just . . . left." She turns back to me. "Mind you. I'd still have been a goner if someone hadn't happened to drive by on the street. But I'll never know why he did that. Why he sliced me up, or why he took off. But one thing I do know for sure"—she looks straight into my eyes—"it was Eric Myers. And there's no question about that."

I nod in response. "I believe you," I say.

With that, we finish up lunch in a semi-awkward silence. It's hard to make small talk about the weather or family after that story. Sadly, the interview hasn't accomplished much except stir up bad memories for Leigh Jones. Her words add some color to the crime, but nothing earth-shatteringly new. And certainly nothing that would make Toby want to rein-vestigate the case. I'm about to turn off the recorder when I remember one more question.

"There was a note in Nicole's notebook," I say. "Revelation 13:18" followed by the name ADAM. Do you have any idea what that means?"

"No idea. Never heard about that. But then again, it's not like I knew her."

"How about Ryan Johnson? That was one of her boy-friends. Or Clare Dibold, her friend? Or . . . Adam Redmond, her stepfather? Do those names sound familiar at all?"

She shakes her head. "Sorry. No. As I said, I didn't know her. I just heard that she got killed after what happened to me."

"Right," I say, turning off the recorder for good now. "I appreciate this. I really do."

"Yup," she says, grabbing her purse. She rummages around, maybe looking for her vape. "I have to get back to work so . . ."

"Yeah. Well, thanks again." I slide my business card toward her on the table. "You have my number if you need anything. Or you want to add anything else. And I'll transfer the money later today." I start to stand up.

"Appreciate that," she answers.

As we walk out of the food court, I think back to her words. *It was Eric Myers. And there's no question about that.*

Maybe it's time to see the man himself, to decide if he's telling the truth or not—not just over the computer, but in person. That might be my last shot of getting any traction with Toby on it.

Which means I need to go to the prison.

CHAPTER SIXTY-TWO

NOW

*M*om *finally asleep. Will come over soon.*

It's from Noah.

"Thank God," I intone. Overcome by relief, I fall back onto the love seat, the sudden movement throbbing my head again. Now that my body can relax, my pounding head wants all the attention again. "I can't believe he found his phone in all that snow."

"I'm writing back so he knows we got it." Melody types, sitting on the arm of the sofa.

"Let's call 911 while we have a signal," I say. "Then I'll call Jay." I slouch down further, exhausted and relieved. Maybe we can find Lainey before it's too late. This nightmare is finally about to end.

But then I see Melody's face.

"It didn't go through," she says.

"How?" I pop up to look at her screen, my forehead banging with pain. "That's impossible. It was just working."

She taps hard on the cracked screen, as if that will help something. "The signal must have dropped again," she says, playing around with some settings.

"Try turning it on and off again," I suggest.

"Okay," she answers, sounding reluctant. "I'm running out of juice here though so . . ."

I grab it from her. "I'm calling 911."

"Yeah, well, I was just trying to do that when you grabbed it," she complains. "I'm telling you, Alex. It's not going through."

I try 911 again. No luck. The phone has no bars once again.

"Jesus Christ," I snap, trying the call once more with the same result. "How can that fucking happen?" My head hurts so much I can hardly see. The Tylenol has definitely worn off. I collapse back into the couch, tears squeezing through the corners of my eyes. "I was going to call Jay too," I say. I didn't realize how much I wanted to talk to him, to hear his steadying voice. Jay is good in a crisis. He would know what to do.

"Listen," Melody says, gently. She takes the phone back from me. "Noah told us he's coming. He's not far. It could be any minute now. Maybe he's calling the police too."

Outside the window, the sky looks like a smudged eraser, gray and pink. I rub my dry, scratchy eyes, the hours without sleep catching up to me.

"You want to take turns resting?" Melody asks, standing from the arm of the couch with a wince. "I can take the first shift if you want."

"I don't know." I rub my eyes again. "Should we do that? I mean. I still feel like we could be doing more to find her."

"What can we do, Alex?" she asks, frustration in the words. "Really . . . what?"

After a pause, I admit, "I don't know. I suppose we don't want to miss Noah."

"And it's almost morning anyway. Power lines will start being cleared. We'll get a signal again." She yawns with her hand over her mouth.

"Yeah," I say. "I just feel like we should stay awake, alert. In case he comes back."

"Okay," she agrees. "I'll try at least."

We sit on the couch together, trying to stay away awake. A crow caws out in the distance outside as pink creeps up in the sky.

Melody smacks her cheeks with her mouth open, making a hollow sound, which looks suspiciously like a drama exercise. "Okay. Let's talk so we'll stay awake better." She sits up straight, facing me. "What's the first thing you are going to do when you get home?"

I think about it. "Shower."

"After that?"

"Eat a huge breakfast," I say. "Or lunch, or whatever time it is."

"Mm," she says. "Chocolate chip pancakes, maybe."

I laugh. "Jay made me pancakes once." He surprised me one morning. He looked sexy as hell in boxers with an apron, spattered with batter, a dab on his cheek. "They were really awful."

Melody lets out a musical laugh that sounds like wind chimes. "No. Don't tell me. Mr. Perfect actually has a fault?"

"Indeed he does. He's a really shitty cook." I stretch out my sore back. "What about you? What are you going to do when you get home?"

She pulls her sweater away from her body. "Fumigate these clothes for one."

With a chuckle, I nod, my eyes closing.

"Hey!" Melody snaps her fingers. "You're falling asleep."

I sit up straight. "Sorry, sorry."

She shakes her head. "Why don't you take a quick rest, Alex? Seriously. You take a turn, then I will. I'll wake you up if I see anything."

"Maybe that's not a bad idea," I admit. Though I pause. Now would be a terrible time to start acting out my dreams again.

"You worried about the REM disorder thing?" she asks, maybe catching my troubled expression. Then, out of nowhere, she smiles and starts laughing.

"What?" I ask, wondering what could possibly be humorous about this situation.

"Remember someone gave Lainey that R.E.M. T-shirt with "Everybody Hurts" for Secret Santa? And she was like . . ." Melody puts on a low voice. "Who the fuck is R.E.M.?"

I laugh despite myself. "I don't know why that was so funny."

"I know, it just was," Melody says, her laughter dying out. "You ended up wearing it, right?"

"Yeah," she says. "It was too small for her anyway."

We don't say anything more for a while. I don't like how we're talking though, remembering Lainey that way. Like we're telling stories at her funeral. After a while, my eyes start closing again, and my head falls forward before I jerk it back up.

Melody stands up. "Honestly. You rest. I'll take first shift."

"I could go first," I offer, feeling guilty. But I can barely keep my eyes open.

"I got it," she says. "And Noah should be here soon anyway."

"Okay," I say, but I'm not even sure that I get the word out before I fall asleep.

CHAPTER SIXTY-THREE

NOVEMBER

"It's time, Boosh," I say, springing up.

Two weeks later, I'm stroking Babushka and checking my email when the word finally comes in. My visit to see Eric Myers got approved. It's just after 4:00 PM and would take six hours to get to Greene County Prison, so it's doable. I just have to pack a few things and rent a car, and I can be there in no time.

In the last couple of weeks, I've been spinning my wheels, lurking on the 666 Killers Facebook site to find nothing new, and waiting for a call back from Adam Redmond. The Twitter conversation has descended into further depths of misogyny and The Armchairs have been diligently digging away at the *A*-girls mystery with nothing to show for it. My six months are nearly up, and with Leigh Jones fingering Eric Myers again and validating none of my other theories,

Toby wants to wrap things up, especially after the cease-and-desist letter. I've been fighting to find the angle, the missing puzzle piece, to no avail.

I'm running upstairs when my cell phone sounds, and I have to run back downstairs and play a game of Follow the Sound before I locate the ringing.

"Hello?" I say, just before it would go to voicemail.

"Hi," a man's voice says. "It's Adam Redmond calling back. I got your message."

"Oh, yes." I rifle around my purse for my notebook and pen, then sit back on the couch. Babushka retakes her rightful spot beside me. "Thanks for getting back to me. I just had a few follow-up questions."

"Okay, but first," he says, "I wanted to apologize for our last meeting. Things have been a bit . . . rough for me lately. I really wasn't myself."

"Oh," I say, surprised at the unexpected apology. "No need. I know this is probably a lot to deal with. I might have stirred up some difficult feelings."

He clears his throat. "Yes. Yes, you did. But that was no excuse for how I behaved. So, anyway. I just wanted to get that out of the way." He takes a breath. "You said you had some questions. Fire away."

"Okay. I understand you led Nicole's Bible study class?" I ask.

He pauses. "Yes. CCD. I was the leader for a while."

"It's just . . ." I jot this down. "I spoke with some of Nicole's friends from the class and . . . they mentioned you had a particular subject matter that you were partial to—"

"Revelation," he answers.

"Yes," I say, again surprised at his straightforward response.

"It's no secret," he says. "I told you I was helping them find the light."

"Helping them find the light?" I repeat, to get him to expound.

"Yes. Warning them against the devil. I know people don't like to speak in those terms anymore. They see it as . . . simplistic, I suppose. Or embarrassing, maybe. But I disagree, on both accounts. There's nothing simplistic or embarrassing about it. Milton was right. This remains the ultimate battle on this green earth. Good and evil. Darkness and light. I'm not ashamed to admit it. I fight this fight every single day."

"Okay," I say, taken aback at his facile theological discussion. "It's just . . . you didn't mention it when we spoke."

He sighs. "As I said, I wasn't quite myself that day, in case you didn't notice."

"Right," I say. But part of me wonders which is the real Adam Redmond, the sober one apologizing or the vulnerable drunk one from the bar.

"I have no qualms about discussing it," he says. "I was open with the police. I'll be open with you too. In fact, I hold myself responsible, to some degree."

"Why do you say that?" I ask, turning another page in the notebook.

Another sigh comes over the phone. "I tried to stop him. I really did. But I couldn't."

"Tried to stop who?" I ask.

Here he pauses. "As an English teacher," he says, a smile in his voice, "I have to tell you that the proper word would be whom."

I bite back annoyance. "Right. Okay. *Whom* did you try to stop?"

"The devil," he answers, simply. "I couldn't stop the devil. And he took her soul."

"You're doing what?" Jay asks, a note of hysteria in his voice.

An hour into the drive, I was still ruminating on my strange conversation with Adam Redmond when I called Jay.

"I'll be back before you know it," I assure him. "And I rented a car so you'll still have yours."

He huffs. "It's not about the car, Alex. You can have the car any time. You know that." A heavy pause comes over the phone. "Did you think to even ask me?"

"Ask you?" The idea piques me.

"Yes," he answers, undeterred.

"You mean, like, for your permission?"

"No," he says, the word measured, reigning himself in. "But just, to let me know, maybe? I would think it's common decency to tell your fiancé you're taking a trip. After all, the wedding is soon, in case you hadn't noticed."

"Still over a month," I argue. We're not quite to Thanksgiving and the wedding is January tenth (a date burned in my brain by now).

"Yeah but," he says, his pitch rising, "the man is a psychopath. He's sending you letters penned in blood, calling you. What if he hurts you?"

I sigh into the phone, softening. So, this isn't about control. He's worried about me, understandably. And he's right. I should have let him know.

"First of all, we don't know where the letter is from yet. And he's not going to hurt me. But I'm sorry. I should have told you. To be honest, I've been waiting for weeks for the warden to agree to it. And it all just came together at the last minute today so . . ."

"It's all right," he jumps in. "I shouldn't have snapped at you. I just . . . I get worried."

On this conciliatory note, we end the conversation, with me promising to call as soon as I get in and as soon as I'm done with the interview. I don't doubt my decision to visit Eric Myers though. If I ever want off this intern track, I have to take some chances.

Glancing at Google Maps, I see I'll be at Greene County Prison around midnight. I grab another celery stick to help me stay awake, and as I search out a mindless pop-hip-hop station, I think about what Jay said.

The wedding does seem close now.

Invitations have been mailed, after the unexpected trouble of finding a calligrapher. I thought a printer would suffice, considering you can 3D print a gun nowadays. But Jay wanted the gravitas of the calligraphy touch, and he was right. The envelopes appear both artful and refined with the hand-drawn black ink. The band has been hired, after Caitlyn sent us various YouTube links. I lobbied for the cheaper DJ option. But Jay found that crass and my mom actually agreed with him on that one. The food items have been chosen: steak, fish, or a vegan/gluten-free option, though food stations would have been less expensive. (I was envisioning Mexican, Italian, Japanese, and Jay said it sounded like Epcot.)

Listing off the items, I can't help but notice how each decision reveals a tiny rift between Jay and me. And since Jay is footing the bill, he always seems to win the battle. On the other hand, I'm no bridezilla. I've been focusing on my job. Most guys can't be bothered to put together their guest list. Jay just took it over for me. I love that about him, how he just takes things over. So I can't complain when he took the wedding worries right off my plate. And it doesn't really matter if the plate has salmon or tacos on it.

And anyway, he let me choose the cake, 100 percent. Caitlyn recommended a "pink champagne" cake, whatever that is, but I wanted one that "tastes like a Twinkie." Jay slightly recoiled at the description but stayed mum. He left that one up to me after all, and a deal is a deal.

I glance at the clock on the touchscreen.

Five more hours to go.

CHAPTER SIXTY-FOUR

NOVEMBER

Sitting across from Eric Myers, my mind jumps all over the place.

I don't sleep well in hotels, so I'm jacked up on caffeine, having main-lined three cups of coffee this morning. Luckily, I came early. The line stretched forever to get in, what with metal detectors and drug-sniffing dogs, but at least no strip searches. The prison has the vibes of a giant men's locker room, with loud male voices, shoes squeaking on shiny tile floors, and banging lockers (cell locks in this case), along with the smell of sweat and antiseptic.

"You get in okay?" Eric Myers asks, bouncing nervously in his seat.

The question sounds oddly genteel, as if I'm a distant relative visiting for Thanksgiving.

"Yes, thanks," I say.

The guard (the beefy one again) quietly scoffs in the corner. I ignore the attitude. After all, I might need his help if Eric Myers comes after me.

"So," I say, after taking a deep breath. "I think it's only fair to tell you that *Crimeline* wants to end things at this point."

"End things?" he asks, baldly crushed by the news. He pushes himself back from the table. "But . . . but . . ." he sputters. "I didn't do it. You have to tell people. You have to get them to reopen the case."

I nod, swallowing. "Listen, I wanted them to. But they don't see it that way."

"Is it the tattoo?" he asks, a screech of desperation in the question. "Because I already explained that. Someone drew that on themselves. I explained that."

"It's more than that, Eric," I say. "There's not enough for me to work with. Your connection to Leigh Jones. The confession. Your DNA on her purse."

"But that was it, right?" He scoots closer to the table again, close enough that if I reached out, I might feel the smoothness of his cheek. "Just on her purse, which I told you was from the date. Nowhere else, right? Was any of my DNA on her clothes? On her skin?" He pauses for an answer, which he knows as well as I do.

"Also the autopsy," I say, not answering his question. "It matches the confession statement very—"

"Come on," he interrupts, with a loud, honking laugh. An incredulous laugh. "You know that's bullshit. I told you that." He throws his hands up in frustration. "Of course it fits the confession. They told me exactly what to say." He taps his fingers on the table, an impatient, out-of-sync rhythm. "The autopsy says someone stabbed her a bunch of times. The cops told me to say I stabbed her a bunch of times. The autopsy says there was THC in her bloodstream, they told me to say that we got high together. They said I tore the butterfly necklace. So I wrote down that I tore off the butterfly necklace."

Everything stops.

The sounds of prisoners walking down the hall, keys jangling, and his tapping, bouncing fingers. It all fades away.

"What did you say?"

"What did I say about what?" he asks, panic spreading across his face, aware he might have made an error. "The necklace?"

"You said butterfly necklace. It was a butterfly necklace?" I confirm.

His eyes rove side to side, as if an answer might be found somewhere out there. "I think?" he says, as a question. "I just remember that she had a butterfly necklace she always wore, so I said that."

"Okay," I say.

He was obsessed with her. He might have recalled her butterfly necklace. But he also just might remember that from when he murdered her. His false confession might just not line up with his real confession, which he just gave me. I thought the heart error revealed his innocence, but maybe it revealed his guilt.

All at once, I want to run out of the room as fast as I can. I start to stand. "So, as I said, they want to wrap things up now."

"Wait," Eric Myers says, the word jumping out. Moving closer, he drops his voice to a whisper. "I have something else to talk about."

"Okay," I say, with hesitation, not fully sitting or standing right now. "What is that?"

He taps on the table twice, a nonverbal command to sit down again. I bristle against the arrogant gesture, but my journalistic instinct wins out and I sit back down.

He leans back now, having won that skirmish. "I think *Crimeline* will be *very* interested in this one."

CHAPTER SIXTY-FIVE

NOW

When I wake up, I am crouching over Melody, my hand above her head in a fist.

She lies on the floor, gazing up at me in shock and fear.

I unclench my fist, dropping my hand like it's on fire, and stand up. I was dreaming. Oh God, I was doing it again.

"I'm so sorry, Melody. Are you okay? Did I hurt you?" I reach my hand out to help her up, but she waves it away.

"I'm okay," she says, breathless. I'm expecting stab wounds all over her, but of course, I didn't have a knife. I could have hit her, but she doesn't seem bruised or anything. The wound on her arm has bled into her shirt, but nothing else.

"Jesus on a motorbike." She slowly stands up and takes a pronounced step away from me. "You weren't kidding about being violent in your dreams. You scared the fucking shit out of me."

I back away from her as well. "I'm sorry."

"You were like, punching the air," she says, still catching her breath. "And I tried to stop you. Which . . . was a mistake." She rubs her forehead in a gesture of exhaustion. "What were you dreaming about?"

I lean against the couch, my arm tired, as if I were just lifting weights. "It was . . . him. In a balaclava." I try to remember who it really was though, when I pulled off the mask, but the face remains fuzzy. I gaze around the room to get my bearings again, still feeling half-asleep. "Sorry," I repeat.

"Well, I did whack you with a tennis racket, so I suppose I can't get too upset." She motions around the room. "As you can see, Noah didn't come yet. It's only been a half hour, but come on, it shouldn't take *that* long."

"I was only asleep a half hour?" I ask, shocked. I walk over to the window to find the sky filling with a rosy pink. "It felt like hours." She's right though. Noah is only a mile away. It shouldn't take that long. "Maybe his mom woke up again."

"Or his car won't start. Or he's snowed in. There are plausible reasons," she admits. The blood on her leg is now leaking through her jeans. "And he probably can't get through to tell us because of the signal."

I chew on my thumbnail. "Maybe we should go out again," I say. "If he's not coming."

"I don't know," she says, through gritted teeth. "Alex, I honestly don't know if I can walk outside right now. My leg is killing me."

"Yeah," I admit. "I'm not feeling so hot myself." My bones still ache back from falling out of the truck, which seems like days ago now. And of course, my head hurts like hell. "Plus, honestly, it doesn't change much if Noah comes or not. We just have to wait it out. Traffic will be back on the street soon enough."

Melody sits heavily on the sofa, her face pale and tired.

"How about you rest this time?" I offer.

"No, that's okay," she says, but I catch a beat of relief in her expression.

"Please," I say. "It's only right. I'll take watch."

She yawns. "Maybe just a little rest would be okay." With that, she adjusts herself to lie down. "Do me a favor?"

"What?" I ask, through a yawn.

"Don't fall asleep and beat me up."

"I'll do my best," I say, trying for humor but sounding grim. "Just get some sleep. I'll be on the lookout for Noah."

"Okay," she says, the word slurred with sleep.

But then a soft crunching noise comes from outside, and her eyes pop open.

"What was that?" she whispers.

"Maybe it's Noah?" I glance outside. "I didn't hear a car though."

"Maybe someone dropped him off?" she asks.

"Wouldn't he just knock?" I whisper back. "Or . . ." I make the sign of a phone with my hand against my ear.

"No signal," she whispers. "But—"

The noise gets louder though, and we stare at each other, eyes opened wide.

They sound like footsteps.

CHAPTER SIXTY-SIX

NOVEMBER

"My cellie's planning to escape," Eric says, leaning back with his arms crossed, as if he just declared checkmate.

I'm not impressed with the chess move though, recognizing it as a desperate attempt to keep me in the room. He would hardly be discussing real escape plans in front of a corrections officer, no matter how uninterested said corrections officer appears.

"Is he," I say, conversationally.

"Yeah, he is," Eric Myers answers, clearly irked by my indifferent tone. "And he's the real deal. Really. They call him the Engineer. Because . . ."

I close my notebook. "He used to be an engineer?"

"Yes, that's right," he says, pulling on the edge of the table, as if telekinetically trying to pull me back in too. "And he got a blueprint of the prison. Someone from home found it for him."

My brain skips ahead now. I have to get the profile done soon, even though Toby won't green-light a show on it. And she shouldn't. Eric Myers slipped up. He accidentally uttered the truth. For the very first time since I took on the project, I'm absolutely certain that he did it.

Maybe I could work on it over Thanksgiving, since Jay will be in Australia and I'll be in Vermont. The wedding will be here before I know it, and despite all my protestations, Lainey and Melody have planned a bachelorette party for the first weekend in December, though they won't tell me where.

"Found the original work permit from 1973," Eric Myers says, breaking into my reverie. His fingers tap a nervous rhythm on the table. The guard yawns into his fist. "The ventilation system," Eric says, again in a low voice, "that's the key. He's just making sure the ducts can support our weight."

The word catches my attention despite myself. "*Our* weight?" I ask. "So that means you're included in this scheme?"

"Maybe," he says, a glint in his eyes. "Maybe not."

Now the corrections officer rolls his eyes.

"Listen, Eric. I was given a very clear assignment with little wiggle room. The 666 murders. I'm sorry, but the Engineer has nothing to do with the case." *Plus, I think it's complete bullshit*, I add in my head.

He moves closer to me, his teeth bared. For the first time, I can see aggression in his face. I can see what Leigh Jones might have seen. What Nicole White might have seen.

"It's about a dangerous criminal escaping," Eric Myers says, a threat running through the words. "Isn't that important?"

I cross my arms, asserting my own boundary. "If that's truly going to happen though," I say. "I would need to alert the authorities, right? They stack on quite a bit of additional time for that, don't they?"

He snorts. "To a life sentence?"

With a slap, I close my notebook. "And then you would just what . . . change your identity? Try to get a job and a house?" I ask, throwing some cold reality on his plan. "And then watch over your shoulder for the rest of your days?"

He shrugs. "I got life in here. If they catch me, I'll get life again. Doesn't seem like much of a risk to me."

"I suppose," I say, out of politeness.

"You could get the scoop on it," he says, with a beat of frenetic excitement, changing tactics from aggressor to helper. "When we escape, you could tell everyone how we did it. Expose all the weaknesses in the system."

I shrug. It's not bad TV. But, and I don't want to come off as jaded and heartless, it's been done before. "I want to thank you though," I say, cutting off this subject. "You've been very open with me, and I appreciate that. So—"

"By the way," Eric says, a lazy grin on his face. "How's Jay doing these days?"

My body jerks in my chair. "What?"

"Your fiancé," he answers, matter-of-factly. "And . . . what's his son's name . . . Greg?"

Unease trickles into dread. *How would he know that?*

A nebulous smile appears on his face. "That would make you the evil stepmother, right?"

I don't say anything. The caged clock ticks on the wall, the sound deafening. I back my seat up. *How could he possibly know this? Did he send the letter? Get someone to call me?*

"That's gotta be tough," he says, leaning back, obviously relishing my discomfort. "Kids don't usually like their stepmothers."

"Thanks for your time, Eric. I wish you the best of luck," I say. And as I abruptly stand up to end the interview, Eric Myers keeps sitting there, smiling.

CHAPTER SIXTY-SEVEN

NOVEMBER

My mind spins on the ride home.

Do I tell Jay? Have I put him and his son in danger? He was right all along. As was my mom. I was taking too big of a chance. I never should have gotten this close to a serial killer. I never should have gone to the prison to see him.

Maybe Eric Myers was just trying to provoke me, to keep me on his case. The move seems counterproductive at best, but he's not the brightest specimen anyway. Maybe it's just an empty threat.

Pictures flash in front of me.

His teeth bared. His cocky grin.

His blue, blue eyes.

But another voice crawls into my head. Clare Dibold has blue eyes. And yes, Ryan Johnson too. But how would he know about the butterfly necklace?

I switch the radio on to drown out the voices, when my phone rings. The touchscreen shows Juanita's number and I push it to answer.

"Hello?"

"Are you sitting down?" Juanita asks.

"Yeah," I say, checking the rearview mirror to change lanes. "I'm in a car, which has seats so . . ."

"Okay. Good news," she says, her tone triumphant. "Got a breakthrough on the letter."

"You got a DNA match?" I ask, with relief. Finally, some positive news.

"Yes," she says. "And we got a picture of him buying the burner phone. And I'll check, but I assume it'll match up with the flowers too."

"A friend of Eric Myers?" I ask.

"Nope," she says.

"Ryan Johnson," I guess.

"Nope," she answers, sounding too pleased to keep me in suspense.

"Well then, who the hell is it?" I ask, getting annoyed now by her song and dance.

"I'm sending you the picture right now."

Hours later, I'm almost home.

I don't know what to tell Jay.

It wasn't Eric Myers sending me the letters and calling me. Nor was it a false flag operation. The letter didn't have anything to do with the case, not directly. Neither did the phone call. The fact that they even had the DNA was just happenstance. He had visited the police station for a school project years ago. The parents signed waivers without really reading them, and the class's DNA ended up on a database.

That wasn't all.

There was the security camera photo. From the phone number, Juanita and her crew managed to trace the serial number of the burner phone, which came from a nearby store. It was bought with cash, but checking the time-stamped receipts, they tracked the time and matched it to the security footage. His face looked young and nervous when he glanced up at the camera, laying out his money. Once they had the suspect, they could easily verify that the fake PayPal account used to buy the flowers belonged to him as well.

The final nail in the coffin: the DNA from the blood on the letter matched his DNA from the database. The letter, the flowers, the texts . . . all him. The grainy picture, now sitting on my phone, which left me gobsmacked, but also left no room for error.

And I don't know what to tell Jay.

Because the person in the picture is Greg.

CHAPTER SIXTY-EIGHT

NOW

The noise stops.

We both stand in the middle of the room by the couch, time hanging over us as we listen, immobile, absolutely silent. A couple of minutes drag by before I run over to the window to steal another look outside.

No one is there.

"False alarm," I say, and start breathing again.

Melody nods, her hand over her heart. "Probably an animal or something." She starts to sit on the couch again.

But then the sound returns.

We both stiffen.

A loud thumping comes up the stairs, creaking on the wooden porch.

Unmistakable footsteps.

We dash against the wall by the front windows, hiding behind the musty green curtain. When footsteps creep on the porch again, my heart bangs in my chest so hard that it hurts. A man's head taps against the window, like maybe he's trying to look in. We stay plastered against the wall. The heat puffs the curtain out though, a half an inch.

"It's him," Melody gasps, her hand flying to her mouth. She drops to the floor, and I plunge down right next to her.

"Are you sure?" I ask, my voice dry in my throat. I lift my head an inch to peek through the slice of window.

But she pulls me back, clinging to my arm. "Stop," she whimpers. "He'll see you."

In a flash, I see him. His figure moves on the porch, then stops at the window. He's tall, thin, dressed in all black. In an instant, I meet his beady blue eyes behind the balaclava.

Blue, definitely blue.

I crouch back down beside her, holding the curtain against the window. "Come on," I say. "We should hide in the basement again."

"No," Melody cries. "Don't leave me." She hugs me, her arms quivering.

A rattling noise jars the room.

The doorknob twists and jiggles, as if turned by a ghost, then his footsteps march on the porch. Again, the knob shakes angrily, and when it stops, time pauses.

We hear nothing, just the soft sigh of the wind and our own breath. But then a horrible banging makes us jump. We crawl closer to each other, embracing. Her heart pounds into her neck.

We can see the shadow of his body through the curtain, slamming himself into the door. The door moves forward by a millimeter. After a pause, he tries again, the door groaning and squeaking. Melody covers her ears as he tries again and again, a slamming sound with every bash. But the door does not give.

After a few agonizing moments, the noise stops. We sit there breathless, clinging to each other, waiting for him to try again.

Silence.

The footsteps sound out again, but this time with the rhythmic clatter of moving down the stairs. I'm praying he's given up. Maybe he'll run away out of anger. Or maybe Noah will come in time to scare him off.

Glimpsing out the tiny window view, I see nothing. I shift my feet, my legs tight and burning from crouching. Melody releases her hands from her ears, her arms barely trembling. I'm about to move to look out the window again when a crash sounds out and Melody shrieks.

A loud cymbal, glass breaking.

Shards sail through the air.

A black-gloved hand reaches through the side window and undoes the lock.

CHAPTER SIXTY-NINE

NOW

The man in black strides in, holding his long knife in the air.

Melody jumps up and grabs the gun from against the wall, then takes a step back, the shotgun shaking in her hands. She is crying, her confidence and poise evaporated. A television pilot does not compare to real life.

"Shoot!" I scream. "Shoot the gun!"

"Please," she says, pleading with him. "Please stop."

He takes another step forward and lifts the knife up high. The gun trembles as tears run down her cheeks.

In the space of a few seconds, I realize the truth.

This is my fault.

If I had taken the engineer thing seriously, if I hadn't worried about my damn scoop, my ambitions, and career so damn much, he never would have gotten out. If I had believed him when he slipped up about the butterfly necklace, he never would have taken Lainey. He wouldn't be here now, with a knife in his hand.

Without thinking, I take a running leap on top of him.

He emits a startled "ooof" sound, the breath knocked out of him, and the knife clatters to the ground. We both scramble for it. I try to grab the handle, but he does too and I can't wrench it away from him. He raises his arm, and I don't even know why, but I bite him, gnawing him like a dog, tasting sweat, fabric, and skin. He grunts in pain but holds onto the knife, and with his other hand, he elbows my head, rattling my teeth. But I don't let go.

I taste his blood, and he lands another punch, which removes me from his arm. So I fall on top of him, laying all my weight on him, feeling like a little kid trying to tackle her big brother. Blindly, I punch at his head, but he dodges my blows, which glance off him.

"Melody," I grunt. "Help me." I catch a glimpse of her standing there in shock, her voice softly keening. "Come on," I yell at her, as we struggle together in an odd wrestling dance. I reach once more for the knife, pushing his sleeve up, and revealing blue looping ink.

666.

"Melody!" I scream.

Eric pushes me off, standing up again, the knife above me. I have a flashback to the black-and-white *Psycho* poster from my college dorm. The poster stuck with putty on the wall. The knife stabbing over and over, the black blood swirling down the shower drain. Lainey making fun of me for it.

How innocent we were. How foolish.

Murder was a ghoulish joke.

"Eric," I say, changing tacks now. "Please don't. You know me." I start crab-walking backward. "You don't have to do this. Please. Let me help you."

This seems to only enrage him though. He bares his teeth. *Is this it? Do I die here today?*

I'll see Lissa. And maybe Lainey.

As he plunges the knife down, my body takes over and I scramble away. He misses me at the last moment. He raises his arms again for another chance, but I leap up too, grabbing the gun from Melody, who stares at me in shock.

Just like she taught me, I lift the gun.

She's right, it takes more force than you would think to pull the trigger. But I do it, closing my eyes and mouthing the pop sound. But the sound deafens my ears. My eardrums shake, scream, blister.

Maybe the way Eric felt when they boxed his ears until they bled, forcing him to confess. But now I know that wasn't true. None of that was true.

Eric's eyes open in shock, in a rude awakening.

How dare I do this? Shoot him? His eyes stare at me, saying this isn't the way it's supposed to end.

But this is the way it's going to end.

Falling down, he holds onto his chest.

And above the aching ringing in my ears, I hear Melody screaming.

CHAPTER SEVENTY

NOW

"Noooo!" Melody screams.

The word echoes in my head, the gun hot in my hand.

"No," Melody cries out again, falling onto her knees. "No, no, no."

I put the gun down and kneel beside her, hugging her. "It's over, Melody," I say, squeezing her tightly. "He can't hurt us anymore."

She just keeps moaning the word over and over again. *No. No. No.* Gripping her head, she rocks back and forth.

"It's over, Mel. It's over." I try to hold her, but she moves away from me.

"You weren't supposed to get the gun," she says, tears in her voice. "I was trying to hold onto it. You weren't supposed to get it." She rubs her eyes, hiccuping, trying to control her crying. "I'll tell them. I'll take the blame."

"No one's going to blame us," I say, realizing she's in shock. "It's terrible that we killed someone. Of course it is. But it was self-defense. Anybody is going to understand that. It was obviously self-defense."

"My prints are on there too," she says, ignoring me, seemingly talking to herself. "So I can say I just showed you how to use it." She nods over and over. "You just touched it, but I was the one who shot it."

"Melody," I snap, wanting to smack some sense into her. "Come on. It doesn't matter who shot him. We didn't have a choice. It was him or us. Let's go. Let's find Lainey now. That's all the matters."

But Melody keeps ignoring me. She stands up and calmly starts walking over to Eric Myers.

"Jesus," I say, baffled, and grab her to stop her. "What are you doing?"

But she keeps going, pulling me toward his body until we stand there inches away from him. Being this close sends fear and revulsion through me, even with him just lying there, not threatening anymore. The knife still sits in his gloved hand, and I kick it away.

But then I see him move an inch.

I pull her back with a gasp. "He's not dead."

But Melody pushes me away. "Thank you, God," she says, relief pouring into the words. She rushes toward the body. "Thank God."

"He might still be dangerous, Melody," I warn her.

But she doesn't listen, crouching down over his body. Blood stains the stomach of his black shirt, the dark circle slowly expanding.

"You don't understand," she says, in a whisper.

"We can call an ambulance for him," I say, gripping her shoulder to pull her back from danger. "Once we get a signal. But please. Stay away from him."

"No. You don't understand," she repeats, and slowly pulls the balaclava off.

CHAPTER SEVENTY-ONE

Melody: Ready for our big weekend?

Alex: WHERE ARE WE GOING?

Melody: We could tell you, but then we'd have to kill you, etc.

Alex: I do NOT want strippers.

Lainey: Um. Have you met us before?

Alex: Haha. Okay, fair enough.

Melody: LOL

Alex: Just us three, right?

Lainey: The three musketeers

Melody: The three amigos!

Lainey: The three banditos.

Alex: The three stooges?

Melody: Pack warm stuff.

Lainey: Yeah, that's right.

Alex: Jay said he knows where we're going. But won't tell me.

Melody: Under penalty of death.

Alex: I tried to get it out of him in all of my seductive ways.

Lainey: I so don't want to hear about your seductive ways.

Melody: I do!

Alex: But I want to know WHERE???

Lainey: Don't worry. You're gonna love it. Honestly.

Melody: Yeah. It is going to be EPIC.

CHAPTER SEVENTY-TWO

NOW

His lips are laced with blood as the mask gently comes up.

I drop to my knees. "No," I say. "No, no, no."

It's impossible.

It can't be.

The face doesn't make sense, doesn't compute. I won't let the face through my eyes, into my head. It's impossible.

"Hey," Lainey whispers.

Melody holds one of her hands, laying her forehead on it. "I'm sorry," she says, "I'm so, so sorry."

"It's okay," Lainey says, though the words come out soft and hoarse. The words take effort.

"Let me see the wound," I say, starting to lift her shirt, but she shakes her head and pushes my hand away. A spent cartridge lies next to her back.

"Hurts," she moans.

"I can help, Lainey," I argue, my hands already sticky with her blood. "We have to stop the bleeding."

"It's okay," she repeats, choking out the words. "You guys." Her eyes close, then open again. "Best friends."

"Don't," I say, barely getting the word out. "Please, don't."

"The three amigos," she says.

"The three musketeers," Melody whispers back.

Lainey gives my hand the lightest squeeze, and her eyes start to close again. "Love you," she says, barely above a whisper, her eyes open just a crack. Then her head turns, going slack.

And her eyes close.

I swallow tears down. "No," I say. I jostle her shoulders. Soft at first, then harder. "Wake up, Lainey," I yell at her. "We can help you. Just wake up. You have to wake up."

Melody checks for a pulse, while I reposition myself.

"Push on her stomach," I order her. "We just need to put pressure on it."

"Alex," Melody says softly, taking her fingers off her neck.

"Just do it," I cry.

Melody puts her bloody hand on mine. "I'm sorry, Alex."

"No," I scream at her. But the word disappears into the room, useless. I collapse beside her, putting my head on the ground, the scratchy hardwood floor digging into my forehead.

And I cry.

In shock, I am sitting beside her now. "I don't understand."

"It was a joke, Alex. For your party. A joke." She bites her lip, fat tears in her eyes. "It was supposed to be blanks in the gun."

Hopping to my feet, I step back from her. "I don't understand," I repeat, louder.

"It was a prank," she says, still kneeling beside Lainey and holding her hand. "They were supposed to be blanks."

"I don't understand," I scream this time.

"There was no intruder," Melody screams back, her voice hoarse, anguished. Then she pauses, her volume softening. "We . . . we made the whole thing up."

"You . . . hold on . . ." My brain tries to compute this and fails. "Nah . . ." I shake my head, not allowing myself to believe it. "That's sick. That's impossible. How . . . how could you even do that?" I consider it briefly, then shake my head again. "I would have heard. I . . . I was just sleepwalking."

Melody sighs. "We sedated you."

I grab my pounding head. "What do you mean you sedated me?"

Her lips twist, her expression dour. "Ambien. We put it in your cupcake."

You get the red cupcake . . . because red's your favorite color.

I stagger back away from her, almost toppling over. "No . . . that's . . . that's sick." I rub the goose egg on my forehead. "No way. You wouldn't . . . you wouldn't do that."

She wrings her hands. "We knew you'd believe it with your dreams and all that."

I shake my head. I feel like I can't stop shaking it, trying to dislodge these thoughts. She could not have done this. Never. "No. No way. That can't be."

"It was a joke," she says, a plea in the words. "Like a true crime prank, you know? Instead of strippers or something. We . . . we put it all together for you."

I stare at her in bafflement. "You mean . . . the whole night?"

"Yes. I mean, no . . . not everything." She scratches her neck. "I didn't know some farm woman was going to shoot at you. And I didn't plan on some rapey guy picking you up."

"But . . ." I say, struggling. "Are you telling me there was no one with a knife? No one who chased you in the snow?"

"Yes," she answers. "There was no one with a knife. There was no one who chased me in the snow."

I glance around the room, taking in the loops of blood, recalling the pool of it in the basement. I wave my finger around the room. "So all this is just . . . what . . ."

"Corn syrup," she says, not meeting my eyes. "I mean, a little better than that. I used the professional grade stuff."

I examine the scene more closely. The "blood" color does have a slight tomato-red tinge, but definitely looks like blood. I'm not a blood expert, but I've examined enough scenes for my internship. I didn't think about it when I first came back to the lodge and washed my hands off. But I was also half-frozen and in shock. Hesitantly, I dip my finger into the blood in one of the pillows and take a taste. Corn syrup.

Then it hits me. "What about your wounds, then?"

Her face falls, abashed. "Makeup." She wrings her hands again. "I took a course in it."

"Jesus fucking Christ," I say, in an exhale.

She hugs herself now, as if chilled. "It was supposed to be funny. Like . . . a lark." Sitting, she stares into the distance. "It was supposed to be blanks in the gun."

I take a step toward her, suddenly furious. "You did this," I hiss. I have never been so angry at Melody. I have never been so angry at anyone. "You fucking did this."

"I didn't mean . . ." she protests.

"You checked it," I say, accusing her. "You said they were real bullets. So you must have known."

"No," she says. "That's the point. I didn't know. I was lying." She throws her hands up. "I mean, I *thought* I was lying. I was pretending they were bullets, but I thought they were blanks. She . . . she told me they were blanks."

"Who's she?" I bark.

"The woman from *Gypsy*. From the prop department. And you weren't supposed to grab it anyway."

I walk away from her again. "I can't believe this. I can't fucking believe this."

"I know." Kneeling there, she starts weeping. "I'm sorry, Alex. I'm so, so sorry."

"That's pretty inadequate, isn't it?" I say, pacing in a circle. "I just killed my best friend, Melody. That's pretty goddamn inadequate."

She wipes her nose. "It just . . . we went too far is all. We took it too far."

I keep pacing, trying to figure out what we're going to do, when I stop short. "Wait a second." I spin around to face her again. "How do I know she's really dead?"

Melody goes pale, her mouth literally falling open. "What . . . you mean . . ."

"How do I know that's not a joke too?" I demand. "That Lainey's actually dead?"

She narrows her eyes. "Alex, how sick do you think I am?"

"Pretty damn sick, it turns out."

But something in her expression tells me she's not lying about this part. I venture closer to Lainey's body but can barely stand to look at her. I also know Lainey. She would have been cracking up by this point. But . . . maybe?

"Prove it," I say.

Melody looks at me, aghast. "How do you . . . I mean . . . Alex . . ."

I can hardly stand to do it, but I force myself to do it fast. I dart in, and touch the wound on her stomach. Melody gasps.

I bring my finger up. But I don't even have to taste it.

The blood is slick and maroon, the scent metallic. Not corn syrup. Blood.

Real blood.

I crumple down next to her body.

Lainey is dead. I've killed her. I've killed my best friend.

"I'm sorry," Melody repeats, rocking, her face in her hands. "I'm so, so sorry."

CHAPTER SEVENTY-THREE

NOW

We sit next to each other, a foot away from Lainey's body. "What are we going to do?" Melody asks, in a small timid voice. Melody has never once sounded timid in our entire friendship.

"I don't know," I mutter, rubbing my temples. My head aches. My body aches. My heart aches. I put my hands over my eyes, willing this nightmare to go away. But the nightmare isn't going away. The nightmare is real. "Maybe we wait for the police to come. Maybe we confess. I don't know."

Memories wash over me.

Lainey breaking the chair swing that one of Melody's moms had installed in our dorm room. We literally fell on the floor laughing, and she was so pissed at us until finally she just started laughing too. The kiss she blew to us midcourt, when she made the buzzer-beater to beat Michigan. When she didn't come out of her room for a week after her father died, and we got her set up with a therapist. When she signed her WNBA contract, and we celebrated all night at the Dead Rabbit and then nursed a shared hangover for three days straight. When she met Ruby after a game against Seattle, and her face lit up every time she talked about her.

And now I've killed her. I've killed my best friend.

How will I tell her mom? How will I tell Ruby?

I won't have to worry about marrying too-perfect Jay, or the live wedding band, or the Twinkie cake, or his fucked-up son who won't say a word to me. Because I'll be in prison. How much time would you get for manslaughter, second degree? Criminally negligent homicide? Five years, maybe, a decade?

A sardonic voice runs through my head.

You might even be on Crimeline.

I can almost hear the Fletcher Fox voice-over. "A bachelorette party prank that went wrong. So very wrong." And the pictures will be of Lainey, lying prostrate in the balaclava. Pictures of us all as roommates. Videos of her on the basketball court. Smarmy half-suggestions about a love triangle between us. And there will be pictures of me, and Melody too, maybe. Pale faced and crying in the courtroom. We will go to prison, but no justice will be done.

No family is avenged. No missing girls are found.

Nobody wins.

"What would Lainey want us to do?" Melody asks. She sits listlessly, hugging her knees. Oddly, the exact same question had popped into my head.

"I don't know," I say, hoarse from crying.

"She wouldn't want us to go to jail," she says, her face streaked with blood and tears. "Would she?"

I keep rubbing my painful head. I need more Tylenol. But a mean little voice breaks in. *You don't deserve it. You don't deserve anything for the pain.*

"It doesn't really matter. It doesn't matter what she would want," I say, resigned. "I'm going to jail no matter what."

"No," Melody says, insistent. "I'll tell them I did it. It's my fault anyway. I'll take the blame."

I exhale, my mind and body absolutely run-down, without an ounce of stamina left. "Melody, do you know anything about a crime scene?"

"Um . . ." She purses her lips, her eyebrows tilting in thought.

"You don't have gunpowder on you," I say, and lay my palms out to demonstrate. "I do. I'm the one carrying the physical evidence."

She blinks, taking this in. "Just rub some on me, then."

"It doesn't work that way," I mutter.

"Then we'll find more bullets," she says. "I'll fire the gun. We can say we were fighting over the gun and you were close. That's why you have residue on you still."

I fold my palms back up, squeezing my hands. "Then we'll both go to jail. What would that achieve?"

She stares ahead in thought. I'm too tired to even think. *Is this the last room I'll ever see as a free woman?* This stupid, cursed hunting lodge, where two women were murdered now.

Melody touches my arm, and I pull away, fighting the urge to shake her off.

"Alex?"

"I don't want to talk right now," I say, my head down, staring at my knees.

"But . . . I might have an idea," she says, a glimmer of hope shining in the words.

Despite myself, I turn to her. "What?"

She swallows. "A way we might not have to go to jail."

I don't say anything for a second. The truth is, as much as I want to punish myself, as much as I know I deserve this, I don't want to go to prison. I don't want Jay on *Crimeline*, talking about what a wonderful person I was. Or . . . maybe that's not even what he would say.

"What is it?"

CHAPTER SEVENTY-FOUR

NOW

"Bury her?" I ask, stunned.

Melody steeples her hands in a prayer position. "Yes."

A hard silence follows this statement, as if neither of us wants to further acknowledge it. Bury our best friend. This would be crossing the Rubicon, admitting murder. This would be me becoming Eric Myers, and all the countless murderers before me who took the unoriginal but often effective way out of murder. Hiding the body.

I swallow down nausea, sickened by the thought.

I don't want to do this. I don't want to bury my best friend.

"We can't," I say.

Melody nods but then meets my eyes. "We can though."

"No," I say, standing up. I can't sit here calmly and consider this. "It's hideous."

"It is," she agrees.

"And even if we were to think about it . . . there's like ten feet of snow outside? The ground would be rock hard." I start pacing again. "We don't have a shovel."

"There is a shovel," she answers, her demeanor unnervingly calm. "In the basement. I saw it in the corner when we were getting the gun." She stands up now to join me. "We can clean up the place. There's bleach in the kitchen."

I turn to her. "You seem pretty adept at this, Melody."

She doesn't respond to my jibe. "We can do it," she repeats.

I keep pacing back and forth. "Okay, let's say we do bury her. Then what? Just hope no one notices that she's gone?"

Melody leans against the wall, like she can barely keep herself up. "Obviously we need a story."

"A story?" I say, incredulous. "What are you talking about? I saw Noah and his mom. I told him about everything. He's probably coming any second now."

She squints, thinking about this. "We take her further into the woods, where he can't see us. And we tell him it was all a joke." She nods to herself. "That could work. They don't know how the night went. They don't know you shot her."

I stop pacing and lean against the wall next to her in exhaustion. "Forget it, Mel. It's not gonna work."

"Maybe," she says, ignoring me, "we tell them it was a prank. And she was doing her part of the prank and was running away but she just . . . never came back. Just a tragic accident."

I don't answer.

A long pause follows her statement. It's simple. It's stupid. But I have to admit it.

That story might work.

Outside, a mourning dove calls, the sound dull and gloomy.

—✦—

"I'm gonna need your help, Alex." Melody tugs at her arm, but the body barely budges. "She's heavy."

I'm standing six feet away from them, trying to pretend this isn't happening.

"Alex," she grunts.

Gritting my teeth, I inch toward them, but then my stomach starts roiling, and I back away again. "I can't do this."

"You have to." She keeps dragging the body, sweating. "I can't do this alone."

I wipe sweat from my own face, not from physical labor but from nausea. I feel physically ill doing this.

"Just . . . give me a second here." I take deep breaths to fight gagging. I get closer to her and reach down, but my hands are shaking too hard.

Melody puts her hand on my shoulder. "It's okay, Alex. We'll do this as fast as we can."

I swallow, my throat so dry that it hurts. "I don't think I can."

"Come on," she prods me, her voice not gentle now. "Do you think she would want you to go to prison? Do you think she would want that for us?"

I shake my head, my eyes filling with tears. I ball my hands into fists, knocking them against my head. "I can't. I'm sorry. I just can't."

"Alex," Melody yells this time, snapping me back into reality. "It's almost daylight. Noah will be here any minute. We need to get this done before someone sees us."

"Okay," I say, breathing deeply. "Okay. Okay. Okay."

"Take one of her arms," Melody says, pointing.

Fighting the heaving in my stomach, I reach down to her arm. Then I back up again and turn away, smacking my hand against the wall. "Fuck. Fuck. Fuck."

"Alex," Melody yells again. "Please stop. You . . . you need to help me. I can't do this alone. Three musketeers, remember? This is what she would want. I promise you. This is what she would want."

I spin around to face them. "Okay," I say. "I can do this. I can do it."

With trembling hands, I reach down for her arm. But first, I brush the hair from her eyes, though that doesn't matter now. She won't need her damn scrunchie anymore. I grip her arm and pull hard, but then her body springs to life, sitting up. I drop to the floor, my heart squeezing in my chest.

"Um," she says, with an apologetic lilt, then offers a sheepish grin. "Happy bachelorette party?"

CHAPTER SEVENTY-FIVE

NOW

L ainey hugs me, but I can't stop crying.

I'm crying so hard I can't breathe.

"I'm sorry," Lainey says, squeezing me tighter. "I shouldn't have done it. But calm down, Alex. Please. I'm sorry. I'm really, really sorry."

"I thought you were dead." I sob. "I thought I killed you."

"I'm sorry. It was stupid." She pats my back. "It was Melody's idea," she gripes, turning to her.

"I didn't even think you'd believe it," Melody says, her tone almost accusing. "Come on. I just told you the whole night was a prank."

"The blood was different," I say, accusing her right back. "The color. The smell. It seemed real."

"Yeah," Melody says, shrugging. "It was real."

I catch my breath from crying. "What do you mean it was real?"

"It was my blood," she says. "Mason the Med Student. Remember?" She points to the crease in her arm. "He drew my blood, and I just saved a few vials."

"I told her that was going overboard," Lainey says, shooting her a look.

"It worked though, right?" she protests. "That was the finale," Melody says, sounding minimally contrite. "We couldn't finish the play without the finale."

I untangle myself from Lainey's embrace. "It wasn't a play. Okay?" I say, exploding at her. I've never wanted to punch someone, ever. But I want to punch her right now as hard as I possibly can. "It wasn't a play. It was my life, okay? It was my fucking life. And I thought I killed my best friend."

Melody puts her arms out in supplication. "But you didn't, right? So . . . that's the catharsis!"

"I didn't need a catharsis," I say, still yelling. "This was a bachelorette party. It wasn't supposed to be some kind of a Greek tragedy."

"But life is a Greek tragedy," she says.

"Melody," Lainey intones, her voice a warning. "Maybe let's hold off on the drama major stuff right now."

"This isn't drama . . ." she argues, but then stops at Lainey's steely expression. She scoots to sit closer to me. "It was supposed to be like cinema verité. A true crime experience like no other. That was . . . that was the gift."

I lean on my elbow, which shakes with exhaustion. "The book was a good enough gift," I say, wiping my nose. "You bringing me here was a good enough gift." I point to them both. "Just being with you guys was a good enough gift."

They answer with guilty silence.

"I'm sorry," Lainey says again.

Outside, the wind still whips through the trees, but the sun shines, brightening the snow.

"There is some good news, however," Melody says, ever hopeful, and we both look at her. "We don't have to bury Lainey?"

I sigh at her pseudojoke.

"Well," Lainey says, "I *am* really heavy. And it is pretty fucking cold out here."

Despite everything, her statement pulls laughter from me.

"Additionally," Melody says, "I proved that I was that good friend who would help you bury a body."

"Right," I say, squeezing my temples. "So I didn't need literal proof of that fact."

Lainey stands up, her knees cracking. "I will say. Alex was pretty quick to agree to the burial."

"Hey," I protest, jabbing Melody in the chest. "It was *her* idea."

"It was the climax," she says, jabbing me back. "Every good story needs a climax."

I jab her yet again. "And letting me think I killed her wasn't the climax?"

"No, no," she explains. "*That* was the darkest night. There's always the darkest night before the climax." She sighs, throwing her hands up. "Don't you people know anything about story writing? Have none of you read *Save the Cat*?"

Lainey gives her a look. "What the fuck is *Save the Cat*?"

"Never mind," she grumbles. "Pearls before swine, I tell you. Pearls before swine."

They debrief me on the night while we clean up. Well, while *they* clean up. I'm just flopped on the sofa like a psychiatric patient, figuring they made the mess, they can clean it up.

"And just so you know. You weren't supposed to walk all the way to the farmhouse," Lainey says. "That part was not planned."

"Oh my God." Melody looks up from scrubbing the floor. "We were freaking the fuck out. I was afraid you were going to get hypothermia."

"Funny." I rub my sore back. "So was I."

"Yeah, well, Steve was supposed to drive by right when you got to the street," Melody explains, dunking her sponge.

"Wait." My mouth falls open. "Steve was you?"

"Yeah, he's my uncle." She grins proudly. "He's a cop. And he was going to pick you up, act all scary, and then incidentally drive you to the farmhouse. But his car got stuck on the way out to the lodge."

"That was my idea, by the way," Lainey brags. "To plant the prison escape story with the CB radio."

"I told him to be nasty and realistic," Melody adds, her voice bobbing with her scrubbing.

I blink my eyes in shock. "He was nasty and realistic, all right."

"Yeah, he's not real thrilled with me," she says, with a shrug. "He had to ice his balls all night."

"I don't think we're getting the blood out of the rug," Lainey says, armed with a spray bottle and sponge. She's in her New York Liberty T-shirt, having taken off the one stained with Melody's blood as soon as humanly possible.

"No big deal," Melody says, flicking her wrist. She has moved on to cleaning the couch. "We can toss it."

"Toss it?" I query. "Aren't the owners going to miss it?"

"Nah, it's ours," she says, with a yawn. "It is fake, by the way. I'm not going to be housed in the same room as an animal skin."

I let out a laugh of utter exhaustion. "You staged the room?"

"Well, duh," Melody answers, seeming offended I might think otherwise. "The rug and the pillows. They're from *Our Town*. They were going to throw them out."

"Right," I mutter, staring at the ceiling. "Of course they're from *Our Town*."

Melody stands up, wet rag in hand. "I think that's as good as I'm gonna get with that couch." She gazes around the room. "At least we didn't mess up the kitchen too much."

"I can't believe Noah and Esther own this place. And you roped them all into this."

Melody spot checks the walls. "It *was* good casting."

I rub my sore elbow, thinking. "Okay, but then how did Steve know where to pick me up after I ran away? To be on the street at just the right time?"

"Eh," Melody says. "Noah called him when you left. And then we just followed your tracker."

"My tracker?" I ask.

"Yeah," Melody says, nonchalant, as she vigorously scrubs the wall. "We had a tracker in your backpack. We weren't gonna let you die out there, Alex."

I stare at her. "Wow, you really thought of everything didn't you?"

Turning to me, she nods in all sincerity. "A good show takes a lot of planning."

"Uh-huh," I say, as she clearly didn't get the sarcasm. "I feel bad though," I say, yawning into my fist. "Noah knew Nicole White. They were friends. I think the whole thing brought back the trauma a little bit." I think of him, so young and sad in the courtroom photos. And now, older, strong, and handsome, but still broken somehow. Like my mom, who was always missing someone she loved. "He's in recovery."

"Yeah," Melody says, sounding sorry. "I felt like shit about that. I only found that out after we told them about the plan." She stretches her arms up and yawns. "The mom didn't seem to like Nicole White much though," she says. "Basically implied she was after her son. It was weird."

My tired brain ponders this. It does seem weird. I figured her over-the-top hatred for Nicole was all part of the act. "What about the map with the red circles?" I ask, rubbing my gritty eyes. I had showed them the map before they started cleaning.

Lainey turns to Melody, who puts her hands up in a surrender pose. "Not me," she says.

Lainey gives an uncertain shrug. "Not me either."

"Huh," I say, wondering about the significance of it, if any. "Probably just someone else who stayed here."

"Yeah, probably," Melody says.

I turn on the couch to take the pressure off my smarting hip. "So I guess it actually *was* Eric Myers who killed Nicole White."

Melody stares at me. "Alex," she says. "He has a freaking 666 tattooed on his wrist."

CHAPTER SEVENTY-SIX

NOW

"I think we are officially ready," Melody says. She has purple rings under her eyes, her expression bleary. She pulls her phone from her pocket. "I'm going to have to get the damn screen fixed."

"Yeah. That was true dramatic commitment," I say, with pseudo-admiration.

"That wasn't intentional," she says. "I just fell in the fucking snow."

Lainey stifles a yawn, peering out the window. "Looks like they finally shoveled the street."

I put my phone on the couch. I want to call Jay, but my phone battery is on red, and they can't find my charger. "Hopefully the Kia can get down the driveway at least."

"Let's go, okay?" Melody asks. "I've got rehearsal tomorrow."

"Wait a second," Lainey says, crinkling her eyes. "Didn't Esther say she was coming here?"

"No," Melody says, pulling on her coat. "She definitely said we should pay at her house."

"I'm sure she said she was coming here," Lainey argues.

"Stop," I say, to them both. "You guys go there. I'll stay here in case she comes."

They glance at each other and nod, both finding this solution acceptable. As they put on the rest of their winter stuff, I start dialing Jay's number when a notification pops up. Their phones chirp in unison.

"Oh my God," I say, seeing it again. "The Amber Alert."

Melody shakes her head. "That wasn't us. I promise."

"No," I say, staring at the message. "But it's crazy. I thought I saw the car when I was hitchhiking."

They frown, looking at me. "You saw the license plate?" Lainey asks.

"No," I admit. "It was too snowy. But I thought it was the same make?" I concentrate, trying to picture it again. "Honestly, I'm not sure. I was half delirious. I thought it was maybe Eric Myers. But now that's off the table."

Lainey tightens the drawstring on her sleeping bag holder. "You should call 911 and let them know just in case."

"Yeah. Maybe so." I peer anxiously at my dying phone battery. "After I talk to Jay."

Melody hitches her rolled-up sleeping bag on her hip and takes a final glance around the lodge. "You ready?"

"Yeah, okay," Lainey says, but frowns when she sticks her hand in her pocket. "Has anyone seen my keys?"

"In my backpack," I answer, starting to call Jay. "Wait. How are you getting out of here? The engine's dead."

"Oh, that." Lainey gives me a guilty smile. "I probably need to reconnect the battery."

It takes me a second. "You didn't."

She gives a little shrug with a fully impish smile now. "We didn't want you roaming too far, did we?"

"I am going to kill you, you know," I say. "I'll do it for real this time and go to jail and everything. Honestly. It will be worth it."

The Tylenol finally does its job, calming the throbbing in my head and my hip, though my elbow still feels sprained. I lie back down on the couch to rest, talking to Jay.

"So did you know about this?" I ask him.

A pause emerges on the other end. "Can I plead the Fifth? That's what you Yanks do in this situation, right?"

"I can't believe you," I say, chuckling. "You kept that secret the whole time?"

His deep laugh sounds out over the phone. "Hey, it was a bachelorette party. We men aren't supposed to get involved."

"I suppose," I grumble, adjusting my hip on the couch. "But I don't see why I needed a concussion as part of the deal."

"Yeah," he says, sounding perplexed. "I don't get that either."

I laugh, though it hurts my head. "She said she didn't realize the tennis racket would do so much damage. And she'd cut it from the script in the future."

"Ah, Melody," Jay says, with fondness, but also a hint of condescension. "So, you all leaving soon?"

"They're paying off the mother and son duo." I reposition myself on the couch yet again. "Then we'll all go." I yawn loudly. "Is Greg still with you?"

"Oh. He never ended up coming," he says, a grumble in his voice. "Emily said he had some sleepover, and I didn't want to get into World War III over it."

"Oh," I say. This is followed by a beat of silence.

"I *am* going to talk to him," he says, to the unspoken question. "I just . . . the time hasn't been right . . ."

"Maybe just forget about it," I break in, considering how awkward all our future interactions will be. "I get that it's a lot for him. So, let's not discuss it. Okay?"

"Okay. Well, actually," he says, "I have to tell you something else." He takes a deep breath, then exhales into the phone. "I haven't been completely honest with you. I didn't want to worry you but . . . we did lose some money on a crypto deal. Eli's not happy, and he's leaving. And he's one of my biggest clients so . . . we might be taking a hit. I didn't give you the whole truth when you asked. And I should have. I should have told you everything."

I smile into the phone. After everything I've just been through, that seems like a *very* little deal. "Don't worry," I say. "I'm sure it'll work out."

He doesn't respond though.

"Jay?"

Still no response, so I look at the phone to see the call has dropped. I'm trying his number again when I notice a voicemail. I figure it's from Jay from earlier, but an unexpected number shows up. I push play, putting the phone up to my ear.

"Hey, Alex. This is Leigh. Leigh Jones." A long pause comes over the phone. "It's probably nothing, but I remembered something. You asked if I knew Adam Redmond and some other folks from anything. I realized it later. I didn't know the other people, her boyfriend and whoever else. But I used to have choir in that church. So, I'd see Mr. Redmond sometimes, leading a class. I never went in, but we'd chat in the hallways sometimes. It's probably nothing, as I said, but . . . it's a connection, I guess." A sigh comes over the message. "Anyway, I got the other two-and-a-half K. Thanks a lot. I hope your project goes well."

I stare at the phone, shocked.

That's it, I think. There's the connection. Leigh Jones knew Adam Redmond. And Adam Redmond was obsessed with the Revelation passage. So, after all this, it's the stepfather? Not Eric Myers?

I'm calling Leigh Jones to get more information when a knock sounds at the door. I twist my head around to see who it is but don't see anyone in the windows.

Lainey was probably right. It's probably Esther coming to collect her money. The thought is beyond aggravating. I picture her tall, stooped figure, her cloudy blue eyes. I really don't want to face her right now.

The doorbell rings again.

"Coming," I moan, getting off the couch.

CHAPTER SEVENTY-SEVEN

NOW

I open the door, squinting at the sun.

It isn't Esther but Noah who stands on the doorstep. He gives me a shy smile, his hands dug into his pockets. For a moment, I get a flash back to him as a fourteen-year-old, cowed by the courtroom proceedings. "Hey."

"Hey," I say back. The interaction feels awkward already. I'm not sure what sort of conversation we're supposed to have. We're not really strangers or friends. And he has just lied to me all night while his mother tried to shoot me.

He peeks in the door. "Your friends around?"

"They went over to your house. They were . . . um . . . paying your mom, I think."

"Oh," he says, befuddled. "Shit. She told me I was supposed to come *here*. I don't even think she's home."

"Yeah," I say. "Wires crossed maybe." As he keeps standing there, I realize my rudeness. "Do you want to come in?" I ask, remembering he actually owns the house.

"Sure, thanks." He walks in and takes a look around.

I must admit, they cleaned the place up pretty good. We stand there stiffly for a moment.

"I know this is a really messed-up situation," he says. "But . . . I'm sorry for lying to you and all."

"Don't worry," I say, leading him into the family room. "It's not your fault."

He wipes his boots on the rug, then follows me. "I really didn't want to but . . . your friends thought you'd think it was funny so . . ."

"No problem, really."

I sit on the couch, and he takes the sofa chair. He puts his hands on his knees, and I feel like I should be offering him coffee. Again, an awkward silence fills the room.

"I . . . I don't have any money on me," I stammer. "My friends should be back though, if your mom isn't there. Or I could Venmo you maybe . . ."

He chuckles with an eye roll. "My mom doesn't get Venmo. But . . . no worries. We'll figure something out." He takes off his beanie hat, his hair springing up underneath it.

"And I'm sorry for . . ." I struggle with the right apology in my half-drunk state of exhaustion. "Obviously I had no idea they were meeting with you. But I know you've worked hard for your recovery. I didn't want to trigger anything."

"Yeah." He shrugs, his smile forgiving. "No worries. It *was* a long time ago."

Sitting there with the coffee table between us feels like a bad first date. Though I don't know why I'm even thinking that way, with my wedding a month away. Putting my hand in my pocket, I startle to feel his paper note, which I had completely forgotten.

"I think you gave this to me," I say, pulling it out to show him. "Did you really have something to tell me? Or . . . was that just part of the act?"

"No," he says, scratching his hair. "I mean, I don't have a ton to say. I just thought if you wanted an interview on him or something, I could do that. I knew him through Nicole a little. Not a lot but . . ."

So, Noah wants to be on *Crimeline* too. I don't know why I find this refreshingly disappointing. I probably should interview him to fill out the profile, but I can barely remember my own name right now.

"I'm kind of beat," I say. "But maybe I can call you next week?"

"Sure," he says, with a noncommittal shrug, then spots the new 666 book on the coffee table. "Whoa. I've never seen this one before." He reaches down, then checks with me. "Do you mind?"

"Of course," I say, leaning back, stifling a yawn as he flips through the pages. "It's out of print. It was a present from Lainey." My body aches with exhaustion, overwhelmed with the desire to curl up and sleep. I wish Lainey and Melody would get back already and pay the man.

Unexpectedly, he laughs. "I don't know why my mom gave them this picture. I look so stupid."

He brings the book over to me, and I move closer to look, as if we're old friends going through a photo album. He's examining the same photo they've always used of him, at his desk in his room, with his unmade bed, video console, and soda cans all over, the scene a sort of biomarker for *typical high school male*. They zoomed in on this one though, emphasizing his unkempt, just-woke-up-on-a-weekend appearance.

"You look fine," I say, politely. "Just . . . young."

"I guess it's dumb to even care about it at this point," he says, about to close the book.

"Wait," I say, jumping forward on the couch. The close-up reveals a detail you couldn't see in the other photo. The monitor shows his video game midplay, a soldier rappelling with a machine gun in hand, fiery bullets flying.

And in the corner, Noah's avatar and gaming name.

Revelation 13:18 MADMAN

A tingle spreads across my neck.

Not Adam. Not Madam.

MADMAN.

Suddenly, names bubble up in my head from Twitter. The names behind the obnoxious comments.

TNT

And Tom.

Thomas Noah Thompson.

"What did you see?" he asks, peering closer.

"Oh, nothing. I just thought it was something." I slap the book shut and stand up from the couch, stretching my arms up to appear absolutely casual. "My friends will be back any minute, probably." I start walking slowly to the door so he will follow. "You don't have to stay though. I'm sure they hooked up with your mom by now."

"Oh, sure," he says, looking surprised at the sudden end of our interaction. Still, he politely stands up as well.

"I'm really exhausted. But . . . I'll call you about that interview next week, okay?" I walk in front of him and open the door.

He takes a step toward the door. "Sure," he says, with a puzzled smile.

He takes another step.

But then he shuts the door.

And he locks it.

Slowly, he turns to face me. "Maybe we should have that interview right now instead."

CHAPTER SEVENTY-EIGHT
DECEMBER

Dear Alex,

I hope you don't mind the handwritten letter. It sounds weird, but you're the closest thing I have to a friend.

They found the Engineer's plans. So, he's in the hole, and might even get more time. Luckily, he didn't say anything about me. When the guards asked me, I said I thought he was joking about it. So far they haven't asked me any more.

But that was my only hope really.

It was a stupid, unrealistic hope, I get that now. And even if we did get out, somehow we'd screw up. I'm not a master criminal. The problem is, I'm not a criminal at all. Just no one believes me. After our last talk, I could tell you didn't either. I don't blame you for that. I'm sorry if I scared you. I was just really upset and didn't handle it well.

You were my only chance. And if you won't push it, or bring attention to the case again, I might as well be dead. I'll just spend my life dying in here.

I know I said something wrong about her necklace. I don't know what I said exactly, but I remember that necklace really well. It was her favorite.

I didn't kill Nicole. I didn't kill the other girls. And I have no idea who did. I wish I did, for their family's sake.

I see their faces sometimes, when I close my eyes at night. Photos from the trial that they showed. School photos, with their hair just brushed. I didn't kill them, but they haunt me anyway.

By the time you get this, I won't be around.

But I want you to know that I appreciate everything that you did for me. Or tried to do.

See you someday, on the other side.

Warmly,
Eric Myers

CHAPTER SEVENTY-NINE

NOW

I run to the kitchen, but he gets there first.

He holds up the long kitchen knife, shiny and clean now after Melody washed it.

Could this be part of the prank? Maybe my roommates planted the picture in the book somehow?

"Listen," I say, "if this is part of the game, I'm done. Whatever they're paying you, I'll pay you more to stop."

"It's not part of a game," he says, in an eerily calm voice, moving closer to me.

I back up again. I don't think he's acting. But that's what he would say, right? Realistic and nasty, Melody's exact words. In the second it takes to debate this, the shine of metal flashes.

The breathtaking shock of pain that follows this seems unrelated somehow. The stab so fast, it appears impossible to connect them. But a surge of blood pops up on my arm, immediately soaking my sleeve. I grab it with my other hand, trying to stop the flow. The pain overwhelms, vibrates. An ice pick through muscle and nerve.

"Jesus," I say, staggering backward. No, this is not part of a game.

"You think this is so funny, huh?" he bellows, darting the knife out again. I just barely avoid the knife point this time. "You and your bitchy friends?"

The next one hits. A punch of grueling pain. Hot blood escaping.

"Please," I say.

A vision floats by—my body overlaying Nicole White's body. The precise, bone-deep understanding now how twenty stab wounds will feel. Knife slicing skin, opening like soft leather. I don't think I could take it.

"Why are you doing this?" I jump past another swipe.

"Why am I doing this?" he asks, spittle coming off his lips. The boy in the courtroom has morphed into a devil. "You *made* me do this!"

"What . . . what do you mean?" I ask, hoping to buy some time with questions. When he's talking, he's not stabbing.

His eyes redden. "I didn't want to kill her. I didn't mean to. But she stopped talking to me." He keeps walking toward me, and I keep backing away. "Because of some stupid shit on a video game. Okay, I said some things I probably shouldn't have. But it was a fucking game!" He sounds incredulous, newly incensed at the injustice. "And I apologized. I tried to explain the Revelation thing too. It was a joke from her dad's class. But she wouldn't listen. And . . . I got mad."

"You were in the Bible class," I say, mainly to myself. I bump into the love seat and nearly stumble. "But what about Leigh Jones? What did she have to do with it?"

He steps forward and I step back. His arm remains fully cocked, gripping the knife. "Nothing, really."

"What do you mean?" I ask, backing up.

"Just that, if I was gonna kill Nicole, I had to get someone to take the blame. Then I remembered Eric Myers, with that tattoo he thought was so cool and scary," he sneers.

Another stab. Another feint.

"You planned it, then? To kill Nicole?"

This belies his claim that he got so mad he just attacked her. It wasn't spur of the moment. Premeditated, not manslaughter.

"I did a good job on it too. I made sure I got every detail right," he says, ignoring me. "Made sure she'd see it when I attacked her. And it worked. They nailed Eric Myers for it." A bitter laugh comes out of him. "It took a while though. No one paid attention to her. I should have picked a White girl."

The blood from my arm pours out gentle spurts with each heartbeat. With every step, my head feels lighter. I don't know how long I have left before I lose too much blood.

"Why the other girls, then?" I ask. My knee hits the coffee table, and blood drips from my palm down my wrist. "If you already got Eric Myers to take the fall."

He doesn't answer right away, tracking me with his eyes. "That was going to be it though. Just them, then I was going to be done with all that." He takes another step forward. "I got better in rehab. They talked about it, the higher power.

And every time I thought about killing someone, I thought about that. And . . . it actually worked. I couldn't believe it. I was getting better. I was getting fucking better," he repeats, tears in his voice. "Then you and your friends had to come back here."

The next swipe catches my palm, fire blowing through my skin.

"Please," I say again. "You don't have to do this. I won't tell anyone."

"Of course you will," he says, simply.

I back up toward the fireplace when, without warning, he plunges the knife into my thigh and I shriek in pain. He pulls it out and my leg buckles. My shoulder hits the hearth.

"They'll arrest you," I say, losing my breath.

"Nah," he says.

"DNA," I manage to say, sputtering.

"All over the place," he says. "I own it." Then he shrugs. "And my mom will cover for me anyway. She did last time."

I am lying half on the hearth and see my mittens drying by the fireplace. *Is this my last vision? Stupid mittens?* Time dissipates. *This is the body they will find. This is how you will die.*

Generalized pallor and evidence of exsanguination, multiple stab wounds, the irides were hazel and corneae were cloudy.

My vision blurs in and out. Ashy, dying fire. Mittens by the fireplace. Charred logs.

Charred logs.

He raises his arm again, but I manage to twist away just in time. With every gasp of life left in me, I reach for the still burning log. I grip it, not even feeling the embers burning my skin, and spinning around, I thrust the flaming end right into his face.

"Argh!" He lets out a guttural moan, staggering back. "You blinded me," he shrieks, sounding almost insulted by the idea. He drops the knife with a clatter, then falls to his knees. "You stupid bitch. You blinded me."

I try to kick the knife away, but my energy has bled out.

Eric Myers is innocent. But I can't let the world know like he wanted me to. The story will die with me. My vision fades, tunnels. Graying in and out.

Noah has somehow found the knife, and I see the arm up again. A horror movie reel. A *Crimeline* episode.

"Son."

The word floats into the room. We both turn to the sound, my eyes flickering open and closed. His mother stands in the doorway with a shotgun pointed right at him this time.

"It's over," she says.

CHAPTER EIGHTY

DECEMBER

NOW

I don't remember much about the hospital.

Hours and days erased.

I remember bits and pieces only. Dizzying, squeaking wheels, bouncing pain. A tube gagging me. Cold water in my veins. Hands rolling me.

Mostly I slept, or halfslept, through a haze of pain medication.

I remember only glimpses of being awake. My mom putting a blanket on me. My dad (my dad?) crying and saying *I'm sorry.* A thought slipping through my sedated, misfiring brain. He was a bad husband, but he was not a bad father.

Jay yelling at the doctors to help me. *Someone help her, please! Why aren't they helping her?* Melody fixing up my hair. Lainey squeezing my hand so hard that it hurt. Even Toby coming by with flowers. Nurses coming and going like ghosts. Beeping and whirring machines.

And one time, Lissa sitting on my bed, her hands on mine, a calm warmth seeping through me, then seeing her fade away. My mouth choking, trying to say her name. Lissa. Lissa. And my mom resting her forehead on mine, saying, *Shh . . . it's okay . . . she's okay now.* And I tried to say her name again, and she said, *It's time to let her go, Alex. I need to you to stay with me now.* And somehow, I did that. I stayed in the room, and I let her go.

I don't remember: the epinephrine. The defibrillator. The units and units of blood. (Thank you, anonymous, good people. Thank you.) Pouch after pouch after pouch of saline hung up on the IV pole, infusion rate wide open.

I don't remember the words hypovolemic shock. Versed. Propofol.

These are words I learned afterward at Melody's house. When I was studying my case, reading two hundred pages of my medical records, researching myself like a *Crimeline* intern.

"Throw away or keep?" Melody asks, holding up red, glossy Louboutin shoes.

"Keep," I say.

"We're not doing a lot of throwing out here, Alex," Melody complains, her hands on her hips.

Lainey is sprawled out on a chair in the corner, which is way too small for her but at least fits in my new apartment.

This is stage two of my recovery.

Stage one I spent at Melody's apartment, healing after my hospital stay. My mom wanted me to come home, but I didn't really want to go back to Vermont. Lainey and Melody both offered to help me, but Lainey only had a week off for her union-mandated December break. Since Melody didn't get the part in the *Guys and Dolls* revival, she took me in.

"Sweater?" Melody lays it over her chest as if modeling.

"Throw away," I say.

She assesses herself in the mirror. "Can I keep it?"

"All yours," I say.

The sweater was snug in the past, though it would probably fit now with the weight loss after the hospital. Ironically, I would fit into the wedding dress perfectly right now, but I won't be wearing it.

Not yet. We decided to delay the wedding for now, while I recuperate and he works on therapy with his son. And I need some more time to figure out who I am, without Chris or anyone else. I need to hear my own voice. So we're living apart for now, but we're still together. In fact, he's coming over "with a curry" tonight.

Melody drops a tangle of metal hangers, and I jump an inch off the couch, my heart racing. She and Lainey look at me, then at each other.

I know I'm jumpy these days, otherwise known as PTSD per my newly acquired therapist. I got another Amber Alert yesterday and leaped a foot off the floor at the sound. Though my own Amber Alert sighting was a false alarm. They caught the ex-husband and brought the child back safely. No *Crime-line* episode, just a happy ending for once.

Lainey blows a lilac bubble with her grape gum. "So," she says, "when do you start the new gig?"

"After the new year," I say, with a nervous but hopeful lilt.

The new gig isn't really *new,* so much as a promotion. It turns out capturing the real 666 Killer and releasing an innocent man from prison lifts you off the perpetual intern track after all. And luckily, they got to the prison before Eric Myers tried to kill himself.

Toby greenlit the anniversary project and wants me to interview him again, but not over the computer this time. A real interview (with a boom operator and everything!). Trayvon did a victory lap on the *Did He or Didn't He* podcast, forcing Shardai to eat crow.

Witness misidentification. He was right all along.

They also want me to do an interview with Noah, who revealed that the map was his. The red circles did not indicate hunting stands. They marked the burial sites for Angela and Amelia. The discovery leaves two families fractured and crushed but at least with some closure, for what that's worth. It would have been worth something for my mom.

Melody arranges the toppling Goodwill pile and rifles through another box. "How's the book going, by the way?"

"Good," I answer, though in truth, I've only written down the title.

"Oh shit," Lainey says, jumping out of the chair. "I was supposed to meet Ruby ten minutes ago." She grabs her coat from the chair. "She's gonna kill me."

"Yeah, I should probably go too," Melody says, abandoning the box. "But I'll come by tomorrow."

"Thanks, you guys," I say, giving them hugs—gentle hugs. My body still feels like a doll that's been ripped apart and sewn back together, the edges rough and jagged.

On the way out, they shut the door, the slam echoing in the silence.

Like a punctuation mark to their visit.

I move over to the chair by the window, resting my elbow on the windowsill. Somebody leans on a horn outside, answered by a barrage of honking in a horn language decipherable only to New Yorkers. Babushka yawns, lounging in a patch of sun on her favorite kitchen rug.

The sounds of the city fill the room, no longer muffled by the thick, gray walls in Jay's penthouse. But I don't mind the noise. Outside, snow falls on the postcard New York City streets, dressed up for Christmas, lights wrapped around trees, wreaths hung over doors, shops flanked with huge red and green candy canes, piles of presents in the windows. My mom wants to visit this year. Maybe I'll take her to Saks Fifth Avenue.

Grabbing my journal from the windowsill, I settle back into the chair. I open it to a blank page, with only the title on top in capital letters, aptly named THE BACHELORETTE PARTY.

I picture Melody and Lainey in the front seats, one head below the headrest, the other above, the wheels of a beat-up Kia skidding on the snowy streets. Then the first line comes to me, and I jot it down before I can forget.

"I yank off the crown."

I pause, smiling at the line.

And then I keep writing.